CRITICAL ACCLAIM FOR LEIGH RUSSELL

'A brilliant talent in the thriller field'
— Jeffery Deaver, bestselling author of *The Bone Collector*

'Leigh Russell is one to watch'
— Lee Child, author of the bestselling *Jack Reacher* series

'Leigh Russell has become one of the most impressively dependable purveyors of the English police procedural.'
— Marcel Berlins, *The Times*

'Taut and compelling'
— Peter James, bestselling author of *A Twist of the Knife*

PRAISE FOR *RACE TO DEATH*

'Leigh Russell weaves a fascinating tale that had me completely foxed. Whilst the mystery is tantalising the characters also fascinate, so clearly are they drawn.'
— *Mystery People*

'As tense openings go, they don't come much better than this'
— *The Bookbag*

'Another first-rate story by the talented Leigh Russell. Highly recommended.'
— *Euro Crime*

'The tension is built up cleverly until the final, shocking, denouement'
— Ron Ellis, *Shots*

'Full of twists, turns and dark secrets. The plot gallops along creating suspense on every page.'
— Shirley Mitchell, *Creuse News*

PRAISE FOR *KILLER PLAN*

'a fast-paced police procedural and a compelling read'
— Carol Westron, *Mystery People*

'Her previous six novels featuring DI Geraldine Steel marked her out as a rare talent, and this seventh underlines it.'
— Geoffrey Wansell, *Daily Mail*

'The plot was excellent with plenty of twists and red herrings.'
— Fiona Atley, *newbooks*

PRAISE FOR *FATAL ACT*

'a most intriguing and well-executed mystery and . . . an engrossing read'
— Sara Townsend, *Shots*

'another corker of a book from Leigh Russell . . . Russell's talent for writing top-quality crime fiction just keeps on growing'
— Amanda Gillies, *Euro Crime*

PRAISE FOR *COLD SACRIFICE*

'A top-of-the-line crime tale and a five-star must-read'
— *Take-A-Break Fiction Feast*

JOURNEY TO DEATH

A LUCY HALL NOVEL

ALSO BY LEIGH RUSSELL

DS Ian Peterson Murder Investigations

Cold Sacrifice

Race to Death

Blood Axe

The DI Geraldine Steel Mysteries

Cut Short

Road Closed

Dead End

Death Bed

Stop Dead

Fatal Act

Killer Plan

LEIGH RUSSELL

JOURNEY TO DEATH

A LUCY HALL NOVEL

THOMAS & MERCER

The characters and events portrayed in this book are fictitious. Any similarity to real persons, living or dead, is coincidental and not intended by the author.

Published by Thomas & Mercer, Seattle

www.apub.com

ISBN-13: 9781503951921
ISBN-10: 1503951928

Cover Design by Lisa Horton

For Michael, who is always with me

Seychelles
June 1977

Prologue

When he first arrived in the Seychelles to take up the post as accountant in the Garden of Eden Hotel, George felt as though he had landed in paradise. Accustomed to the grey skies of England, he was bowled over by the beauty of the landscape and the changing colours of the Indian Ocean. The sunsets were spectacular. It was hard to believe anything malevolent could flourish under the tropical sunshine. Young and inexperienced, he soon learned that beneath the surface, life on the island was far from ideal. After two months he was still struggling to learn the ropes in his job. He was even contemplating giving up and going home to England. But that was before he met Veronique.

One evening he was sitting at his desk writing a letter home when he heard a faint tap at the door. He twisted round to see a woman silhouetted in the open doorway.

'Shall I come in?' Her voice was low and warm.

'Who is it?'

'I come to clean for you.'

'Oh, all right, come on in then.'

He returned to his writing. Noticing a faint scent he looked up from his letter. A small vase of white frangipani blooms had appeared on his desk. With flowering shrubs proliferating wherever he went it was hardly necessary to bring them into the house. All the same he was touched by the gesture, and went to the kitchen to thank his maid.

Whatever happened afterwards, George never forgot the first time he saw Veronique. She was standing in his cramped kitchen, pushing a loose strand of curly dark hair off her forehead. Years later he would experience a similar thrill, like an electric shock, when he saw his newborn daughter's face for the first time; a visceral knowledge that this encounter would change him irrevocably.

An oval face looked back at him, framed by hair that tumbled down her back in casual disarray. He felt a sudden intense longing to cup her smooth golden shoulders in his hands. Beneath finely arched brows her black eyes seemed all pupil, as though she could see more than other people. Her small nose was slightly flattened, her olive skin glowed with health and her lips, reddened with lipstick, formed a childlike pout. She lowered her eyes under his scrutiny and when she raised them George gave a tentative smile. Her face relaxed in a momentary complicity, changing the balance of their nascent relationship. No longer the master of the house, he was a supplicant, and when she smiled he felt as though he had received a precious gift.

He cleared his throat nervously. 'My name is George.'

'I know.'

In that instant he had the uncanny impression she knew everything about him, could see his darkest desires, with the understanding only a woman could possess. If he had stopped to think about what he was doing he would never have had the nerve, but it felt natural to follow her into the bedroom without a word passing between them.

Afterwards he told her he came from England. With a sleepy smile she said she knew that too. He quickly found out that she knew next to nothing about the world beyond the Seychelles.

'The island is my home,' was her only reply when he expressed surprise at her ignorance.

'Don't you want to travel and see the world?' he asked.

'Why?'

He started to explain that the world was a large place full of fascinating landscapes and cultures, but his speech petered out. The world beyond the island no longer drew him.

All his life George had longed to explore exotic places far from home, but it was next to impossible without any money. When the opportunity to work in the Seychelles had arisen, he had jumped at the chance to explore the region. In the weeks leading up to his departure for Mahé he had been busy making travel plans. Veronique's lack of curiosity about the world seemed spiritual, as though she had discovered inner peace. If he had been born on an island paradise, instead of an island with a chilly wet climate, perhaps he would not have wanted to leave either. By loving a woman from a foreign culture he felt he was learning to know himself. If it had not been true, it would have been corny, the kind of romantic slush his sister liked to watch on television. He could have slept with other women on the island but he needed Veronique. It was so much more than sex.

Cocooned in happiness, George paid little attention to the gossip that flew from ear to ear at the hotel bar. Rumours spread like lightning across the island. The political pressure was building up until a coup seemed almost inevitable. Yet nothing happened. President Mancham went to England on holiday. On his home territory other holidaymakers carried on snorkelling and burning in the unaccustomed heat and splashing in the pool, oblivious of the islanders holding their breath, waiting for news. The weather remained oppressively hot, bougainvillea still bloomed dark pink and purple, and the sun continued to set in resplendent colours.

Aware only of his love for a beautiful woman, George hardly noticed the growing political unrest. All he wanted from life was right here on this island. For the first time in his life he felt truly happy.

'We'll get married and I'll take you away with me to England,' he promised.

Veronique smiled, alluring as the island. 'Mahé is my home.'

'Then we'll stay here on the island and never leave.'

George was driving along the coastal road after work one day when he heard a burst of gunfire. His first instinct was to put his foot down and get away from there as quickly as possible, but realising he might make an easy target, he swung the wheel and pulled in at the side of the road. Bent almost double, he climbed out of the car. Crouching down behind a large boulder he waited, listening. The sound of a gunshot startled him, so that he yelled aloud in fright. Fortunately his cry was masked by shouts and laughter coming from the beach. Terrified, he peered round the rock at a group of young men sprawling on sand still warm after the fierce heat of the day. George dodged back out of sight, and listened to their exchange with growing unease. There was an atmosphere of pent up aggression in the group, and they were armed.

'Shit, he was just giving guns away,' one of the young men cried out.

'He told us not to use them,' another voice replied. His response was greeted with laughter.

'What's the point of putting a gun in a man's hands and telling him not to shoot?'

'It's like putting a beer in his hand and telling him not to drink.'

'It's like putting a naked woman in his bed and telling him not to fuck her.'

Cautiously George edged forward until he could see the men, chattering excitedly. Only one member of the group remained silent. He sat apart from the others, scowling. A small crab was crawling across the sand. The solitary man watched its laboured progress for a few seconds before crushing it slowly between his thumb and forefinger. His expression of callous intensity made George shiver.

'There's a world of difference between hearing stories of revolution in the capital, and the cold feeling of a weapon in your hand,' one of the men said cheerfully, weighing his gun in his hand.

A thin youth jumped up. Grinning, he aimed his gun straight at the man who was sitting on his own. As the other man ducked his head, the rest of the group roared with laughter.

The man who was the butt of the joke sprang to his feet. 'If you make a fool of me again, Jean-Paul, you will not live long enough to regret it.'

The prankster slapped his angry friend on the back. 'There is no shame in being afraid of a gun, Baptiste. Your courage is well known on the island.'

The sullen man sat down again, muttering to himself.

Another man stood up and aimed his gun at a massive granite boulder jutting out of the clear blue water of the bay. With a loud retort a bullet flew upwards into the air. 'Ah, shit!' he cried out, jerking backwards at the recoil. He gripped the gun in both hands and his second bullet hit the grey rock with an echoing crack.

They all cheered. A second man jumped to his feet, shot, and missed the target. His friends jeered. Then they were all on their feet, bullets cracking against the boulder, water spraying wildly as they embarked on an impromptu contest. Only the sullen man remained sitting apart from the others, watching.

A scraggy dog came limping along the beach towards the men. It stopped and eyed them suspiciously.

'Must be deaf as well as lame,' one of the men said, 'or the shots would've scared it away.'

Still morose, Baptiste rose to his feet and raised his gun. Steadying it with both hands, he aimed at the creature's head, right between the eyes. The dog jolted as though it had been electrocuted. It let out a short yelp of surprise before collapsing on the sand where it lay twitching for a moment. Then it was still. A thin trickle of blood showed dark against the yellow sand.

The other men shouted, congratulating their friend on his skill with a gun. Laughing and joking they returned to their boulder. Only the man who had shot the dog stood still, observing the others at their game.

After a moment he turned away and spat on the sand again. 'Guns were not made for shooting at rocks,' he muttered.

His menacing words terrified George, cowering a few feet away. He needed to get away from there while the men were occupied. Once they lost interest in their shooting competition they would leave the beach and discover him, hiding behind a rock. They might mistake him for a British spy. While he lingered, he risked suffering the same fate as the dog. Silently he stole back to his car and drove off. He did not stop shaking until he was inside his house.

He had just sat down in his garden among the bougainvillea and hibiscus to watch the sun set over the ocean, when his phone rang.

'It's happened.' The hotel manager's voice was hoarse with excitement. 'The coup. Over in Victoria. Mancham's been ousted while he's away in England.'

They had been expecting political conflict to break out for so long, it was almost inconceivable when the moment finally arrived.

'René's henchmen have been handing out weapons like candy to all his supporters. They've announced a twenty-four-hour curfew, so stay at home and keep out of sight. It's mayhem out there. God knows what they're doing, putting deadly weapons in the hands of untrained men. There's pockets of violence breaking out all over, not just in the capital, young lads with guns getting drunk and out of control. It's dangerous on the streets.'

'I saw a group of lads playing about with guns today. They killed a dog.'

'You had a lucky escape. A man was shot dead this evening on Beau Vallon Beach.'

George laughed nervously. 'The locals are getting a bit hot under the collar about their politics.'

'Politics had nothing to do with it. A fisherman had a row with his neighbour over a lobster pot and shot him. If enough guns are handed out, some of them are going to fall into the hands of people who want to use them.'

For several days George waited, not daring to leave his house. As soon as the curfew was lifted, he went back to work. The five-mile journey seemed to last for ever. He prayed his car would not break down as he drove past armed soldiers on the road. Once before, his car had packed up on his way home. As he set off on foot, a low growling had alerted him to a pack of wild dogs trotting along the road behind him. He heard them panting as they drew closer, and forced himself to keep walking. Then the howling had begun, one dog after another, clamouring to attack. The pack had run with him all the way back to his house, yelping and slavering, but they had not attacked him.

The dogs were nowhere near as frightening as the men with guns he passed on the road. But no one took any notice of him as he drove to the hotel on that hot strange day.

'You heard about the chief of police?' the hotel manager asked him. 'They bundled him into a car and put him on a flight straight to England. Do yourself a favour, George, and get the hell out of here while you still can.'

George did not answer. He had no intention of leaving the island without Veronique.

That evening, he joined a group of ex-pats for a drink at the bar.

'They're much better off without Mancham,' the fat chef was saying.

The manager nodded. 'Corruption was rife when he was president.'

'Too much power in the wrong hands is always a disaster,' George chipped in.

'They're much better off with René,' the chef insisted. 'At least he's sober.'

'You really think René is going to be any different?' George challenged him.

The others huddled together uneasily as George continued. 'What makes you think René is going to be any better than Mancham? They're tinpot politicians in a banana republic and one leader or another makes no difference when the whole system's rotten. They're saying it's an ideological coup, but it's just a quest for power. First the British, then Mancham, now René – and none of it makes any difference to the ordinary people on the island. Things aren't going to get any better under René. If you ask me, they should bring back Mancham.'

George was just getting into his stride when the manager shuffled closer to him.

'Keep your voice down,' he hissed.

The manager looked around the room, smiling, and nodded at an acquaintance, but he spoke sternly.

'Don't look round now. They're watching you.'

Following the others across the poolside area away from the bar, George noticed a couple of brawny men standing by the door, their eyes fixed on him. He turned away and gazed out over the ocean.

When he looked round, the strangers were still staring at him. A chill crept down his back.

'Who are they?' he asked the chef, nodding in the direction of the two strangers.

'What's that, sunshine?'

'The two stooges by the door.'

George glanced over his shoulder. The two men had gone.

'The way things are going, I may have to leave,' he told Veronique that evening. 'You know what the new regime thinks of the British. Marry me and come back to England with me.'

'This is my home. Stay here.'

'It's not like I'll have any choice if they come for me, and it could happen at any time.'

'I cannot leave Mahé . . .' She faltered.

Her eyes grew troubled as he told her he might have been overheard criticising the new president. 'It was stupid of me, I know, but there's nothing I can do about it now.'

She put her hands lightly on his shoulders and he could smell her perfume.

'Take me with you, George,' she whispered, her eyes shining.

'Get your passport.' He paused, seeing her bewilderment. 'You have got a passport, haven't you?'

But he already knew the answer. She had never left the island.

'That's it then, I'll stay here one way or another.'

She pulled back out of his embrace. 'No, you must leave. It's dangerous for you here.'

'Well, if they insist on sending me packing then I suppose I'll have to go. In the meantime, you need to apply for a passport straight away. Hang on.'

He ran over to his desk and pulled out his stash of emergency cash.

'Here, take this. All of it.'

Her eyes grew round. She had probably never seen so much money in her life, let alone handled it.

'Take it,' he repeated, thrusting the notes into her hand. 'It will help you get hold of a passport. If they send me away before you can get out, I'll send you more money, from England. Where shall I send it?'

'Send it to Veronique Hall, at the Post Office in Victoria.'

He smiled, hearing their names linked on her lips.

'If you can't get a passport, I'll come back for you. You have to wait for me, no matter how long it takes.'

She put her finger on his lips. 'You do not need to say this.'

On the surface, life at the hotel continued as before. The British government had issued no recommendation for tourists to leave. Holidaymakers carried on burning in the sun, walking on the beach and enjoying the water sports. The chief of police was not the only one to have disappeared. Those who remained became staunch supporters of the new regime, wherever their previous sympathies had lain.

Without a word spoken on the subject, George and his friends no longer felt comfortable talking in public areas where everyone seemed to be constantly looking over their shoulders. More pressing was the problem of how to get hold of a passport. At a loss, George went to see the hotel manager.

'I want to ask your advice.'

'Fire away old boy.'

'How do I go about obtaining a passport?'

The manager leaned forward and squinted into George's eyes as though trying to read something there.

'Don't tell me you've lost your passport? Jesus, what a time to go—'

'No, no. It's not for me. It's for a – a friend.'

The manager put his arm round George's shoulder and propelled him towards the door.

'A woman?'

'I can't say.'

'Not here,' the manager murmured. 'Come and see me later on. My office. Six o'clock.'

As George was walking away, a burly man stepped into the corridor right in front of him. A second thug came and stood behind him. Trapped, George cringed, waiting for a fist to land in his face.

'Come with me.'

The voice was stilted, as though the speaker had learned the words without understanding their meaning. At the same time, a large hand gripped George by the elbow and pushed him towards a side exit. A black car was waiting outside, parked in the shadow of palm trees. A hotel porter was lolling against the wall near the exit, smoking. He glanced up, tossed his cigarette away and scurried back inside. There was no one else to witness George leave the hotel.

'Where are you taking me? I can't just walk away from my desk like this. I have responsibilities. At least let me speak to the manager—'

'Shut up.'

Smoothly the car slid away from the hotel. George stared out of the window. He wondered if the view of the ocean speeding past was the last sight he would ever see.

'Where are you taking me?' He was embarrassed to hear his voice wobbling.

No one answered.

He was relieved when they drew up outside his house. One of the thugs pushed him out of the car and onto the path. He had to scramble to keep his footing.

'Get your stuff.'

'What stuff?'

'Get your stuff,' the man repeated in a flat tone. 'You going home, boy.'

'Home?' George repeated stupidly, staring round at the driver's mirrored sunglasses. 'I live here.'

The driver leaned back against the side of the car, legs crossed, and blew a smoke ring into the humid air. 'You best do like he say and get your stuff or you going home without it.'

'You move your ass, boy. The plane leaves in two hours and you gonna be on it.'

'I can't possibly be ready so soon.'

Careless of the danger he was in, he insisted they give him more time. He did not explain that he needed to contact Veronique. It might put her life at risk if they knew she was involved with a British man, a known supporter of Mancham. He cursed himself for having spoken out against René in public, in a moment of thoughtless stupidity. He did not actually give a toss who was president. He cared only for Veronique.

'No,' the brute replied. 'No more time. The plane leaves in two hours. Go get your stuff.'

He stepped forward, reaching George in one stride. Grabbing the front of his shirt in one huge fist he yanked him forwards, almost pulling him off his feet.

'It's a small island. Don't try no funny business.'

He shoved George roughly down the path to his front door. With only two hours before he was due to leave, he could not hope to find Veronique. He did not even know where to look for her.

'My home is here with you,' was the only answer she had given when he had asked her where she lived. At the time, that had been enough.

There was nothing he could do but pack his suitcase before the men returned. Carefully he wrapped a specimen of delicate black coral in a shirt and laid it in the case with his clothes. In his panic he nearly missed a note that had been slipped under his back door. Written in a childish scrawl, with deep indentations made by the letters as though the paper had been resting against the palm of her hand, at one point the biro had gone clean through the paper, leaving a tiny tear for a full stop at the end.

'I cannot come today. It is no longer safe.'

The note was signed 'V'.

All too soon, he heard loud banging at his front door. Without a word, the thugs bundled him out. As the car accelerated away from the small white house by the ocean, the thought of abandoning the woman he loved cut through him like a physical pain. His only consolation was the knowledge that she would understand his hasty departure had been forced on him. He trusted in her constancy as surely as he knew the sun would set over the ocean the following day, although he would no longer be there to witness its dying light.

Seychelles
Present Day

1

From her seat by the window Lucy stared past the edge of a wing. As the plane descended below a carpet of grey cloud, she saw the Indian Ocean far below, surprisingly turquoise in the early morning sun. They dropped closer and she saw the surface, crinkled by waves. Fluffy white clouds floated underneath them, resembling dollops of whipped cream. Two long islands came into view, one larger than the other, like a whale with a calf swimming alongside. They flew on and she saw a large green island with a wide bay. As they descended she could make out tiny angular flecks of boats. The plane wheeled until she could see nothing but water, and then they were flying over the bay, white surf edging the land like ruffled lace. They were almost on the ground, close enough for her to see white buildings with terracotta roofs dotted along the coastline. More buildings flashed past, at the foot of green hills dwarfed by a high grey mountain. Apart from that one stone outcrop the island looked lush and green. Lucy tried to look excited, but she felt numb with misery.

'Ladies and gentlemen, welcome to Seychelles. The local time is seven thirty a.m. and the outside temperature is twenty-seven degrees Celsius. Please keep your seat belts fastened . . .'

Lucy leaned back in her seat and closed her eyes. It would be a relief to get off the plane and stretch her legs.

'Are you OK?'

She opened her eyes and nodded at her mother, forcing a smile. 'I'm fine, really. You don't need to worry about me any more.'

Unwilling to leave her alone, her parents had whisked her off on holiday with them, taking her five thousand miles away from her devastating break-up with her fiancé, Darren. She had not been away with them for several years, had not spent longer than a weekend in their company since she had left home at eighteen.

As the plane touched down, she struggled to maintain a cheerful façade. She was doing her best, determined not to ruin the trip for her parents, who had been looking forward to spending sixteen days in the Seychelles. For as long as she could remember, her father had told them anecdotes about the time he had spent working there when he was younger: bananas and coconuts growing on trees, orchids sprouting like weeds along the roadside, and sensational sunsets over the ocean.

Her mother returned her smile. 'We're going to have a wonderful time.'

Lucy nodded and gazed out of the window. Already she was regretting her acquiescence, but her parents had made it impossible for her to refuse their offer. Her mother had flatly refused to go away and abandon her daughter to deal with her emotional crisis alone. It was unlike Lucy to be so despondent. Clearly her parents thought a change of scenery would help her to move on. She hoped they were right.

Her father leaned over. 'Look, didn't I tell you we'd be landing right at the water's edge?'

'I thought you were exaggerating when you said it was like landing in the sea,' she replied.

'The airport's built on reclaimed land,' he replied. 'We are on the sea.'

She smiled at him, wishing she could share his enthusiasm. But as the plane raced along the Tarmac towards the end of the runway, she sat back in her seat, wondering what Darren was doing.

It did not take long to collect their luggage in the tiny airport, and they found a taxi easily. The driver spoke in a thick French accent, pointing out local sights as they skirted the town of Victoria in the early morning rush hour.

Lucy's father stared out of the window. 'There were no traffic jams here in my day. It was all mini-mokes back then.'

'That was over thirty years ago, George,' her mother said.

'It's all much more built up than I remember it.'

'You been here before, sir?'

'My husband worked at the Garden of Eden Hotel, where we're staying,' Lucy's mother said.

'You worked at the Garden of Eden, sir? Very nice. When were you here?'

'I was here in 'seventy-seven.'

''Seventy-seven? Ah, a year after independence, that was when they got rid of Mancham and made René president.'

'Yes, that's right. I was here when that happened. I suppose things have changed a lot since then?'

'Yes, sir. Back then life was very different. Now we have fast roads, and many more tourists come to the islands. Anyone who wants to work can get a job. Everyone has a house, TV, mobile phone, car. The children go to school, not like in my day. Everything has changed. Now they sell much land to Russians and Saudis. You can see the palace of the Prince of the United Arab Emirates on top of the hill there. They even got a gas station and a hospital up there. They got everything. Before the airport was built, the world didn't even know we existed. Now everyone wants a piece of the island.'

'Still, tourists bring money in,' Lucy's father pointed out.

'Yes, but with the hotels owned by foreign investors, where does all the money go?'

'Are there still wild dogs here these days?' her mother wanted to know. 'My husband used to see them.'

'Not any more, madam, not many,' the driver reassured her. 'They used to be everywhere, before Chinese construction workers came.'

There was a pause while the visitors absorbed the implication of his comment.

'The Seychelles certainly have an interesting history,' her mother said.

'That's true.' The driver resumed his patter, pointing out a seafood restaurant and a bar popular with tourists. They drove past white buildings, mature palm trees and dark green shrubs with startlingly bright flowers, orange, red and pink.

'It's beautiful,' Lucy said.

The driver laughed. 'This is only the town. Wait till you see the beaches.'

They reached Beau Vallon and passed a row of small supermarkets.

'Why are there so many of them all together?' Lucy's mother asked.

'Is because of the hotels. The guests come here for water and whatever else they wish to buy. You can shop here any day. Is good for food if it's convenience you want, but the market in Victoria is better and is only a few rupees to get there on the bus. Or you can get taxi. Is easy. You ask in reception. Or better, you call me. I give you my number.'

The Garden of Eden Hotel was stunning, with marble floors and a beautiful tropical garden. Having checked in, Lucy was impatient to look around. Her parents wanted to retire to their room to rest after their journey.

'It's going to get hot soon,' her mother said. 'I'm going to have a rest and unpack. I'll be up and about later on when it cools down. Why don't you go and have a rest too? We've been travelling for eighteen hours.'

Lucy shook her head. 'Not bloody likely. Don't worry, I won't go out of the hotel grounds, but I'm going to check this place out.'

'Well, make sure you keep out of the sun.'

'Stop fussing.'

Lucy began to walk away, regretting her irritable tone. Her mother was only showing she cared. She turned to apologise but her parents had already closed their bedroom door.

Later it would begin to cool down and they had arranged to meet for a drink by the bar before dinner. In the interim, Lucy had time to herself. The prospect made her apprehensive, but also excited. Since she had left home, Darren had made all her decisions for her. Now she was alone, for the first time in her life, she was determined to make the most of the holiday. Darren was not going to ruin this for her as well. Changing into a blue bikini and matching sarong, she strode to the lift and set out to explore the hotel.

Barely three weeks had passed since she had walked in on Darren and his other girlfriend, in bed together. For a moment Lucy had been too stunned to speak. Darren had refused to apologise. He seemed to think he had done nothing wrong.

'Yes, I know we're engaged,' he had responded to Lucy's tearful challenge, 'but you can't control everything I do. I thought we agreed that we both need our freedom. We don't want to be shackled by conventional rules. That's not who we are. Being engaged doesn't mean you own me.'

'It means you shouldn't be shagging some random cow. Get out of my bed!'

'Who are you calling a random cow? Fuck off!'

When Darren had attempted to introduce his 'other girlfriend', Lucy had run out of the flat. She had not seen him since. He had called her several times at her parents' house, but she refused to speak to him.

'He's not worth it,' her mother had insisted.

All her friends had said the same. It did not help. Since the break up, all Lucy had wanted to do was to sit at home by herself and hide from the world.

'You're twenty-two,' her mother had comforted her, 'you've got your whole life ahead of you. I know it doesn't feel like it now, but it will get easier.'

Her mother was right. She had to start building a new life for herself. Kicking off with a dream holiday in the Seychelles was not a bad way to begin.

The pool area was surrounded on three sides by huge flowering shrubs. She recognised scarlet, purple and startling pink of frangipani, hibiscus and bougainvillea. Set in the midst of this profusion of lush greens, the clear blue water of the pool sparkled in brilliant sunshine. As she wandered past the pool she was startled by an old man who emerged without warning from the shrubbery. Heavy-lidded black eyes peered out from under the brim of a tattered straw hat. She turned away and walked over to the bar, ignoring white loungers laid out around the pool inviting her to sunbathe. Beyond them wooden tables and chairs were dotted around in the shade of huge parasols. Combined with palm trees and flowering shrubs, a thatched roof over the bar area created an exotic ambience. Perching on a bar stool, she sipped cool lemonade and fell into conversation with the barman, a blond guy from Nottingham called Eddy.

'I came here eighteen months ago for the snorkelling and haven't been able to drag myself away from the island since. Once you get hooked on this place there's nowhere else, no other life.'

Lucy smiled, picturing herself breaking free of all her ties: parents, grandparents, friends, her boring job, leaving England behind for a new life on this paradise island. That would show Darren she had forgotten about him.

'There must be a downside,' she replied.

Eddy leaned his elbows on the bar, his face suddenly serious. 'You mean the flesh-eating tarantulas, or the snakes that can swallow a living man whole?'

Lucy laughed. Her mother had been nervous, but her father had reassured them none of the species on the islands were poisonous, and there were definitely no snakes.

'The worst you might see is a rat,' he had added, grinning at her mother's grimace. 'Come on, Angela, there are just as many rats in London.'

And I was stupid enough to want to marry one, Lucy thought.

'What's the night life like round here?' she asked the barman.

'Are you here on your own?'

'Yes – no – that is, I'm with my parents.'

'Ah.'

Lucy wasn't quite sure what his exclamation signified. As though in justification, she explained that her father used to work at the hotel. Eddy looked interested.

'That so? What's his name?'

'You wouldn't remember him.'

'Try me.'

'No, really,' Lucy laughed. 'It's over thirty years since he worked here.'

The barman whistled. 'Before I was born.'

'Me too.'

'Yes, I can see that.'

They chatted for a while. In the course of the conversation Lucy told him her father had been employed as the hotel accountant in the seventies. A couple of girls came over to the bar and Lucy wandered off to find a free sunbed. The heat was intense as she strolled to the far side of the pool where a row of sunbeds were shaded by palm trees. She lay back and closed her eyes, deciding to give herself half an hour at most before she went inside. Even in the shade the heat was vicious and her naturally fair complexion burned easily.

A shadow fell across her face and she looked up to see Eddy the barman and another man walking towards her. She sat up and tucked her sarong around her thighs as the barman introduced his companion. Tall and broad shouldered, Adrian looked about thirty. His black hair was parted on one side and fell over his forehead, almost hiding eyes so dark she could not distinguish pupil from iris. He flicked it back with a jerk of his head but it slipped down again as he leaned forward to talk to her. His skin was swarthy from the sun, giving him a Hispanic appearance.

'Adrian's the hotel accountant,' Eddy explained, and Lucy smiled.

'So your father used to be the accountant here?' Adrian asked, as he pulled up a chair and sat down beside her.

'A long time ago.'

Lucy told him about her father and learned that Adrian had been working at the hotel for just over a year. He had no plans to leave, although he said he had studied in England and might go back there one day.

'It must have been strange returning after being away for so long,' she said. 'How did you manage to settle in again? It's all so different here. Did you feel like you were on holiday when you came back?'

He shook his head. 'It wasn't really like that. People are very accepting here. And in any case I attended an international school, so friends came and went all the time. Nothing was ever permanent for me, not where people were concerned.'

Even when you believed relationships were permanent people still let you down, Lucy thought bitterly.

'But I always knew I'd come back. How do you settle for the cold and the wet when you've grown up with all this?' He waved his hand towards the palm trees and the sky. 'It's beautiful here and the longer you stay the more you fall in love with the place. If you like I can show you the sights. There's a coastal road that runs round the island, and paths over the mountains if you fancy a hike.' He took a swig of his beer. 'Or I could take you into the capital, Victoria.'

Lucy thanked him and explained she was there with her parents.

Adrian smiled. 'Bring them along too. The more the merrier, and it will get me out of the office for a few hours if I'm showing English visitors around. Especially if it's someone who used to work here at the hotel.'

It might have been the sun, or the distance from home, or perhaps it was because he was a stranger, but Lucy found Adrian was easy company. For the first time she was able to talk about the break up of her relationship without any embarrassment.

'Turns out he was a complete shit,' she concluded her sketchy narrative. 'He'd been seeing his other girlfriend on and off all the time and I didn't even know anything about it. Can you believe it? I was completely taken in by him. What an idiot!'

'I reckon he needs his head examining as well as his morals,' Adrian replied and she smiled, acknowledging the compliment.

Adrian had to return to work but he promised to look out for her later on. Lucy went up to her room to escape from the heat. Worn out after travelling, she fell asleep without even starting to unpack. When the phone shrilled beside the bed she sat up, wondering where she was. She did not recognise the plain white walls and brown curtains, or the unfamiliar hum of the air conditioning. Only when she looked over towards the window and saw the ocean with its low lying islands did she recall where she was. Her phone was still ringing, so she rolled over on the bed and grabbed the handset, glancing at her watch as she did so. It was half past six.

'Lucy, where are you? Is everything all right?'

Lucy winced at the note of alarm in her mother's voice. Although she was grateful for her parents' support since she had returned to them, distraught, she was beginning to feel hemmed in by their protectiveness, and she hated the thought of them worrying about her.

'I'm fine, really. You don't need to worry about me. I fell asleep, that's all. I'll be down soon but I want to get changed and I really need a shower. Why don't you and Dad have a cocktail together and I'll see you soon?'

'Well, all right, if you're sure you're OK.'

'I'm fine, Mum. Don't spoil your holiday by worrying about me. You go on ahead and I'll join you. Just give me half an hour.'

The buffet dinner was excellent. Lucy had never seen so much food. Restraint was unthinkable after several cocktails. She sampled dish after dish until she simply had to stop.

'You have to pace yourself.' Her father's warning came too late.

Feeling sick, and regretting her indulgence, Lucy felt a surge of anger. At her age, she should have been on holiday with a boyfriend, not her parents. Accusing her of being needy and dependent, Darren had blamed her for the failure of their relationship, but he was the one who had lied and cheated. She struggled to keep her composure.

'It really is perfect here, isn't it?' her mother said.

They were sitting over drinks when Adrian wandered over and greeted her. With a glance at her parents she invited him to join them. He pulled over a chair and sat, insisting he had already eaten. Just then a waiter came over to clear their table and tell them about the desserts.

'Not more food,' Lucy groaned.

The waiter nodded at Lucy's father as he stacked their plates with quick, practised movements.

'You used to work here, sir.'

'I did indeed. Now how on earth did you know that?'

'Eddy the barman told me.'

Adrian smiled at the waiter's retreating back. 'Tell one, tell all,' he said.

'That hasn't changed then,' Lucy's father replied, leaning back in his chair.

Adrian shook his head and his long black fringe flopped forward over his eyes.

'If you want to keep anything secret in this place you have to keep it very close to your chest. The islanders are the most dreadful gossips.'

Her father fiddled uneasily with his glass. Lucy wondered if she had spoken out of turn in telling the barman about his past connection with the hotel, but that was more than thirty years ago. What harm could it possibly do to mention it? And in any case, if she had not told the barman about her father, she might never have met Adrian who was good company and had offered to show her around the island. It occurred to her that her father might resent a stranger stepping into his role, but just then her father threw his head back, laughing at a joke Adrian had made, and Lucy dismissed her qualms. The holiday had only just begun. She was determined to make the most of it.

2

Listening to gossip in the bar, he overheard the long-awaited news. Without betraying his interest, he paid careful attention. A conversation on the patio later confirmed his suspicion. It was as well to make sure. He doubted he would recognise the Englishman after so many years. The dark angel would know if he was the one. She had been waiting for his return for a long time.

Without warning, the patio was crowded with people, chattering and laughing. He slipped into the bushes, irritated by the noise. Ignoring the path he wound his way through dense shrubbery until he was completely hidden from view. Making his way back through the gardens, he followed the path down the side of the hotel to his van, and set off. Along the coastal road he stopped. Clambering down from the driving seat, he leaned back against the side of his van, heedless of the small flowers crushed beneath his feet. Moonlight shimmered on the ocean a few yards away, beyond a stretch of golden sand. He closed his eyes, seeing another scene in his mind, another beauty.

A few holidaymakers were walking along in the shallows, parallel to the shore. He barely heard their brief bursts of laughter. Other figures stood with their backs to him, gazing out over water glimmering in the moonlight. He hardly saw them. Two scrawny brown-skinned children hared past, giggling as they chased one another. Their game came to an abrupt end when they spotted a ghost crab. They crept forwards, circling around it. The crab vanished into the sand and they ran off, shrieking. He observed their antics, without really seeing them. He had no recollection of his own childhood games; he remembered only the life he had forged for himself.

His thoughts began to race. With trembling fingers he rolled a cigarette and stood staring at the sea, his mind in turmoil. His arms hung loose, the cigarette dangled from his bottom lip. As a thread of smoke rose fluttering in the air, he tried to recall exactly what he had heard. It was growing dark, but he was not ready to talk to her yet. First, he wanted to think. Whatever happened next, he must not fail her. At last he climbed back in the van, muttering under his breath. With a sudden jerk he put the engine into gear.

Leaving the road after a few miles, he drove up a wide track and turned off onto a narrow path. Even with his window wound down, he could hardly hear the sounds of the forest above the whine of his engine. The van laboured up a steep incline, the terrain increasingly rugged. A couple of times the engine growled and knocked loudly and the vehicle juddered. He took no notice. Even when the path was completely hidden beneath overhanging branches he did not brake, but followed every twist of his route until he could go no further. Continuing his journey on foot, he reached the hut where she was waiting for him.

He burst in, eager to share his news. 'He has returned! And he has a wife and daughter with him.'

He could not read her expression. She had waited so patiently for this moment. Closing the door, he crossed the room and took her in his arms, gently stroking the top of her head as it rested against his shoulder.

After a moment she pulled away from him with a crafty smile. 'You want to know what I'm going to do.'

He waited for her to speak again.

'I'm not going to tell you,' she said. 'Not yet.' Her grin broadened, stretching her pale face.

He lowered his head in silent homage.

3

THE NEXT MORNING, LUCY'S father hired a car as soon as they finished breakfast. They wanted to drive to the capital, Victoria, before the heat became unbearable. At the far end of the bustling street a granite hill dominated the view, a reminder that the island had been there long before the road with its ramshackle shops and crowded pavements. Everywhere Lucy looked she saw brightly coloured apparel, as though the people were striving to outdo the brilliance of the flowers that grew on the island. They negotiated their way through a forest of brown limbs, flowering shrubs in large terracotta pots, cars, children trotting along the street, the whole scene buzzing with the noise of people and traffic. Despite having passed a restless night, Lucy felt fresh and alive. Admittedly she had been tipsy when she had gone to bed, but walking along the busy street in the daylight it seemed ridiculous that she had gone to sleep crying about Darren. The exuberance of the dirty street was infectious.

Blue railings enclosed the market. As they walked through gates twice as tall as a man a powerful smell reached them, an indeterminate blend of vegetables, raw fish and the zingy scent of fresh fruit. Garbage bins and buckets of mouldy food detritus stood just inside the gate. Lucy held her breath at the stench. A cloud of tiny birds flew up from a mound of spilled flour, startling her. Following her father in the shade of a corrugated metal ceiling, her senses were assailed by vibrant colours and pungent aromas, and a hullabaloo of clamouring voices. Stout women with large bags slung over their shoulders haggled with stallholders beneath the shade of umbrellas. All the fruit and vegetables were massive compared to the ones Lucy was accustomed to seeing in England. Only the tiny bananas were smaller than those at home. Oranges, purple cabbages, green peppers, white cauliflowers, yellow bananas, red watermelon – produce of every colour was there on display.

'I don't remember the market being on two storeys,' her father said, staring at the bright fabrics hanging over the first floor railings in a second level of colourful display.

'Maybe you never noticed the upstairs because it was clothes,' her mother replied. 'You were probably more interested in the food.'

He chuckled and began pointing out different fruits: guava, papaya, lime, star fruit and fresh coconut. All available now in supermarkets at home, thirty years ago they had been virtually unheard of in the UK.

'The place is definitely more upmarket than it was when I lived here. And I definitely don't remember it being so colourful.' He looked around. 'No, it was more downbeat then.'

'You can see the paintwork isn't thirty years old,' Lucy said.

She squinted up at wooden struts supporting a corrugated iron roof, the whole edifice held up by metal pillars painted red and blue and yellow to match the railings up the stairs.

'Nothing stays the same,' her mother said.

Lucy thought about the granite mountain they had glimpsed beyond the town, and the orchids they had seen growing wild along the side of the road.

They wandered on past stalls displaying huge avocados, bunches of green and yellow bananas, red tomatoes bigger than apples. Fish lay side by side on a grey slab: whole silver tuna, mottled grey groupers, red snappers that were bright pink with silvery scales, grey fish emblazoned with astonishing red dots, and a stunningly beautiful turquoise fish with purple scales.

Lucy gazed along the row of glistening cadavers laid out in a morgue bursting with life. 'It's enough to put you off eating fish,' she muttered, but no one was listening. 'And we think London's cosmopolitan,' she added, gazing around at the market packed with local people of every ethnicity.

Alluring scents of spices and fruit were superseded by odours of garbage and fish. A large white bird perched on a railing, eyes fixed on a brawny man chopping heads off fish with a cleaver, while women clustered around waving their hands and chattering shrilly.

They watched a man cut the end off a coconut so that it stood upright on his table. With rapid swipes of his knife he peeled back the husk at the other end, pierced the flesh, and poked a straw through the hole. Finally he decorated the coconut with a small bright flower before handing it to a waiting customer. Lucy was tempted to buy one, just so she could watch the speed at which the stallholder transformed the coconut into a drink.

'I wonder if it's nice?'

'You can bet on it,' her father answered. 'Coconuts here are nothing like the dried up versions you get at home.'

'Coconuts are very high in saturated fat,' her mother said.

'Don't be boring!' he scolded her and they both laughed at some private joke.

With a faint shriek Lucy's mother pointed to a large spider, its thin yellow legs crawling across a cobweb.

Lucy's father laughed. 'That's a comparatively tiny one.'

While her parents were chatting, her attention was caught by a figure standing in front of some cardboard boxes on the far side of the market. She was almost certain he was the same bowed old man who had startled her by the pool the previous day. He stared intently at her from beneath his battered straw hat. As she watched, he grabbed another man by the arm and the two of them engaged in animated conversation before the second man turned towards her. He also seemed to gaze straight at her, eyes narrowed, while the first man continued speaking. She was convinced they were talking about her. Losing interest, the second man shrugged and turned away while the first man pulled his shabby straw hat lower over his corrugated forehead and crossed his arms. His eyes almost hidden beneath the brim of his hat, he leaned against the wall, motionless, his face still turned towards her.

'What's he looking at?' she asked her father.

'What's that?'

'That man over there, I just wondered why he was staring at us . . .'

She looked round but the old man had vanished into the crowd.

'What's the matter?' her mother asked, instantly wary. Automatically she checked that her bag was zipped shut.

Lucy shook her head. 'Nothing. It's nothing. I just thought a man was staring at us, that's all.'

'The Creoles often stare at tourists,' her father reassured her.

He turned to feel the guavas at the next stall. The vendor yelled at him in Creole and he replaced the fruit quickly, as though it had stung him.

'You wanna buy? You wanna buy?' the stallholder shrieked. 'For you, special price.'

'But he was staring at me,' Lucy persisted, troubled.

Her father turned to her. 'Don't worry. It's natural. You're a beautiful girl. Of course you're going to get admiring glances.'

She nodded, forcing a smile. 'Yes, I suppose so.'

The old man had not appeared to be admiring her good looks. On the contrary, there had been something menacing in the way he had glared at her. Not normally anxious or paranoid, after Darren's betrayal she did not think she would ever trust anyone ever again. With a sigh, she shook off her feeling of disquiet. Maybe she had misinterpreted his glance. And if local people resented foreigners coming to their island, there was nothing she could do about it. She was on holiday with her parents. All they had to do was enjoy the market before they followed the coastal road back to the Garden of Eden.

4

THEY DID NOT DRIVE straight back to the hotel. On the way her father had agreed to show them the house where he had lived in the seventies.

'It's only a house,' he said when Angela asked to see it. 'It's not very interesting. It's just like any other house. It might not even be there any more.'

'But it was your house, George,' Lucy's mother replied, 'and that makes it interesting to us. Come on, you've talked so fondly of sitting on your verandah watching the sun set over the sea and now we're actually here, I don't want to leave without seeing it. I know we probably won't be able to go inside, but we can just have a look at it from the outside, can't we? It was part of your life, wasn't it?'

They drove around the north point of the island and left the car in a shaded passing bay. Walking the final hundred yards, they saw the sea in the distance as they descended a small slope. Reaching a clearing they gazed down a steep incline at a two-storey white house, and the corner of a verandah that overlooked the ocean. Even from a distance Lucy could see the garden was beautiful. Flowering bushes grew there in profusion, shades of pink and red, purple, yellow and brilliant white, their stalks bowed under the weight of huge blooms.

'How could you bear to leave all this?' Lucy asked.

Her father stared at the house, a distant look in his eyes.

'What do you miss most?' her mother asked, smiling at her husband. 'The sunsets or the sensational buffets?'

'Or the water sports?'

He turned abruptly away from them without answering, and walked slowly down the path. Stopping beside an ancient frangipani bush, he picked one of the white flowers. Holding it to his lips, he closed his eyes and breathed in its perfume, rubbing the soft petals between his fingers.

Lucy started to follow him but her mother laid a restraining hand on her arm.

'Give him a moment,' she said softly. 'I think he wants to remember. He never really had a chance to say goodbye when he left. I don't know if he ever told you but it was all rather dramatic and sudden.'

'What do you mean?'

'He was sent home at a moment's notice by the authorities.'

'Why?'

'Oh, just for being British. It happened to a lot of them at the time. The British were very unpopular with the new regime.'

'Did he keep in touch with anyone he knew here?'

Lucy thought about her fellow students at university, already drifting apart now they no longer lived close to each other. Her friends had been Darren's mates and their girlfriends. Her affair with Darren was the only relationship she had expected to outlast her student days. Without that, she had nothing much to show for her time there.

'I don't think he had many real friends here,' her mother replied. 'But he loved the place, the house and its views, and the garden. I think he was lonely but he was still happy here.'

'Who wouldn't be?'

Lucy thought how well her mother looked. Her fair hair was swept off her face in a ponytail because of the heat, and the style made her look younger than her fifty-three years. She was already beginning to look slightly tanned, although she had been careful to keep out of the sun, and she seemed more relaxed than she had been for a long time. Lucy felt a stab of guilt as she wondered how much her own distress after the break up of her relationship had affected her mother. It could not have been easy for her parents to witness her meltdown. For weeks she had been too immersed in misery to think about anything but her own disappointment. She smiled, but her mother had turned away and was gazing down at the ocean.

For a long time Lucy's father stood in the shade of the tall frangipani bush. At last they followed him back up the hill to the car. He sat for a moment, his head resting on his arms on the steering wheel.

'It's beautiful here, George,' her mother said at last, as though her husband was personally responsible for the setting.

He looked away and nodded his head without speaking.

'It's fabulous,' Lucy chimed in enthusiastically. 'I love it! It must have been absolutely amazing, living here.'

'Time for lunch?' her father asked.

Although he had always been keen to reminisce about his experiences in the Seychelles, now they were there it seemed he no longer wanted to talk about his life in the white house by the sea. Lucy thought about his sudden enforced departure. It must have been difficult, being sent home like that.

'I'm starving,' her mother said.

Her father drove off without a backward glance.

After lunch her parents went for a siesta, out of the sun. Bored in her room, Lucy went down to the pool hoping to see Adrian. He was not there. She wandered over to the bar where a girl was talking to Eddy.

'Hi there, Lucy,' he greeted her.

He jerked his head towards the girl he had been chatting to and introduced her as Judy.

'So you're Lucy.' Judy smiled, speaking with an Australian accent. 'It's nice to meet you. Eddy was just talking about you, because he thought I was you. I'm flattered,' she added politely.

Lucy nodded. 'I suppose we do look a bit alike.'

'You could be sisters,' Eddy said.

The two girls looked at one another and smiled. From behind they might easily be confused, but apart from their slender build and spiky short blonde hair they had little in common. Fair and delicate, Lucy's turned up nose made her look younger than her twenty-two years, while Judy was more tanned with dark eyes and sturdy features. She was wearing a red and blue bikini. Lucy asked Judy if she was staying at the Garden of Eden and the other girl laughed.

'In my dreams. No, I've got a room.'

She gestured vaguely towards the beach, and a charm bracelet on her wrist jangled delicately.

'She's here looking for a rich man,' Eddy teased and Judy nodded.

'Too right,' she laughed.

Lucy was not sure if they were being serious.

While the barman fetched Lucy a lemonade, she fell into conversation with Judy, who told her she was going parasailing.

'Why don't you come along?'

Lucy admitted she had never tried it.

'It's a breeze,' Eddy assured her, joining in the discussion. 'You'll love it. You can't come to Mahé and not go parasailing,' he added when she hesitated.

He winked at Judy who grinned at him. On impulse Lucy asked how much it cost.

'It sounds a lot, but it's worth it,' Eddy assured her.

Judy took Lucy along the beach. They chatted as they walked, and Lucy admired her companion's bracelet. Every time she moved her arm it tinkled.

'Thanks,' Judy smiled. 'It's got little bells on it, with gold letters in between. Not real gold, of course. But they are real bells. How cool is that?'

'What do the letters spell?'

'Oh, they're all J. For Judy.'

She took Lucy to a narrow wooden jetty where a small group of people were waiting. A lithe young man was issuing instructions and giving demonstrations, while another man strapped the next customer into a harness and lifted the parachute in the air to catch the wind. The queue of people watched as each one was swept off their feet into the air, some elegantly, some awkwardly, depending on their level of expertise. As one girl raced forward, the wind dropped unexpectedly and she ran straight into the water. The boat spun round to pick her up but she was close enough to the shore to stand up and wade back to her friends who were laughing and applauding her failed attempt.

Rehearsing the instructions in her mind, Lucy ran along the wooden jetty leaning backwards, clutching the straps of her safety harness. Her pounding heart seemed to skip a beat as she was lifted off her feet and she closed her eyes in terrified exultation. Everyone else on the beach had been so relaxed about the exercise: the young men who had provided her with a rudimentary training and strapped her into the harness, and the other holidaymakers who were waiting their turn to be towed out over the ocean. Her guts churned as she kicked her legs helplessly in the air.

After what felt like hours, she opened her eyes and glanced down. The boat towing her along looked absurdly small. With its engine inaudible at that height, all she could hear was the wind rushing past her as she soared above the water. The beach looked miles away. Wheeling above the ocean like a bird, she felt detached from the world. She wished she could stay up there forever, floating serenely away from her life. All too soon she began to descend until she tumbled into the warm water, the boat approached and she clambered aboard. Her harness was removed and she was driven back to the beach where Judy stepped forward for her turn.

Returning to the hotel, she went for a shower and changed before meeting her parents for a drink in the bar area. They watched the sun set over the sea. Almost a spiritual experience in its beauty, it seemed to put Lucy's petty disappointments into perspective. She felt at one with the sky, watching the colours of the sunset and remembering her experience parasailing. Her fiancé's betrayal seemed so insignificant that her recent distress seemed incredible. She was alive and the world was a beautiful place. A sense of well-being flooded through her. When Adrian joined them for dinner, she could not tell if she was falling for him or just intoxicated with the magic of the island, and the alcohol she had drunk. He was not the kind of man she usually went for, but maybe that was a good thing. He was certainly attractive and eligible but she was not looking for another relationship yet, and was not sure she had recovered enough from her break up to contemplate a holiday fling. Nevertheless she heard herself flirting with him and knew she was laughing too much, but no one else at the table seemed to mind.

After being so unsociable at the white house that afternoon her father was back on form, relating stories of near disasters in the hotel accounts when he had been working there.

'Of course we didn't have computers back then,' he told Adrian. 'We had to do all the calculations by hand.'

'You had calculators.'

'Yes, but we still had to do all the computations ourselves. Nowadays the accounting programmes do everything. All you have to do is enter the figures. I'm not saying it's any easier now. It's just very different, that's all.'

Adrian inclined his head in recognition of the acknowledgement.

Her mother asked for ice in her white wine, and Lucy did the same. She had already drunk too much, and her head was beginning to spin.

'We used to have the ice delivered,' her father said. 'It took a long time to fathom out why there was always a discrepancy between the delivery note and the amount we received. I thought the supplier was diddling us. There was a bit of barney about it but we never got anywhere. Then I discovered the kitchen staff used to leave the delivery out in the sun, so it wasn't so heavy for them to carry inside.'

They all laughed. Once he started, her father had a collection of anecdotes to share, and Adrian added a few of his own when pressed.

'Still keeping Rentokil in business?' her father asked and Adrian chuckled, putting his finger to his lips.

Her father whispered to his wife, 'There's a reason why the staff prefer not to live on site.'

Her mother smiled. 'I'm going to the ladies. I'm not sure I want to hear this.'

'Wait for me,' Lucy said. 'I'm coming with you.'

On the way back to the table, Lucy noticed an old man perched on a low wall, smoking. She was surprised to recognise the old man from the market; the same face scored with deep lines, hooked nose and penetrating eyes peering out from beneath his straw hat. She gave a tentative smile but he stared straight at her without blinking.

'I saw that old man again,' she said as she sat down.

Her three companions looked at her blankly. She saw her parents exchange an anxious glance.

'What old man?' her mother asked. 'I didn't notice anyone on the way back.'

'Oh, it's nothing,' she mumbled.

Embarrassed, she reached for her glass of wine. Her cheeks felt hot and she felt slightly dizzy. She could have been mistaken about what she had seen. The conversation moved on.

5

HER PARENTS HAD BOTH fallen asleep in the shade by the pool. Lucy wandered over to the bar but Eddy was talking to a couple of young girls who were giggling and flirting with him. The whiteness of their skin proclaimed them newly arrived on the island. Lucy bought a cool drink and strolled back to her lounger. The afternoon was overcast so she decided to take advantage of the drop in temperature to explore the coast. Although the sky was cloudy the atmosphere was so humid that she turned back after about ten minutes, tired out. As she drew parallel with the hotel someone called her name and she saw Adrian waving at her from the beach.

'Fancy having some fun? I've got the afternoon off.'

They walked along by the water's edge until they reached a small bay deserted apart from one wiry brown-skinned man of indeterminate age. His white hair hinted that he was older than his sprightly movements suggested. As they approached him Lucy saw that he was Caucasian with bright blue eyes, tanned as brown as an African Seychellois. Probably well into his sixties, he was still a good-looking man. Adrian introduced him as Tim, a former diving champion from Australia, now living on the island earning his living with his boat.

'What do you do, exactly?' Lucy asked.

'A bit of fishing, take a few trips, nothing official,' he winked at her and tapped the side of his nose with one finger before leaning over to lift up a pair of waterskis. 'Come on, Adrian, show the young lady how it's done.'

Adrian demonstrated the correct way to balance on the skis and hold onto the bar.

'Tim taught me everything I know about water sports.'

Lucy watched as Adrian swept out to sea, riding the water in the wake of the speedboat. They wheeled around a few times. When they returned Adrian was dripping with spray, his eyes bright with exhilaration.

'Your turn,' he told her.

Her arms trembled as she took the bar.

'You have to be confident,' he warned her, 'or you're likely to come a cropper.'

Easier said than done.

She leaned right back as Adrian had shown her and nodded. With a wave from Adrian and an answering shout from Tim the boat accelerated away, jerking her straight off her feet. She clung helplessly to the bar as she was dragged through the water, struggling to keep her head above the surface. Tim spun the boat around and brought her back to the shore, shaken and drenched.

'What the hell is out there?' she demanded crossly, gazing at a small red mark on her shin that stung like a nettle rash.

'Sit tight.'

Tim fetched a bottle and she read on the label 'Jellyfish Sting Relief'.

'Great,' she muttered.

Adrian watched, frowning, as Tim calmly applied the gel. 'Any allergies?'

She shook her head. 'None that I know of. But I'm not too partial to jellyfish.'

'You'll live,' Tim replied cheerily, putting the bottle away. 'I've seen worse. This little blighter hardly touched you. By tomorrow you won't even be able to see where he got you.'

'Are you sure?'

He grinned at her. 'That's nothing. You should see some of the whoppers I've come across. No, believe me, it'll soon be gone. It's not a disaster. Apart from the waterskiing. Are you ready for another go?'

'What about the fish? Aren't jellyfish supposed to be dangerous?'

Tim laughed. 'Dangerous? The creatures out there are so tame I could send my mother-in-law into the water to scare them away. Just watch out for spiky black sea urchins. It won't do you any good to step on one of those blighters. And with your delicate skin you might want to get sunblock with jellyfish repellent. There are some great products around these days.'

Lucy glanced at the barely discernible red mark on her leg and shook her head. She felt like a fool for having made a fuss about it. On top of her humiliating attempt at waterskiing, she could not have made more of a hash of trying to impress Adrian.

'Maybe another day,' she replied.

The clouds had gone, leaving a clear blue sky. Adrian took her further along the shoreline to a secluded cove surrounded by gigantic boulders. High overhead, the sun pounded down on them as they walked.

'It's lovely here,' she cried out.

'There are a number of these little bays,' he told her. 'This is one of the quietest but to be honest they're all like this most of the time. There's another one a bit further along, but it's quite tricky to get to so it's always deserted. Anyway, we can go there another day,' he added, as she wandered over to a shady spot and sat down.

'Are you all right?' Adrian asked, as she closed her eyes and allowed her head to droop sideways.

'I'm fine,' she replied, opening her eyes and squinting up at him. 'I'm just a bit hot.'

He passed her some water and she gulped it down.

The sand of the deserted beach was smooth, and partly sheltered by palm trees. Lucy wanted to lounge in the shade, losing herself in wonder at the breathtaking scenery. With a sharp pang, she caught herself wishing her ex, Darren, was there at her side. It was the most romantic setting imaginable. Blinking back tears, she made a conscious effort to shake off her sudden melancholy, determined not to blight her enjoyment of the beautiful beach. Assuring her he would keep a sharp eye out for jellyfish, Adrian ran into the water, splashing and laughing, so she kicked off her sandals and raced across the sand to the sea.

They swam along the coastline where the water was shallow for a few minutes. Still smarting from her humiliating attempt to waterski, Lucy pointed at a large grey boulder sticking up about a hundred yards out to sea.

'Race you to that rock,' she shouted and set off swimming as fast as she could before he had a chance to react. She laughed out loud as a shoal of little fish passed below her, tails flicking, black and silver bodies twisting from side to side as they glided through the clear water. The rock was further away than she had realised. Her legs, already tired from the walk in the sun, felt heavy. As she swam on the water grew deeper until she could no longer feel the bottom. She had the impression there was a sharp dip in the ocean floor as the water suddenly became colder, but she was a strong swimmer and besides, she had challenged Adrian to a race. She kept going.

Without warning, something gripped her left ankle, dragging her downwards. Spluttering with alarm, she struggled to wriggle out of the thick tendrils of seaweed wrapped around her leg. It felt as though a hand was clutching at her, tightening its grip as she gulped for breath and fought to free herself. Then something trapped her other ankle so she could not kick. Looking down she glimpsed something moving. She felt sick with terror in case a shark had caught hold of her legs. About a year before there had been reports in the media about a shark attack somewhere in the Seychelles. She seemed to remember a man had died on his honeymoon. As she was pulled under, she looked down again. Through the clear water she made out a blurred outline. It looked as though a woman was swimming beneath her. Looking through the wavering water, she realised her eyes must be misleading her. With no one else there, it could only be Adrian pulling her down.

Cursing him for playing such a dangerous prank she struggled frantically as he tugged her right under the water. She held her breath until her lungs felt as though they would burst. The sea roared in her ears. Her eyes stung from the salt, and a bitter taste of brine in the back of her throat made her gag. Gathering all her strength, with a desperate burst of energy she kicked down with all her might. Her feet hit against something hard. On the impact her legs were abruptly released and she thrashed her way to the surface, choking and gasping for breath, her vision blurring as she became dizzy.

Strong hands gripped her under her arms and she was aware that Adrian was towing her towards the shore. Reaching shallow water he half carried, half dragged her onto the sand where she lay, gasping and shivering, her eyes stinging painfully.

'What happened to you out there?' he asked, his black eyes wide with concern. 'Are you OK?'

'What the hell do you think you were you doing?' she demanded.

Her throat felt tight and she almost choked with the effort to speak.

'What was I doing? I thought you got cramp. One minute you were swimming ahead of me, then you just disappeared.'

Lucy was trembling with anger and shock. It was hard to credit his cheek. It struck her that she did not really know anything about the dark-skinned stranger who had brought her to this isolated spot, led her into the water and then nearly killed her. More than anything, she was furious with herself. Off guard, she had fallen for a stranger, misplacing her trust once again.

'Next time you go playing a stupid game like that—' She broke off, coughing. 'You nearly drowned me out there. What the hell were you thinking?'

Adrian pulled away from her, a startled expression on his face. 'What are you talking about? It was your idea to swim out to the deep water. I was following you when you went under. If it was dangerous you've only got yourself to blame. How was I to know you weren't up to it?'

'Don't pretend it wasn't you.' She was furious now. 'You pulled me under. It wasn't funny.'

Adrian looked surprised. 'What are you talking about? I just saved your life!'

'After you nearly drowned me!'

'There's no way I pulled you under the water. What kind of an idiot do you take me for? You really think I would play such a dangerous trick on you out there? That's crazy.' He stared at her in consternation. 'Look, Lucy, I'm sorry you caught a fright out there, but there's no need to get in a state over it. You're not the first person to get into difficulties in the waters round here, and I don't suppose you'll be the last. However strong a swimmer you are, the currents can catch you out, and there's seaweed and fish down there, and it's easy to get confused when you're frightened. Just don't ever go out there on your own. That's when accidents happen.'

'I'd know if it was cramp and it wasn't,' she muttered. 'Someone pulled me under.'

'Could it have been a fish?'

Lucy shook her head. 'A fish? It wasn't a fish. I think I know the difference between a human being and a fish.'

It sounded so ridiculous, she could not help laughing. Adrian smiled, seeming relieved that she had recovered from her alarm. As they walked back to the hotel, she mused over what had happened. In the sea she had been convinced that Adrian was messing around under the surface. Now she doubted her own senses, particularly as she had been out in the sun all day. She had been sure that someone had pulled her under the water. Who else could it have been but Adrian? Yet to begin with she had thought a woman had been swimming below her in the water. Maybe it had just been a shoal of fish that had caused her to panic. Perhaps she had imagined seeing a figure in the water below her. Her memory of the incident had already begun to blur and she was confused about what had happened.

'So if it wasn't cramp, and it wasn't a fish, where could this mystery attacker of yours have gone?' Adrian asked.

Gazing out over the turquoise ocean, Lucy refrained from suggesting that someone could have swum round out of sight behind the rock. It was possible, but it sounded absurd. There was no reason why anyone would do that.

'And why would anyone behave like that?' Adrian went on, voicing her own question.

'I guess it must have been cramp,' she mumbled, embarrassed. 'Thank you for rescuing me. It was lucky for me you were there.'

'It could just as easily have been the other way round,' he replied. 'Only an idiot would swim out here alone.'

6

ANGELA DOZED OFF, WAKING to see George snoring gently on a lounger at her side, legs outstretched, hands resting comfortably on his paunch. Sometimes she was caught off guard, startled by how old he looked, his hair still thick but completely white, his limbs somehow shrunken. Only seven years older than her, it was odd how her husband had become an old man when she did not feel any different to the young woman who had fallen in love with him, except that she tired more easily than when they had first met over a quarter of a century ago. Preoccupied with Lucy's disappointment in love she had not been paying George much attention recently, but looking at him now she could see that their daughter's trouble had taken its toll on him too. Family tragedy was supposed to bring people closer together but Angela and George had dealt with the situation independently. They had hardly been able to discuss it. At least they had agreed it would be a good idea to insist Lucy accompany them to the Seychelles. They had both hoped the change of scene would do her good, and Angela had been pleased to see Lucy enjoying Adrian's company.

'Adrian seems very nice,' Angela said as they sat down to dinner that evening.

'We don't know anything about him,' Lucy said without looking up from her plate.

Angela sighed. Naturally warm and trusting of others, Lucy had become distrustful. It was understandable. Having been so badly let down, she was bound to be more circumspect in future. Angela just hoped she would not allow her painful experience to prejudice her against every man she met.

'It's over,' she said softly. 'Not every man is untrustworthy. Where's the harm in giving someone else a chance . . .'

Always protective of Lucy's feelings, George gave his wife a warning frown.

'I don't know what you mean, give someone else a chance,' Lucy protested in a furious whisper. 'Please tell me you're not going to start fantasising about any man who happens to talk to me.'

'Let her sort herself out in her own way,' George agreed.

Lucy turned on him. 'What do you mean, sort myself out? I'm fine. I don't need sorting out.'

They sat, heads down, studying their food.

Angela broke the silence. 'This fish is so soft.'

'It's gorgeous,' Lucy agreed, and Angela relaxed.

In spite of Lucy's lukewarm response to him, Angela was disappointed when Adrian did not join them that evening. They had all been getting on so well. George had clearly enjoyed the exchange of entertaining anecdotes about hotel life. Angela could hardly go looking for him, but as they were leaving for a stroll in the gardens after dinner she spotted him seated in the bar.

'Oh, look, there's Adrian,' she said brightly.

Lucy looked away.

'You two go on,' Angela said, pausing in her stride as they left the hotel. 'I've eaten way too much and I need to sit down for a bit.' She patted her stomach with a moue of regret. 'I'll go and sit by the pool and you can come and find me when you get back.'

Promising not to be gone long, George and Lucy wandered off into the gardens, lush and mysterious in the moonlight. Angela watched them go. As soon as they were out of sight, she hurried back to the bar and accosted Adrian.

'Come and join me for a drink.'

He exchanged a glance with the group of men he was sitting with but followed her without demur as Angela led him to a corner table.

'Adrian, I'm not going to pry,' she began.

He raised his eyebrows with a guarded expression.

'Mrs Hall—'

'Please, hear me out. I won't keep you long.'

He nodded but looked uncomfortable, or perhaps bored, as Angela leaned forward and spoke rapidly, glancing towards the gardens every few seconds.

'Adrian, I was wondering . . .' She hesitated before plunging on. 'I wondered if you might like to take Lucy out on a trip, sightseeing somewhere? She's making the best of things, stuck here with us, but George and I are happy sitting around the pool most of the time – we're not that young any more – at least not compared to Lucy – and I'm sure she'd appreciate someone younger showing her around.'

She felt her face go red, and hoped it did not sound as though she was trying to palm her daughter off on him. Not that Lucy ought to need any help in finding a boyfriend. She was undeniably pretty, with a small nose that turned up at the end, like a little blob of putty, and pale blue eyes, large and round as though the world never ceased to amaze her. Considering both her parents were blond, it was not surprising that her hair had been almost white when she was a child, and she remained a natural blonde.

Adrian's eyes narrowed. He cleared his throat nervously.

'Mrs Hall—'

'Please, call me Angela.'

'Angela. I took Lucy to one of the lovely coves along the beach this afternoon. Did she tell you?'

Angela shook her head uneasily, wondering what she had blundered into. The last thing she wanted to do was embarrass her daughter.

'Thank you. I'm sure she had a lovely time,' she replied, suddenly formal, uncertain what had happened between Lucy and Adrian.

'We went for a swim. It was fine, but she's – well, she's a little highly strung, isn't she?'

'Highly strung?'

'She was disturbed by an encounter with a fish in the water. It wasn't a shark or anything like that. I mean, there was no reason for her to be scared. But she became – well, upset. I'm not sure it would be a good idea, my taking her out for a day. She seems—' He stopped abruptly as though he had just remembered he was talking to Lucy's mother. 'I mean, absolutely nothing happened, it really was nothing, but at first she seemed to blame me for what happened. I'd be happy to take you all out, show you around—'

He broke off again, clearly afraid of sounding rude in refusing to take Lucy out alone.

Angela nodded, suddenly serious. 'You might not think it, seeing her now, but normally Lucy's very level-headed, and always so positive about everything. But she's not herself at the moment.'

She only paused for a second. Lucy might thank her one day for telling Adrian about her disastrous love affair.

'They had been living together for two years and it came completely out of the blue that he'd been two-timing her for so long,' she concluded. 'I think it was the betrayal of trust that upset her the most. We were all shocked. He seemed so nice. It was going on right under her nose and she knew nothing about it.'

Adrian nodded awkwardly, but said nothing.

'The thing is,' Angela resumed, 'I think it's made her wary of men. She's not usually one to make a fuss about anything. She's – well, she's good fun, as a rule, but this has hit her very hard.'

'I can see that such an experience might have that effect.'

'She used to be so trusting. And now . . .' She sighed. 'She's so vulnerable. But she's getting back to her old self. She just needs time. I know she'll bounce back. That's why we brought her here with us. She needed to get away. She thinks she's over him but it's not always so easy to recover from something like that.' She shrugged. 'I'm talking about love.'

'Yes – I mean, no, I'm sure it isn't.'

Adrian stifled a yawn and Angela wondered if she was making a fool of herself, confiding in a complete stranger. He seemed very young. He probably did not understand what she was talking about, but she had to voice her concerns to someone and she did not want to worry George. He would pretend to dismiss her anxiety as a fuss about nothing, and then fret in silence. She pondered what else to say, while Adrian fidgeted in his chair, no doubt waiting for an opportunity to extricate himself from his position as unwilling confidant.

George and Lucy approached, laughing together. Angela thought how fragile her daughter looked, how young she was to have been so hurt. They caught sight of Adrian sitting with Angela and came over, George smiling, Lucy trailing behind her father.

'Hello, Adrian,' George called out.

The young man rose politely to his feet and greeted George and Lucy.

'Let me get you a drink, Adrian,' George said, smiling.

The two men chatted easily as though they were old friends. They had a lot in common. Angela watched Adrian but he barely glanced at Lucy who was listening to their anecdotes and laughing.

'The gardens are lovely in the moonlight, aren't they, Lucy?' George tried to describe how the place had changed since he lived there. 'The rooms, the gardens, it's all so different, and yet it's all just the same. The hotel's been extended, of course, but the beach hasn't changed. The gardens have been developed. We had a lovely walk just now, didn't we? Seeing the gardens in the moonlight.'

'I can't get over how early it gets dark here,' Lucy said.

Adrian did not even turn to acknowledge her remark. He drained his glass and stood up, thanking George for the beer. Then he walked away without a backward glance.

'He's a nice chap,' George said, watching him go.

'Yes,' Angela agreed.

She glanced furtively at her daughter, wondering what had really happened between Lucy and Adrian while she and George had been sleeping by the pool.

7

The following morning Lucy felt her mood lighten as she dressed for breakfast. She had slept well, despite her fright when swimming in the sea the previous afternoon. Walking along the beach chatting to Adrian it had been easy to lose track of time. On the way back to the hotel she had been surprised to see how far they had walked on their way to the cove. On reflection she concluded she must have been suffering from heatstroke when she had panicked in the water. She remembered how weak she had felt. It could only have been a fish below her, with seaweed flapping around it, or perhaps a large octopus had caught her in its trailing tentacles. The movement of the water could be deceptive, making sea creatures appear human.

Whatever the truth of it might be, she recalled with embarrassment how she had accused Adrian of dragging her under the water. He must think she was a paranoid fool. Remembering how he had totally ignored her attempt at conversation the previous evening, she resolved to apologise properly for her outburst the next time she saw him. She would prefer to avoid him altogether, but it was only the fourth day of the holiday and with ten days to go she was bound to bump into him again. Her parents had latched onto him, and it might become uncomfortable if the coldness between them persisted. There was nothing else for it but to humble herself and acknowledge she had behaved badly.

After breakfast she decided to return to the quiet cove she had visited with Adrian. It would be easy enough to find, straight along the shore, and this time she was careful to pack sunblock, a hat and a bottle of water, before slinging her canvas beach bag over her shoulder.

'I'm going for a wander,' she announced cheerfully and her parents smiled up at her from their sun loungers by the pool. 'I'll be back in time for lunch.'

'Where are you going?' her mother asked.

'Just down to the beach and I might walk along the shore. I won't go far.'

'Don't stay in the sun too long.'

'No, I won't. I've got my sunblock, and my hat,' she added before she set off.

She walked slowly, admiring the deep turquoise ocean that broke softly against the shore, sparkling with froth. Once she had left the hotel behind her the beach was deserted, smooth and golden. It was idyllic. The online descriptions she had studied before the trip had failed to do the place justice, their hyperbole unable to match the reality of the natural beauty around her. Beyond the sandy beach the land was fertile with palm trees towering over lush vegetation, magnificently green and vibrant, dotted with startling splashes of colour. Reaching an outcrop of massive boulders lying across the sand, she saw a cloud of midges buzzing around a dead fish and almost turned back. Instead she looked away and held her breath as she clambered past the stinking carcase. Glistening grey stone towered ten feet above her. She left the rocks behind and kept going. Just as she was beginning to suspect she had missed the bay it opened out before her in an almost perfect semicircle of shoreline.

Sitting on a low boulder in the shade of a gnarled takamaka tree she had a long drink, the water in her bottle already tepid.

Taking out her phone she took a series of pictures, although no photograph could reproduce the feel of the sea breeze on her face, the colours of the palm trees and glorious flowering bushes, or the sound of waves on the sand. Her pictures would serve as souvenirs, something to cling to when her recollection faded. Over the past few weeks, so many people had assured her that the memory of her pain would fade in time. It was true. Here on this beautiful morning she had barely given Darren a thought. Frothy white water raced up the beach. As each wave drew back, the sand appeared to dry instantaneously. She was not sure if that was due to the heat drying out the sand, or if the water seeped down rapidly to leave the surface dry.

She could have stayed there all day, lazing in the shade, watching the ocean, but she had told her parents she would be back for lunch and she knew her mother would fret if she was late. Reluctantly she gathered up her belongings and started on her slow trek back to the hotel. It was too hot to hurry. Instead of walking along the edge of the sea where she would be exposed to the sun, she kept to the dappled shade of ancient trees that formed a backdrop to the beach.

Reaching the stretch of massive grey boulders she picked her way between the smaller ones, again avoiding looking at the dead fish. She lost her footing on the smooth surface of a boulder and nearly slipped over. Her heart thumped as she regained her balance. Placing her feet with care and advancing laboriously, she stepped out from the rocky terrain onto soft sand. This was too beautiful a setting to abandon to memory completely. As she rummaged inside her bag for her phone, the rhythmic crashing of waves breaking against the rocks was disturbed by a loud thud. Spinning round, she saw a large boulder lying on the sand only a couple of inches away from her. It had not been lying in her path a few seconds earlier. If she had not stopped to find her phone, her blood would now be seeping into the yellow sand, her bones crushed by the huge lump of granite. Her phone slipped from her hand. She took a step back on trembling legs, as though the inert rock was threatening her.

Shading her eyes with one hand she stared up at the huge wall of rock, but could see no signs of disturbance. It must have been a random boulder that had fallen in her path. She wondered if the vibrations from her footsteps could have dislodged it from some precarious perch high above her. It was hard to believe the rock had fallen by coincidence, exactly in the spot where she was walking. Dazzled by the light and dazed with shock, she thought she saw the silhouette of a person outlined against the sky. In the time it took her to blink, the outline had disappeared. A few seconds later she spotted a figure loping away towards the road. No sooner had it appeared than it vanished, leaving her wondering if her eyes had been playing tricks on her.

Terrified that the boulder at her feet could be followed by more, she stuffed her phone back in her beach bag, and tottered down towards the sea. Kicking off her sandals, she splashed through the shallow water, making her way back to the hotel as quickly as she could. She seemed to be walking forever. Her shoulders were turning red and slightly sore to the touch as she drew near the hotel. She expected her parents to be on their feet demanding to know where she had been all that time and was surprised when they both just smiled up at her from their sun loungers as though they had not missed her at all. Lucy smiled, relieved, although her face felt strangely taut. She did not want to upset her parents on their dream holiday. She kept her sunglasses on, afraid her eyes would reveal her consternation.

'Are you all right?' her mother asked, sitting up. She stared closely at Lucy, frowning. 'You look a bit red. Did you get burned?'

'No, I don't think so. I'm fine, really. I think I'll go up to my room for a bit.'

'What about lunch? We waited for you.'

Lucy shrugged. She was no longer hungry.

'I just want to lie down for a while.'

'Are you sure you didn't get too much sun?'

'No, I'm just tired, but I'm fine, really. You go ahead and have lunch and I'll see you later. And stop worrying. I didn't get too much sun.'

'Too much ice cream, more likely,' her father grinned.

'Yes, I think that's it,' Lucy lied and turned away, relieved to have escaped further interrogation.

Back in her room she wondered whether to report what had happened. If there was a serious risk of rock falls along that part of the coast, perhaps the authorities should be alerted. But away from the beach she was no longer convinced a rock had actually fallen in her path. It might have been there all the time without her noticing it. There were so many granite boulders lying around on the sand. The sound she had interpreted as a thud could have been a wave crashing against the shore. And the figure she thought she had discerned on top of the rock could have been a creation of her overactive imagination, like the fish woman she had imagined the previous day. She closed her eyes and tried to block out the disconcerting thought that she was imagining dangers where none existed. With shock and distress over her failed relationship distorting everything, she was starting to lose confidence in her own sanity.

An alternative occurred to her, equally disturbing: someone on the island was attacking her.

8

That evening Lucy and her parents went to the buffet for dinner. Once again, the food was superb: a long table covered with mounds of fresh seafood, dish after dish of colourful local vegetables, a bewildering variety of curries, different rice dishes, and more fruit than could possibly be eaten in one evening by the residents and staff of the hotel. It was like returning to the market in Victoria, and frustrating that there were too many wonderful dishes to sample everything. Lucy tried a tiny fat banana. Not as sweet as the ones she had at home, it was far tastier, moist and almost lemony in flavour.

'The bananas are gorgeous, but it's all too much,' Lucy groaned, smiling.

'At least it's all healthy,' her mother replied.

'I told you the food would be sensational,' her father said complacently, as though he was personally responsible for the catering.

Lucy felt a little awkward when Adrian approached their table, remembering how dismissive he had been the last time she had seen him.

'Adrian, nice to see you. Come and join us,' her father greeted him effusively.

Adrian glanced at Lucy before taking a seat. The conversation flowed easily between the two men and before long Lucy began to relax, watching her parents enjoying themselves. Her father leaned back in his chair and roared with laughter over some reminiscence of hotel life while Adrian protested that a new system had been introduced to improve the running of the hotel. Her father was sceptical about the progress, Adrian defensive, and they sparred good-naturedly for a while.

'How about you, Lucy?' Adrian turned to her civilly.

Describing her return to the cove where they had gone swimming together, Lucy held back from telling him about the rockfall, so as not to alarm her parents.

'Just enjoying the weather,' she replied vaguely, and Adrian turned back to her father.

After dinner, Adrian invited Lucy to accompany him on a stroll outside. Catching a smug expression on her mother's face, Lucy felt herself blush but it was a beautiful evening and she could not resist the allure of the floodlit gardens. She wanted to follow up on her resolution to apologise properly to him and clear the air. It would also give her an opportunity to mention the rock fall to Adrian without worrying her parents. She did not really care if he thought she was barmy, but if there was a chance it could be dangerous to walk along that stretch of beach, she ought to mention it to someone.

They walked in silence for a while, the night air cool on her bare arms. Reaching the edge of the garden they sat on a bench and gazed at the ocean, rippling in the moonlight.

'It's so beautiful here,' Lucy said at last.

At her side, Adrian murmured assent.

'Adrian . . .'

She paused, aware that he had turned to look at her. He did not speak and she was grateful for his patience, or perhaps it was indifference. Either way, it was not important. Before confiding what had happened that morning, she needed to apologise. In ten days' time she would be leaving and they would never see one another again. Her apology was for his benefit, but also to make her feel better about herself. She wanted to behave like her old self, and not like a sour cynic.

'Adrian, I owe you an apology.'

'An apology? What for?'

Lucy gazed up at the stars piercing the darkness, clear and bright. Palm trees swayed above her, silhouetted against the sky. She listened to the soft swishing of waves against the shore. Behind her faint noises drifted out to them from the hotel: voices, laughter, music.

'Thank you, but you know very well what I'm talking about. I behaved like an idiot yesterday when we went swimming, and I'm sorry. I don't know what came over me but I – well, I got a fright in the water. I thought I was going to drown, and I just lost it. But I had no right to take it out on you and I'm sorry. I overreacted and I'm sorry.'

In the darkness it sounded as though he was chuckling.

'OK, I get it, you're sorry,' he said. 'Enough apologising. It's not necessary.'

'And,' she ploughed on, 'I want to thank you for saving my life.'

'Like I said, it could easily have been the other way round. Forget it.'

'But—'

He interrupted, and his voice sounded warm, as though he was smiling. 'You're on holiday. Relax and enjoy it.'

Adrian stretched his arms above his head and brought them to rest crossed behind his head. He leaned back and heaved a contented sigh staring up at the sky.

'Take it from me, this place is perfect.'

'Nothing's perfect. There must be a downside. What if there's a hurricane?'

Adrian explained that the Seychelles lay outside the cyclone belt and consequently avoided the hurricanes that struck the region.

'Tropical storms then?'

'It certainly rains a lot. That's why it's so green here. But it's nothing like rain in England. It's never cold here so when you get wet you just dry off again. It's no big deal. Actually the rain can be quite a relief from the heat and the humidity.'

'What about rock falls?' she hazarded, trying to bring up the subject of the rock that had nearly crushed her. She might love the island, but it did not seem to like her very much.

Adrian laughed. 'Must you really insist on talking about imaginary dangers?'

Haltingly, Lucy told him about the rock that had fallen in her path. 'The thing is, I think I saw someone on the rocks above me—'

'Is this your mystery assailant again?'

'You're laughing at me.'

'Not at you, but at your imaginary dangers. Look, Lucy, you're perfectly safe here. Watch out for pickpockets in the capital, and don't go swimming on your own, and you'll be perfectly safe. Give yourself a chance to relax. It'll do you good.'

Lucy had wondered whether to mention the rock fall to her father when her mother was not around to panic. Adrian's scepticism decided her. While her father would no doubt dismiss her fears as unfounded, he might tell her mother, who would almost certainly be thrown into a tizz over something Lucy had imagined. The incident was best forgotten. Grateful for Adrian's common sense, she was pleased she had confided in him before speaking to her father.

'You're right,' she said, smiling at him in the darkness. 'Thank you.'

After a short walk around the gardens they went back past the pool to the hotel. As they approached the patio they saw an old man in a straw hat sweeping the floor tiles with a large flat broom. His hunched shoulders might have been the result of years of some particular physical activity distorting his posture or it could be a congenital developmental defect that caused his spine to curve in that way. A cigarette hung off his bottom lip. He glanced up at them and Lucy recognised his weather-beaten face.

'I've seen that man before,' Lucy muttered.

Adrian told her that was hardly surprising. The old man was often seen around the hotel, sweeping the paths.

'He doesn't talk much but he's willing to work, which is more than you can say for most Seychellois.'

They watched him for a few seconds as he carefully swept fallen petals into a small white heap in a corner of the patio.

The old man glanced up. Seeing them watching him he nodded across the pool, calling out in a strong Creole accent.

'You taking good care of the English girl?'

Adrian called back that he was.

'But can you take care of yourself?'

The old man seemed to be addressing Lucy, peering at her from beneath the brim of his tattered straw hat, before he turned back to his sweeping.

'Who is he?'

'Just one of the locals who hang around the place sweeping. They're everywhere. You'll see them raking seaweed off the sand in the mornings. That's why the beaches look so clean.' He nodded at the old sweeper. 'He's completely batty but quite harmless, and very willing to work in exchange for beer and food.'

'Doesn't he get paid?'

'He gets a pittance, but it's not as if he spends much time here. It's not a bad way to live, sweeping in the hotels, with no responsibilities and no worries.' He heaved a sigh.

'Where does he sleep?'

Adrian shrugged. 'I've no idea. He just comes and goes. He's a bit of mystery really.'

Lucy looked round, interested. 'What do you mean, mystery?'

Adrian laughed. 'I wouldn't let your imagination start running wild again. There was some story about him, some tragedy in his life, but I don't know what it was. Anyway, he seems to like sweeping the patio. He's harmless.'

9

THE NEXT DAY, GEORGE and Lucy went for a trip in a glass-bottomed boat with a group of Americans. It was a half-day trip but they would be gone for most of the day, embarking in Victoria.

'The fish are spectacular!' George enthused. 'You're going to love this, Lucy.'

To her parents' surprise Lucy had lost interest in snorkelling, although she had been looking forward to it before the trip. When it came to it, she seemed nervous of going in the water, but she was very keen to view the multi-coloured marine life from a boat, and George was happy to accompany her.

'I haven't been out in a glass-bottomed boat for years,' he grinned.

Angela had decided to stay behind and spend the day reading by the pool. She did not admit as much to George and Lucy but she was keen for the two of them to spend time together. Like his wife, George had spent hours listening to Lucy agonise over the breakdown of her relationship with the rat she had planned to marry. It would do them both good to spend time together just having fun. Angela reached for her chilled lemonade, lingering over the feel of the glass, cold against her fingers. There was no doubt the holiday was doing Lucy good, and George seemed more relaxed than he had been in a long time. Already the experience of the past month was drifting away; they would return home revitalised and ready to move on. She picked up her book, tossing the thought aside. She did not want to think about England yet. The end of their holiday would come around soon enough. In the meantime, she wanted to enjoy every moment on the island.

She must have dozed off because although she had no recollection of time passing, her glass was no longer cold. Glancing at her watch she saw that the morning was not yet half over. Slinging her bag over her shoulder, she strolled back towards the hotel. Pausing on a narrow pathway between dense bushes of purple-flowering hibiscus and frangipani trees with delicate white blooms, she breathed in their perfumes, closing her eyes to shut out any other sensation.

George and Lucy would not be back until late afternoon. Fully awake now, Angela wandered back to the air-conditioned bedroom and looked around for the book she had been reading. Realising she had left it in the pool area, and too lazy to venture out in the heat again, she decided to lie on the bed and read something on George's Kindle instead. He was unlikely to have taken it with him on the boat trip. Not seeing it anywhere in the room, she opened his case to check if he had left it in there. It would be just like him to hide his Kindle, so none of the hotel staff could be tempted to pinch it.

'I'm not suspicious, just careful,' he would say, whenever she laughed at his caution.

Rummaging through his shorts and shirts, she found his Kindle and put it on the bed before going to shower. Returning to the bedroom, she noticed an envelope on the floor just inside the door. She was sure it had not been there a few moments earlier when she had gone into the bathroom. Wrapped in her towel, she opened the envelope and was surprised to see a letter in George's handwriting.

She was intrigued. He never hand letters by hand. As she sat on the bed reading, her curiosity turned to disbelief.

Dear Veronique

I hope my last letter reached you. It's been a long time, but I promised you I'd return to see my dark angel. I'm back on the island, staying at the Garden of Eden. Please send a message if you'd like to meet.

I've not forgotten our time together.

It was signed 'G'.

A second sheet of paper had a note scribbled in capital letters.

Meet me on the beach today if you want to know the truth about George. I'll be waiting for you.

It was signed 'the dark angel'.

As Angela re-read the letter her shock gave way to fury while her mind raced through the implications of the message. Lucy had been unhinged when she discovered Darren had been cheating on her for two years. George had been keeping a secret from her throughout a twenty-five year marriage. She read his letter again. Clearly George had been having a relationship with a woman called Veronique when he had lived on the island over thirty years ago. He had promised to return, and now he was back, ready to resume their affair. He had 'not forgotten' their time together, indeed! Leading Angela to believe he was bringing her to the Seychelles for a romantic holiday, in reality he had come back hoping to hook up with a former lover he called his dark angel. It was unforgivable. After tearing up the note from Veronique and throwing the tiny scraps of paper in the bin, she thrust George's letter in her beach bag, packed her make up and purse, slipped her phone in her pocket, and left the room, slamming the door behind her. George had returned. She would not.

Reaching the ground floor of the hotel, she hesitated. The note had only said Veronique would be waiting for her on the beach. It had not specified where, exactly. Her legs were shaking as she turned and made her way past the pool and down towards the sea. She wondered if Veronique was looking out for her. Perhaps she was watching her as she left the hotel and began to cross a deserted stretch of beach. Still trembling with rage, she walked through an area of overgrown trees at the top of the beach, keeping in the shade as much as possible.

Despite her caution, she must have been exposed to the sun for too long, because her head was pounding. When she tried to open her eyes, she could not focus on anything. She closed her eyes again and waited for the fog to lift.

She must have passed out because when she came to she was lying on her side. Terror gripped her. There was a smell of body odour and stale tobacco. When she tried to look around everything was dark. Slowly she opened her eyes and felt her eyelashes brush against something. She tried opening first one eye, then the other. She was not mistaken. Something touched her eyelashes, almost imperceptibly, as they moved. Instinctively reaching up, she found that she could not move her hands.

'Is anybody there?' she called out, terrified. 'What's happened? Have I had an accident?'

The last thing she could remember was walking along the beach, furious after reading George's letter. Perhaps she had wandered up to the road and been knocked down. She wriggled her limbs. Her legs moved freely. She could raise her elbows, but her wrists felt as though they were securely tied behind her back.

'Am I in an ambulance? Why can't I move my hands? What's happened to me?'

A dry, husky voice whispered close to her ear, startling her. 'George's wife.'

Angela felt a stab of fear hearing her husband's name. 'Veronique? Is that you?'

There was no answer.

Angela tried to sound firm. 'Who are you? What do you want with me? I want to see my husband.'

There was no answer. A door slammed shut, making the floor shake. It vibrated as an engine spluttered into action.

'Where are we going?'

No one answered.

Fighting to quell her panic, she tried to work out what was happening. It was difficult, when nothing made any sense. She was tied up, blindfolded and lying down in a moving vehicle. Scrabbling on the floor beneath her with her fingers, she clutched at what felt like small soft petals spread out on a metal floor.

'Where am I? Where are you taking me?'

Overwhelmed, she broke off, sobbing helplessly. Her bag was no longer over her shoulder. Cautiously she shuffled around the floor, searching for it. If she could find her phone, she could call for help. They drove for what seemed to be hours while she searched the floor in vain, finding nothing but a thick layer of petals. Without warning the vehicle turned sharply and slowed down. The floor tilted as they jolted wildly along a bumpy road. They appeared to be climbing. Rolling over, she felt her phone pressing against her leg. It had been in her pocket all the time but, with her hands tied behind her back, she could not reach it. At last they juddered to a halt. Angela tensed as she heard the door creak open.

'It has been a very long time,' the dry voice whispered, close to her.

'What has? What are you talking about? I demand to know who you are. If it's money you're after, you've chosen the wrong person to kidnap. We're not rich people. All our money's tied up in our house—'

Beside her, she heard a sound like spitting. 'I do not want your money.'

With a sick feeling in the pit of her stomach, Angela understood. 'I know who you are. You won't get away with this. And you won't get him back. Not like this. He'll hate you for it. Do you really think he'll want you back after you've mistreated me so atrociously? You're insane!'

Her voice broke as she realised the truth of her own words. She was in the power of a woman who saw her as a rival. And that woman was mad.

10

It seemed to take ages for the excursion to set off from the port area, given that the hotel had booked their seats on the glass-bottomed boat trip and they had paid in advance. As they were sitting around waiting to board, a large American woman dressed in garish orange and yellow accosted Lucy.

'Do you speak English?'

'Yes. I am English.'

'Oh my. I just love that accent. Do you mind if I join you?'

Before Lucy could respond that she was keeping the chair beside her for her father, the woman sat down and introduced herself as Gloria from Texas.

'I'm Lucy.'

'And where are you from?'

'We're from London.'

'Oh well, what do you know? Did you hear that, Billy? She's from London, England. We just love London.'

Lucy looked up and saw her father buttonholed by a stout man in gaudy Hawaiian shirt and Texan hat, an outsize camera hanging on a leather strap around his thick neck.

'I'm Billy from Texas,' he boomed in rich bass tones, 'and that's my Gloria over there, talking with your young lady. And those are our two girls, Tess and Paula.'

Lucy looked over at two well-built girls with curly fair hair and plain faces who looked about the same age as her. They were identical apart from their hair which they wore at different lengths, perhaps to distinguish themselves from each other.

'Tess is the one with long hair,' Gloria confided. 'Aren't they just something? Come with me and I'll introduce you. Come on, don't be shy. I know they'll be dying to meet you.'

Without waiting for a response, Gloria seized her by the hand and led her over to the twins. Lucy stood flanked by the girls who smiled warmly at her. Out of the corner of her eye she saw Billy wink at George as they passed.

'Ah, she's your daughter. I thought that must be it. There's a definite family resemblance. But you can't go jumping to conclusions these days. I didn't want to go putting my foot in it,' he boomed conspiratorially. Leaning forward, he lowered his voice. For a moment Lucy could not hear what he was saying. 'He wasn't best pleased, I can tell you, being mistaken for his new wife's father!' Billy bellowed suddenly. He threw his head back and guffawed, the veins in his thick neck standing out.

His laughter was infectious, and Lucy's father joined in. Meanwhile Gloria had gone to sit down, leaving Tess and Paula vying for Lucy's attention. The Americans were all stereotypically loud and brash, and immensely affable.

At last the captain ticked their names on his list and they climbed aboard and took their seats. Their guide was wearing a dirty sling inside which they could see his bandaged forearm.

'Don't tell me that was a shark took a lump out of your arm?' Billy from Texas wanted to know.

Gloria slapped her palms against her cheeks, her mouth gaping in mock horror. 'Oh my!'

The guide shook his head and stared out at the sea without answering.

'He was fishing,' the captain called out, 'and a tuna grabbed a mouthful.'

'It happens,' the man in the sling said, adding that it was a bloody big tuna. He grinned and smacked his lips with a loud sucking sound. 'He made a good dinner!'

Seated around the glass window in the bottom of the boat, Lucy watched fish swimming very close, easy to see in the clear water. She was sitting between the twins who screeched with delight at every sighting of a fish. They all cooed with excitement when a small turtle swam past. Her father looked more relaxed than she had seen him since her break up with Darren. Lucy felt a pang of guilt. She had barely considered the effect of her own distress on her parents and made a silent vow to try and keep her misery to herself from now on. She had dragged them into her depression for long enough. It was time life returned to normal for them all.

It was easy to engage in conversation about the brilliantly coloured tropical fish that swam in the seas around the islands. Her father recognised many of them from his previous stay in Mahé although he could not remember all the names. Lucy listened intently as their guide pointed out stripy silver-and-black zebra fish, long thin trumpet fish that looked like small eels, brilliant blue-and-yellow emperor fish, and lion fish with their orange stripes and bizarre turquoise crests fanning out along their bodies like the spokes of a giant comb. Her father identified orange-, black-and-white clown fish, and a red snapper floating lazily past.

'That would make a decent plateful,' Billy laughed when George told him what it was. 'Have you tried the fishing yet, George?'

Her father shook his head. He seemed too preoccupied with watching the sea creatures to mention that he had lived on Mahé, many years ago.

'Look at that!' Paula called out suddenly, pointing towards the horizon. Lucy looked up just in time to catch the tail end of a shoal of flying fish leaping out of the water in graceful formation.

'There must be a shark chasing them,' their guide explained.

They all scanned the sea in vain for the tip of a black fin travelling in the wake of the speeding fish.

'As long as it's only fish they're after,' Billy said, with a meaningful nod at the guide's bandaged arm. 'You wouldn't want a shark taking a bite out of you. A tuna's bad enough.'

The guide shook his head. 'I been swimming in these waters nearly forty years, and I never had a problem with sharks yet.'

'There were two fatal shark attacks in these waters last year, off Praslin Island,' Tess piped up eagerly. 'I read up about it before we came. The first victim was a Frenchman.'

Paula gasped audibly and the guide interrupted quickly.

'That was an isolated incident with a rogue shark. It didn't come from round here. It killed a Frenchman, yes, but that was—'

'There were two deaths last year,' Tess corrected him. 'That's two people killed by sharks, the Frenchman and an Englishman. The Frenchman's arm was bitten clean off – or was that the Brit?' She turned to her sister. 'He was on his honeymoon.'

'That's so terrible,' Paula wailed. 'The poor girl he was married to. Can you imagine?'

The guide turned and spat over the side of the boat. 'Those were random attacks, the first in over forty years,' he insisted. 'The waters here are completely safe for swimming and diving. That was a freak accident last year. We don't have any problems here. Believe me, there are no dangerous creatures where we go diving. It's like an aquarium. You can see for yourselves.'

He nodded at the glass bottom of the boat and they all looked down.

'Check out the size of that monster!' Billy called out as a large sting ray glided past. They watched it sashay through the water oblivious to their exclamations of delight.

'Do any of the fish look like women?' Lucy asked the guide.

'A fish like a woman?' he repeated, sounding surprised. 'Do you mean mermaids?'

'Bless you, dear, there's no such thing,' Gloria burst out, throwing Lucy's father a sympathetic glance. Clearly she thought Lucy was some kind of half-wit. George just shrugged his shoulders as if to say, what can you do? Lucy ignored them.

'Manatees, that's what she means,' Billy called out.

'Manatees?'

Billy's huge brimmed hat wobbled as he nodded energetically. 'Manatees look like sea lions but they're large fish that are supposed to resemble human beings.'

Gloria reached across to pat his belly and laughed. 'You speak for yourself, Billy Warton.'

'Manatees are mammals, not fish,' Tess pointed out.

Ignoring the interruptions, Billy continued his dissertation, keen to share what little he knew. 'According to some historians they were responsible for the whole mythology that grew up about mermaids, because sailors mistook them for half-naked women with fish tails.'

An octopus drifted past their window, part of their own world yet utterly alien, its tentacles weaving the water.

'They're so weird,' Lucy commented to no one in particular.

'I've always said that if there is life on other planets it won't be half so different from us as the creatures we have here on earth under the sea,' one of the twins agreed.

'You know octopuses can distinguish between horizontal and diagonal planes?' Billy told them.

'What he doesn't know about marine life,' Gloria said, tapping his fleshy arm. 'It's a hobby of his. Now don't you go boring all these good people with your useless information.'

'It's not useless,' he protested.

Lucy's father agreed, assuring Gloria he was interested in hearing more. Billy's two daughters exchanged bleak glances.

'What's the biggest octopus anyone's ever seen in these parts?' Lucy asked.

The question sparked some desultory speculation but no one knew the answer. They passed over a reef of knobbly white coral. A few rainbow-coloured fish darted in and out of sight. A whole group simultaneously changed direction with one flick of their tails. The colours were breathtaking, seeming to glow and sparkle in the water like living gemstones. Shoals of bright red-and-yellow fish slid among the corals and others passed by, blue fading to yellow, and anemone fish, black, white and yellow. Their guide pointed out a giraffe crab, its long claws resting on the ocean floor.

In one place they saw a bank of fine black strands swaying in the water. At first glance it looked like human hair. Lucy leaned forward, transfixed.

'What's that?'

'What?'

The black weed drifted out of view.

'I just saw something that looked like black hair. What was it?'

'That was Tess's hair getting in the way,' Paula joked.

'No,' Lucy insisted. 'It was some kind of weed in the water that looked like black hair.'

'What you just saw was black coral,' the guide told her. 'It's very rare now. It looks like a small tree, but it's actually coral, one of the oldest continually living species on the planet.'

'Wow!' Gloria exclaimed.

'Black coral,' Lucy repeated.

'I had some once but I don't know what happened to it,' Lucy's father said. 'It got lost after I took it home to England.'

The guide turned to him with a frown. 'I wouldn't try to take it out of the country if I were you. It's internationally protected as an endangered species. You could get yourself in serious trouble.'

'Oh, I'm going back more than thirty years ago,' he assured him.

'You've been here before?' Billy seized on the remark. 'Well, you're a dark horse, George. So you were actually over here thirty years ago, eh? You must have seen a few changes since then.'

'I had a contract to work here for a year but had to leave when there was a coup in 'seventy-seven, not long after the islands became independent.'

Billy nodded. 'I read about that before the trip.' He turned to his wife. 'You hear that, Gloria? George was living right here in the Seychelles when they had a coup d'état back in the seventies. So,' he turned back to George, 'what made you come to work here all those years ago?'

Her father inclined his head at the question. Young, newly qualified and broke, he explained how he had decided to take advantage of the tax exemptions available to those working abroad. Within a couple of years he had planned to have enough put by for a deposit on a flat of his own. Billy nodded in approval as George explained his youthful plans.

With a show of reluctance, Lucy's father began telling his new acquaintances about his life on the island. Lucy could tell he did not really mind. On the contrary, once he started he clearly enjoyed relating anecdotes from what he called 'the old days'. Billy and Gloria were a gratifying audience, fascinated by everything he told them. Lucy and her younger companions were happy to listen while they scanned the water beneath the boat for fish. Watching her father's animated face, Lucy decided the outing had definitely been worthwhile.

11

THEY LURCHED TO A halt, and Angela heard the door creak open. A gust of fresh air wafted into the vehicle. Stumbling forward on her knees, she felt her way to the open door and clambered out onto turf, springy after the metal floor. It was a relief to leave the stinking interior of the van. She straightened up, breathing deeply. The air smelt damp and green, like freshly cut grass.

'Where are you?' she called out softly.

No one answered. This could be her chance to escape. Frantically she pulled at the cord that bound her wrists, but only succeeded in making it chafe painfully. Stretching out behind her back, her fingers felt the dry rough surface of a tree trunk. Carefully she turned and leaned forward until her forehead was touching the bark. Twisting her neck, she kept her eyes tightly shut as she rubbed the side of her head against the tree. The blindfold slipped off easily. Straightening up, she turned to gaze at a green world.

In front of her stood a dilapidated hut, almost completely concealed in thick shrubbery. Bewildered, she took a step towards it. The door was bolted on the outside which meant Veronique could not be inside. Walls of moss-covered wooden planks supported a corrugated metal roof almost completely shrouded in thick ivy.

There were no windows or chimney visible. She scanned the area without seeing any sign of the woman who had brought her here. A thick mist hovered overhead, brushing the tops of the trees which surrounded her, gnarled and twisted. A reluctant intruder in an alien environment, she was lost in a forest that had put down roots in primeval times.

Fine rays of sunlight found their way through the interlocking foliage but the atmosphere was cool in contrast to the searing heat of the coastline. Hearing water cascading nearby, Angela shivered in her flimsy skirt as she squinted at the dense vegetation surrounding her. Terracotta-coloured earth was almost completely covered in a tangle of overlapping roots and ferns. Ivy or bindweed with huge leaves had wound its way around many of the ancient trunks of trees that grew incredibly high, their flat branches forming a dense canopy high above her. Even if George managed to persuade the authorities to carry out a search of the whole island, there was no way she would ever be spotted from a helicopter. Without a guide to lead her back to the road she might never find her way out of the maze of undergrowth. With her heart beating faster in terror, she forced herself to stay calm and think of a plan.

The island was only about three miles wide. The ground sloped very steeply. By walking downwards she must eventually reach the coast. Even if she failed to hit upon a direct route, the island was twenty miles from end to end. Since she was probably at least five miles in from the northernmost tip, the furthest she might possibly have to walk would be about fifteen miles, as long as she could keep going in one direction. Given that she might take a circuitous route, the coast must still be within walking distance. She just had to keep going. The terrain would be tricky to negotiate but at least she knew she had to make her way downhill. It was imperative she set off without delay. She would feel safer when she had put some distance between herself and the maniac who had brought her to this remote spot against her will. However difficult it would be with her hands tied behind her, she preferred to take her chances on her own.

Telling herself there were no poisonous snakes on Mahé, she began to pick her way between luxuriant bushes and tall trees. She reckoned she had at most six hours to find her way out of the forest before dusk. The ground was damp and the air uncomfortably humid. The Tourist Board warned visitors to avoid walking barefoot on moist soil and vegetation on the island, and she hoped her open sandals would offer sufficient protection against parasites and infection.

Everything in this strange world was green, not only the foliage but trunks and roots of trees, granite boulders, even the light. Somewhere close by she could hear running water and a faint high-pitched whistling. She had to watch where she put her feet on the uneven stony ground. A dense network of moss-covered roots and trailing woody stems threatened to trip her at every step. Creepers straddled green branches alongside strands resembling pale green hair. Inching her way forward, she lost her balance. Stifling an involuntary shriek she reached out with her elbow in an attempt to steady herself against a granite boulder covered with irregular olive-green circles of mould. It felt slimy and she slid forwards, grasping helplessly at the air behind her as she sank to her knees. Close up, she noticed a sweet aroma from a fleshy-leaved plant growing on the surface of the rock. The fragility of its tiny white flowers flourishing in so dark a place made her want to weep.

A bullet-shaped black beetle crawled across the rock on spindly legs. She drew back with a low cry and clambered to her feet, ripping her skirt. Her legs shook as pain stabbed her knee where she had fallen on it, and she struggled to suppress a growing sense of despair. Sodden with sweat and the humidity of the atmosphere, she had no idea where she was. As she began to edge forward again, the silence was disturbed by a shrill sound. It took her a second to realise that her phone was ringing. George must be calling her. Perhaps he was already on his way back from Victoria. If she managed to retrieve the phone from her pocket, she might be able to answer, and tell him what had happened. The police might even be able to pinpoint her exact location if she kept the phone switched on. Frantically she struggled to reach her phone with her elbow. With her hands tied behind her back, her efforts proved futile. Bending forward as far as she could, she tried to knock the phone out of her pocket with her chin. She lifted one knee and jiggled it about, but it was no use. The phone was impossible to dislodge. Frustrated, she watched the fabric of her skirt vibrate with the ringing. After a moment it stopped. The ensuing silence seemed to close in on her, suffocating her.

As she gathered her strength to move on, a clump of giant ferns rustled to her left. She spun round and froze, unable to breathe, wondering what had disturbed the ten-metre-high fronds. Too late she heard shuffling, and an intake of breath that was not her own. As a rough bag was thrust over her head, she took an involuntary step forward and felt her feet slide beneath her. A hand grabbed her by the arm, preventing her from falling. Her phone was snatched roughly from her pocket. The hand on her arm shook with the movement as a foot stamped repeatedly on the ground beside her. She knew her phone was being smashed.

Ignoring her demands that she be released, her captor grasped her tightly by both arms and pushed her forwards, holding her upright every time her feet skidded on the wet leaf humus that carpeted the ground. She had no idea where she was going. All at once she was shoved violently in the back, and she heard a door slam shut. For all her struggle across difficult terrain, she had not travelled any distance at all from the ramshackle hut. Before she could gather her wits, her wrists were shackled in what felt like handcuffs. The cold sharp edge of metal pressed into her flesh when she wriggled her hands.

From behind her, the bag was lifted off her head. She caught a fleeting glimpse of a green gecko motionless on the wall, before the blindfold was pulled back down over her eyes. Without warning she doubled over and retched gobbets of sour-smelling vomit. She straightened up, her teeth chattering and her whole body shaking uncontrollably.

'You can't keep me here,' she protested. Shaking her arms, she heard chains rattle behind her back. 'They'll be searching for me. The police will find me. You won't get away with this. My husband will be here soon. Take me back right now and we can forget all about it, pretend it never happened.'

Thirst gripped her so she could no longer speak. She was aware only of the bitter taste of vomit in her throat.

'If this is some kind of sick joke . . .' she began.

Her voice cracked and she struggled to swallow, her mouth was so dry. She thought she was going to be sick again. Hearing the door slam shut, she started forward. Chained to the wall, she found she could only shuffle a few steps in any direction.

'Don't leave me here,' she called out, terrified she had been left there to die alone in the darkness.

12

THE BOAT TRIP ENDED half an hour later than scheduled but no one minded. They had all enjoyed the outing. By the time they disembarked, Lucy felt almost sorry to be leaving the company of her cheery American companions. Billy and Gloria's hotel was the first stop. As the bus trundled them back along the coastal road, Gloria invited George and Lucy to join them for dinner.

'They do a wonderful buffet here,' she insisted. 'The food in this place is to die for!'

'Too true,' Billy concurred, glancing ruefully down at his sizeable paunch.

The hotel where Gloria and Billy where staying with their daughters was only a few miles along the coast from the Garden of Eden.

'That's decided then! You'll join us. You can take a cab back from our place later. How far can it be on this tiny island? The bus driver won't give a damn. If he doesn't have to drop you off, he'll be able to scoot off earlier. Come on, George, let Billy and me treat you and Lucy to dinner. We're longing to hear more of your stories.'

Lucy's father thanked her, explaining that although he and Lucy would love to spend the evening with them, they had to return to their own hotel where his wife would be waiting for them. The bus rattled on between lush slopes and the blue expanse of the ocean stretching away to the horizon. Sandwiched between the twins, Lucy listened to the discussion.

'Give your wife a call and tell her to come along. She can grab a cab from the hotel. We'd love to have her join us.'

George wavered but Lucy could see he wanted to carry on talking to the Americans.

'Why don't you give Mum a call?' she said. 'It might be fun.'

'That's decided then,' her father said. He sounded pleased. 'I'll call my wife right away. I'm sure you'll get on well together.'

He tried a couple of times but Angela's phone went straight to voicemail.

'Come on, George, we're nearly there,' Billy called out. 'What do you say?'

'I can't get hold of my wife, but I'm sure she'll get in touch when she wakes up and she can come and join us if it's not too late.'

The buffet was similar to the one laid on in the Garden of Even every evening.

'What's this one?' Gloria asked a passing waiter. She pointed at one of the dishes. 'I don't remember seeing this before.'

'That is octopus curry, madam.'

Gloria grimaced as the waiter walked away.

'Octopus curry?' she repeated, laughing. 'Is it any good?'

George shrugged. 'I don't know. I never tried it.'

'You lived here and you never sampled the octopus curry?' Billy said.

'Well, you can let me know what I've been missing.'

'Not bloody likely!'

'If you dream about eating curry, it means you're worried about someone you love, and you're going to face difficult times ahead,' Paula informed them earnestly.

Behind the American girl's back, Lucy raised her eyebrows at her father who grinned.

'Oh, stop with all your dream interpretations,' Gloria scolded her daughter. 'As if anyone in their right mind would dream about eating curry! I can't recall ever dreaming about curry. How about you, George? Did you ever dream about eating curry?'

Paula shook her head with a resigned shrug. This was clearly not the first time she had discussed the interpretation of dreams with her mother.

The initial excitement at their meeting palled with the fading light. As soon as they finished their main course Paula and Tess made their apologies and disappeared, promising they would call Lucy and arrange to see her again soon.

'Young women these days,' Billy said with a complacent shrug of his huge shoulders. 'They're off to Victoria with a couple of guys from Boston. Would you believe they met right here in the hotel?'

Gloria and Billy were sampling desserts.

'You've got to try these, Billy,' Gloria insisted, as she tucked into a banana cake dripping with syrup. 'It's the best yet! Out of this world! Even better than those pancakes.'

'Just let me finish this panna cotta and I'll be on it. How about you, George? What are you having?'

Lucy yawned and glanced at her father to try and indicate subtly that she was ready to leave, although it would be rude of her to say anything before their hosts had finished eating.

Lucy's father had a signal and could not understand why he had not heard from his wife.

'She's probably lost her phone, or forgotten to charge it,' Billy assured him. 'Gloria does that all the time. I mean, all the time.'

'Oh, stop it, you big bully.'

Gloria flicked his arm with her napkin.

'I lost my phone once,' she explained earnestly. 'And he hasn't let me forget it.'

Lucy's father did not reply. He looked tired. Lucy could not care less whether Gloria had lost her mobile once or fifty times. After this evening they would never see the American family again.

They had not discussed with Lucy's mother what time they expected to return from the outing and she probably assumed they were still involved in the boat trip which, in a manner of speaking, they were. In any case, she clearly was not concerned about them or she would have been in touch by now. She could always call them from the hotel even if she had lost her phone which was, of course, possible.

Just as Lucy thought her father was about to stand up, Billy began pumping him about his experiences during the coup and Gloria asked to see the photographs Lucy had taken on the boat trip. She seemed surprised that all the pictures were of marine life. Gloria showed Lucy her own photographs, each one of Billy or their daughters, at the hotel and the beach, and on the boat trip and even on the bus. There were pictures of Tess and Paula with Lucy, and Billy with George. Gloria offered to send them to Lucy who thanked her weakly.

'Come on, George, just one more night cap,' Billy insisted, when Lucy's father finally stood up to leave.

It was nearly eleven by the time they returned to the Garden of Eden. Lucy agreed when her father suggested they go straight to bed.

'I hadn't realised how tired I was till we got in the taxi,' she fibbed. 'But thanks, Dad. It's been a lovely day.'

'I'm afraid we allowed ourselves to get a bit swamped by the Americans.'

'Not at all. They were sweet. Well, OK,' she added, seeing the expression on his face, 'they were a bit overpowering. But they were nice with it. And it was worth it to see those fish! I got some brilliant photos.'

He nodded, pleased. 'You can show us in the morning.'

'Yes, good night, Dad. And thanks again.'

Lucy went to her room and kicked off her shoes. For a few minutes she sat on her bed, too weary to move. The heat had been debilitating during the day. She was looking forward to taking a shower before falling into bed, when there was a knock at her door.

13

'DAD? WHAT'S UP? YOU look as if you—'

Her father opened his mouth to answer but his eyes suddenly welled up and he could not speak. Shocked into action at seeing him so emotional, Lucy pulled him into her room and sat him down on the bed.

'Dad? What is it? Tell me. Are you ill?'

He shook his head.

'Is it Mum? Something's wrong with her, isn't it? Tell me!'

'I can't find her.'

She did not answer straight away but watched his face, frowning, as he stumbled through his account.

'When I got back to the room, she wasn't there. She wasn't in the room. I went and had a look around downstairs but I couldn't see her anywhere. I checked everywhere, by the pool, in the gardens, the bar, but she isn't anywhere—'

'Perhaps she went for a walk—'

'It's half past eleven, Lucy. You know your mother. She'd never wander off without letting us know where she was going.'

'She must have got lost then,' Lucy said, suddenly brisk. 'Have you tried her phone?'

Head in hands, her father told her that her mother's mobile phone was still going straight to voicemail. She had taken it along with her purse. Accustomed to relying on her father to assume control of any situation, Lucy surprised herself by taking charge. Always wanting to protect her, her father had never before turned to her for support. Ashamed of a fleeting sense of pride at taking on the responsibility so readily, she wondered what Darren would say if he could see her now. She dismissed the thought fiercely. There was no room in her mind to dwell on that scumbag right now. Her father needed her. He was all over the place. She had not realised he had drunk quite so much. He sounded close to tears.

'If it wasn't for me, we'd never have come to Mahé, and your mother would still be safely at home in England right now.'

'Don't be silly. You weren't to know she'd wander off and get lost.'

'I don't know where to look,' he mumbled.

They went to her parents' bedroom and Lucy began checking her mother's belongings systematically. She started with the bedside table then moved on to the wardrobe.

'What are you looking for? I told you she's taken her purse, and her phone. She didn't take her credit cards.'

Her father sat on a chair helplessly watching her flicking through her mother's clothes.

'She probably went to sit by the pool and dropped off.'

'She's not by the pool. I checked.'

'The point is, she didn't intend to be gone for long so she must have fallen asleep somewhere, while she was waiting for us. She left her passport and credit cards, so we know she wasn't intending to run off and not come back.'

Her father scowled at her. 'Of course she wasn't going to run off. What are you talking about? You're not helping, Lucy.'

'Yes, I didn't expect you to like the idea, but we have to be logical and consider everything. Now, we know what she left behind but what did she take with her?'

'What?'

'If we can find out what she took with her, we might be able to work out where she went. What's missing? Think, Dad! What did she take with her?'

She stared earnestly at him. He frowned, making an effort to focus on the question. Rubbing his forehead he looked anxiously round the room as he listed what was missing.

'Her purse with her cash, and her make-up bag. As far as I can remember, that is. And her key's not here, but that's about it as far as I can see.'

'So she was definitely intending to come back.'

'Of course she was going to come back. This isn't bloody *Shirley Valentine*. For God's sake, Lucy, what the hell are you trying to say?'

Ignoring his outburst, Lucy pursued her train of thought. 'What else is missing, Dad? Think!'

'She was reading a thriller and I can't see it by the bed. Then there's her sunglasses, and the sunblock that she kept in her beach bag.'

'That's a point. Where's her beach bag?'

He shook his head. 'It's not here.'

'So that's her room key, sunglasses, sunblock, book, make-up, phone, purse and beach bag. If she wasn't by the pool then she must have gone to the beach.'

They stared at one another, aghast at the possibility that Angela might have met with a terrible accident. Looking at her father's pale face, Lucy tried not to think about the fatal shark attacks that had taken place off the coast of Praslin only a year ago. The American girl's voice seemed to bray inside her head: 'The Frenchman's arm was bitten clean off – or was that the Brit . . .'

'Mum would never have gone out swimming by herself,' she

protested. 'Would she? Oh my God! The coastguard. There must be a coastguard here.'

Lucy raced from the room with her father hurrying at her heels. The receptionist in the hotel stared at them vacantly, flicking shoulder length black hair off her heavily made-up face.

'You want to report a problem, sir?' she asked with as much animation as if Lucy's father was ordering a newspaper for the morning. The phone rang and she reached for it.

'Leave that,' Lucy snapped. 'This is an emergency. It can't wait.'

'An emergency?'

'Yes, it's my wife—'

'Your wife?'

'She went to the beach this afternoon—'

'Your wife went to the beach this afternoon?'

'Yes.'

Lucy's father slapped the counter impatiently, struggling with the effort to speak calmly. Lucy took over, explaining that she and her father had been out all day and had only discovered on their return that her mother was missing.

'Your mother is missing?'

Suddenly grasping the seriousness of the situation, the receptionist called the night duty manager who immediately took them to his office where he took down a few details and promptly contacted the coastguard.

'They're on their way.'

Blinking rapidly he removed his spectacles and wiped them fussily on a large white handkerchief. A local man, he looked very young and inexperienced. He hardly inspired confidence in a crisis. Lucy insisted he instigate an immediate search of the hotel and the grounds. Replacing his glasses the manager rubbed his hands together nervously and cleared his throat.

'The coastguard will be outside soon. Any minute now, in fact.

And I'm sure – I'm sure everything will turn out well in the end. That is, I'm sure your wife is fine. It's – I'm sure we'll find her safe and sound.'

He gave a tense rictus that barely passed for a reassuring smile and rose to his feet.

'Can I offer you a drink? Courtesy of the hotel. This must be very difficult for you just now. Until we find your wife, that is.'

'Never mind the sodding drink, wake up all the staff and start looking for my wife. She could be lying unconscious somewhere in the hotel grounds.'

The manager coughed and picked up the phone. Lucy was relieved that something was being done, but summoning the coastguard gave the situation a reality she did not want to believe. When they left the manager's office she scanned the hotel foyer, hoping to see her mother, then borrowed her father's key and ran back up to the room in case she had returned. Praying under her breath, she opened the door, but her parents' room was empty. Leaving a note asking her mother to call her father at once, she hurried back downstairs. Together she and her father went down to the beach, looking around them as they went, desperately hoping to spot her mother fast asleep on a sun lounger. Meanwhile, the hotel manager had mobilised available staff to search the premises. It was possible Lucy's mother had passed out, or fallen and hit her head. The idea of her lying, unconscious, somewhere in the hotel grounds, was less terrifying than the thought that she might have been swept out to sea, and lost for ever.

As Lucy and her father reached the beach below the hotel, they heard the roar of a helicopter overhead. At the same time a powerful beam of light swept along the sand beside them and out across the vast expanse of water. Lucy followed it with her eyes, scrutinising the waves for any sign of movement.

'If she's out there, they'll find her,' the hotel manager said, joining them on the sand. Disconsolately they watched the beam of light as it circled continuously above the dark water, searching.

'Is she a strong swimmer?'

Lucy's father shook his head. 'Not a strong swimmer, no.'

'But she can swim,' Lucy added quickly. 'She can swim.'

'She would never have gone out in the water by herself,' her father said emphatically, as though he was trying to convince himself.

Lucy and the hotel manager looked at him but neither of them spoke. It was a clear night. A small crowd of spectators gathered on the beach, attracted by the helicopter. Lucy's father put his arm around her. Together they watched a rescue boat zoom out across the waves to vanish into the darkness.

The waiting was excruciating. After about half an hour Adrian joined them, enquiring if there was any news of Angela and whether there was anything he could do. Lucy shook her head. There was nothing any of them could do but wait and pray. No one mentioned drowning. But as time went on, and there was no news, the likelihood of finding her mother alive grew increasingly remote.

14

Angela crouched on the floor, listening intently. The next time her captor returned to the hut, she would be ready. In the hushed mountain forest she thought she could make out the distant drone of an engine, followed by footsteps shuffling through leaves. She waited. For a long time nothing happened. At last she heard the bolt slide across and the door swung open. Leaping forward, she kicked out as hard as she could. Aiming at where she thought her captor was standing, her foot jerked uselessly in empty air. An instant later a crack on the side of her head knocked her to the floor where she lay, writhing and terrified. A head injury could cause serious damage. A few seconds later the door banged shut and she heard the bolt slide across. She was alone, frightened and in pain, and desperate for the toilet. So much for her attempted escape.

She tugged at the chain, using all her weight. It was firmly attached to the wall. Clearly someone had been preparing to use this isolated place as a prison. She wondered whether other gullible tourists had been chained up in the hut while demands for money had been issued, or if this had all been set up just for her. She might be the random victim of a kidnapper, but her abductor had referred to her as 'George's wife'. It was hard to avoid the conclusion that her abduction was linked to Veronique, the mysterious woman from her husband's past. She sank to her knees and tried to analyse her situation objectively. If killing her was the purpose, she would already be dead. The fact that she was being kept alive indicated that money was the real objective, despite her kidnapper's protestations to the contrary. George had probably already been contacted with a ransom demand. Unless something different lay behind her capture: vengeance.

She sat back on her heels and did her best to think clearly. Through the flimsy fabric of her skirt she could feel springy moss beneath a thick layer of petals. Their cloying scent mingled unpleasantly with an odour of damp and decay, and the all-pervading odour of her own vomit. Through her hazy confusion she tried to remember everything her assailant had said. There had been a reference to George, and a comment to the effect that it had been a long time. From the reference to George to the insistence this was not about money, everything suggested her attacker was a jealous ex-lover. It could only be the woman George had written to.

'Who is Veronique?' she shouted out.

No one answered.

There was no point in dwelling on the ramblings of a lunatic. She had to focus on making her escape before her strength faded. It was not going to be easy. Her last attempt had ended badly. Clambering to her feet she was dismayed at how weak she had already become. Her legs trembled so much she could barely stand. She took a few deep breaths in an attempt to calm herself. The intake of warm humid air made her cough. In a sudden fit of desperation, she shook the chain that tied her to the wall. It rattled violently but remained firmly embedded in the wood. Leaning closer, she felt her way along the wall and found where the ring was attached to it with a gigantic metal staple. There was no way she could hope to yank it out. Her next thought was to work her hand free, but that was impossible. The manacle gripped her so tightly she could barely move her wrist inside it. There was not even enough space for her to slip the little finger of her other hand in between the metal and her trapped flesh. She bit her lip and tasted blood on her tongue, reminding her that she had drunk nothing since leaving the hotel. As though she had pressed a switch, her brain began to pound and she felt lightheaded. When she closed her eyes bright spots of light pierced her mind like needles, forcing her to keep her eyes open.

Sharp splinters pricked her fingers as she felt her way along the wall to the extent that her shackles allowed. Her area of exploration was limited. The side of the hut was made of solid vertical planks of wood, the surface of the wood pitted and rough. She scrabbled and scratched at it in a desperate attempt to pick away at the wood, succeeding only in breaking her nails and tearing the flesh from her fingertips until they were raw and stung painfully. In a corner she discovered a metal grid nailed into the wall. She slid her fingers through the holes and tried to shake it. The grid would not budge. She felt around the frame with her fingers. It was nailed to the wall. There was no way of moving it. She leaned back against the wall, shaking with disappointment. Slowly she slid down the wall until she was crouching on the floor, squatting on a bed of petals. In a frenzy of disgust, she dug a hole in the earth, sobbing as she buried her own excrement. Although she patted the earth down and covered it with petals the stench persisted, clinging to her skirt and hands, permeating the foul air.

She must have fallen asleep because when she opened her eyes, she was lying on her front. She propped herself up against the wall, dazed, until a noise startled her into consciousness. The bolt was being slid back. As the door opened she scrambled to her feet. The defiant speech she had rehearsed during the night evaporated on her parched lips as she heard the sound of pouring water. The cold rim of a cup was pressed against her bottom lip. Greedily she drank. The water tasted brackish, but she gulped it down regardless. Ignoring water spilling down her shirt, she kept swallowing until the cup was empty. She took a deep breath. She was not going to die.

'Thank you. I was thirsty. Now, please, let me go. My hands hurt.'

The only answer was a burst of hoarse laughter. Angela shuffled backwards until her shoulders hit the wall.

'Who are you?'

There was no reply. Desperately, Angela repeated her question. This time the dry voice rasped close to her ear. She felt the warmth of a breath on her skin.

'Veronique.'

'What do you want from me?' she cried out in exasperation, too weak for anger.

'The dark angel does not forget.'

A moment later she heard the door close. As the bolt slid across, she gave way to helpless tears. Her legs shaking, she slid down to the floor and squatted on her haunches. She wished the madwoman would either let her go, or else kill her quickly. This slow torture was unbearable.

15

THE MORNING WAS HALF over. Despite the trauma of her mother's disappearance, Lucy had slept deeply when she had finally gone to bed, exhausted by the night's troubles. Now it was time to face whatever the day had in store. Encouraged by the news that the coastguard had found no sign of her mother at sea, she called on her father and they went down for a late breakfast together. He tried to remain practical as they turned over all the possibilities. They both agreed that the most likely explanation was that Angela had wandered off and fallen ill, or lost her memory, perhaps as a result of falling and sustaining a head injury. Those were the only ways they could account for her failure to contact them. At least twelve hours had elapsed since she had disappeared, and maybe as long as twenty-four hours. It was frustrating that they had no idea what time she had left the hotel.

While her father spoke to the hotel manager, Lucy questioned everyone she saw. She approached other hotel guests, as well as porters, receptionists, security guards, bar staff and cleaners, but no one had noticed her mother leave the hotel. A couple of the guests recognised Angela's photograph and thought they had seen her by the pool the previous day, but they were not sure exactly what time they had seen her. Other than that, no one could remember having seen her on the day she had vanished. At last Lucy ran out of people to ask. She phoned Adrian to ask if he had heard anything, but none of the hotel staff he had spoken to that morning remembered seeing her mother the previous day.

'I really need to work,' he apologised, as though he was somehow letting her down. 'But call me if there's anything I can do. Just ask for me at reception and I'll come over straight away.'

The hotel manager had already contacted the hospital. Nevertheless, Lucy's father wanted to go there himself to make sure his wife had not been admitted as a patient. On the way, he said he would go to the police and report his wife missing. There was so much to be done. The previous night he had given way to despair. Now his plans, combined with the daylight, seemed to have put him in a more positive frame of mind. Lucy understood that he needed to keep busy. After a brief discussion, they agreed she should accompany her father. She had a feeling he was reluctant to let her out of his sight. Leaving instructions with the hotel manager, the staff at the reception desk and the security guards that George was to be contacted the minute Angela showed up, they set off.

They went first to the regional police station, only a short distance from the hotel on a junction just beyond the row of supermarkets. A large clear sign identified the police station. Beautiful well-tended flowering bushes grew on either side of large double doors. Inside, a woman was sitting behind the counter, chatting to a young police officer in uniform. Glancing around, Lucy saw a door with a notice, 'Detainees WC', just past a row of wooden lockers, and a sign on the wall: 'Service without fear, favour, affection or ill-will'. There was a photograph of the president on the wall, and another of the commissioner of police. As she looked around, she listened to the young policeman who noted down what her father was saying. The officer said he would pass the details on to the

Central Police Station in Victoria, which would organise a search if her mother failed to return very soon. He gave her father a card and urged him to contact the station as soon as his wife turned up.

When they left, Lucy suggested they go to the police headquarters after stopping at the hospital, just to make sure the message had got through.

Her father replied that he had been thinking the same thing himself. 'It's not that I don't trust that young officer,' he added. 'He only has to call the central station, but we might as well check, just to be on the safe side. And I know the hotel manager contacted the hospital, and Adrian said he called them as well, but it won't do any harm for us to go there. We leave no stone unturned. If she's lost her memory, she might be there without anyone having identified her. And I want to leave my number with them myself in case she turns up in a few days. If she's confused, anything could happen.'

'Yes, let's not trust this to anyone else.'

Lucy hoped her father was not taking on too much, but she realised that keeping busy helped them to stay positive. They clung to the idea that her mother was suffering from some form of temporary amnesia. It also meant she might make a full recovery. Anything else was too painful to contemplate.

They spoke very little on the way to the hospital. Worried about her father, Lucy had suggested they ask Adrian for a lift, but her father was not sure how long their various visits would take, and Adrian's time away from his desk would be limited.

The hospital consisted of a complex of white buildings with different coloured roofs set against a dramatic backdrop of dark green hills. The woman on reception was attentive and helpful but adamant that no blonde English tourist had been admitted within the past twenty-four hours, with or without any memory loss.

'Are you sure?' Lucy asked several times, until the receptionist became annoyed. 'Can you just double check?'

'I already told you we had no one admitted in the last twenty-four hours who isn't accounted for. We know the identity of every one of our patients, even the very elderly who don't always know their own names. We know who they are, all of them. If your mother was here, we'd know about it.'

'Well, it's a good thing she's not there,' Lucy said as they walked back to the car in the blazing sunshine. 'At least now we know she's not been taken seriously ill.'

Her father agreed. She could tell he was trying to sound positive, but his voice wobbled. Lucy understood why. If Angela was not ill, the truth might prove to be far worse.

'Where to now, Dad?'

'Next stop the Central Police Station. I'm sure they'll sort out this mess in no time. I expect we'll find she's been there all along. She probably had too much to drink and they picked her up, or something. Perhaps she spent the night in a cell at the police station.' His laughter sounded unconvincing to both of them. 'I'm sure they'll be able to help anyway.'

'Yes. After all, she's only been gone overnight.'

They stayed doggedly optimistic, each aware they were they putting on a show for each other's benefit. Neither of them wanted to be first to crack and admit out loud that they thought Angela might already be dead. Remembering her fears for her own safety, Lucy wondered if the person who had attacked her had now turned on her mother, with fatal consequences. She did not mention that possibility to her father. Telling herself her own fears were unfounded, she took his arm and assured him they were bound to find her mother soon.

It took them a while to find the car park in Victoria from where it was a only short walk to the police station. They went into an office marked 'Reception'. A woman behind the desk directed them to another entrance further along the street. This office was marked

'Enquiries'. The mission statement on the wall in Beau Vallon police station was displayed here too: 'Service without fear, favour, affection or ill-will', as was a photograph of the Commissioner of Police. A smiling young officer greeted them. On hearing the reason for their visit, he looked instantly concerned and asked Lucy's father to fill in a form to register his wife as a missing person. While her father was writing down the details, Lucy checked her mobile for the twentieth time that morning. As she was looking at it, they overheard the policeman talking on the phone.

'. . . An Englishman . . . Yes, a call from Beau Vallon. The wife's done a runner . . .'

Lucy interrupted angrily. 'My mother hasn't run off, she's gone missing.'

A few moments later a tall dark-skinned officer joined them. Inspector Henri asked them to follow him across an open courtyard into a different building. They followed him up several flights of stone stairs into a small office with three polished wooden desks. When they were seated, the inspector confirmed he had received a report from a regional police station.

'You say she's been missing overnight, no more than twelve hours?'

'Well, it's anything from twelve to twenty-four hours.'

The policeman glanced up from his notes. 'You can't say how long your wife's been missing? Forgive me for asking, but was there an argument, sir?'

'No. Look, I took my daughter out for the day yesterday, and when we got back to the hotel, my wife had disappeared. So she could have gone missing as early as yesterday morning, I just don't know. But either way, she's missing, and you need to do something about it.'

The inspector looked from her father to Lucy and back again.

'This is my daughter.'

'Yes, I can see that she looks like you.'

The inspector turned to Lucy. 'I hope you are enjoying your stay on Mahé.'

'Look here, Inspector, we came here to report that my wife is missing. The coastguard searched for her last night but there's no sign of her along the coast or out at sea. We've searched the hotel and she's not there, and she's not at the hospital, so we've come here to report that she's missing. We want you to find her.'

The policeman turned back to him. 'Your wife, indeed yes, sir. So, you reported the incident to your closest regional police station at Beau Vallon, and they passed the message on to us.'

With a sigh of exasperation, Lucy's father confirmed that they were staying at the Garden of Eden Hotel and had been to the local police station on their way to Victoria. The policeman consulted his watch.

'Let me see. You made your initial report nearly three hours ago, but your wife has actually been missing overnight. Right.' He nodded his head, suddenly brisk. 'We have a description. Tell me again, where was your wife last seen and at what time exactly?'

He took down a few more details and told them he would set up an immediate search of the area.

'Is there anything we can do?' Lucy asked.

'Leave it to us. We will conduct an extensive search of the whole island. I assure you the station commander takes such reports very seriously. We are not as sophisticated as the British police force but believe me, sir, if your wife is still on the island, we will find her. Our command centre will circulate a message to all the police stations on the island, and all patrols, and our media office will send out a description to the local radio and television stations. We will do everything possible to find your wife, if she has indeed suffered some misfortune, and not decided to leave the island of her own accord.' He gave an apologetic shrug. 'It has happened.'

'Of course she hasn't—' Lucy's father began.

The inspector raised his hand. 'In the meantime, let us hope she returns to you soon. Here is my number. Call me immediately if she comes back.'

Lucy was furious but she kept her outrage to herself until they were back on the street. 'Who the hell does he think he is, speaking to you like that? How dare he suggest she's run off and left you!'

Her father gazed at her helplessly.

'Oh, Dad, this is awful,' she wailed, losing her grip on her composure and struggling not to cry. 'What can we do?'

'We press on,' he replied with forced cheerfulness.

He turned away too late to hide the sight of his own eyes watering.

'Where to this time?' she asked, wiping her nose on her sleeve.

'The British High Commission.'

'Good thinking, Dad. At least they should take it seriously when we tell them a British woman's gone missing.'

They walked the short distance across the square, past the clock tower. From her father's descriptions Lucy had imagined it rivalling Big Ben, but it was actually quite small, dwarfed by the buildings around the square. The British High Commission was situated in a tall glass-fronted building, the sky reflected off the mirrored windows of its elegant façade. They climbed the steps and entered the building. Inside, a notice advised them the British High Commission was open 8.30 to 12 Monday to Thursday, with an emergency number. They crossed to the desk where a helpful security man directed them to the third floor. Stepping out of a small mirrored lift, they saw a large well-lit crest displayed on the wall facing them, with a motto 'Dieu et Mon Droit'.

'I wonder why it's in French?' Lucy muttered.

Her father spoke to a uniformed security guard sitting in a corner by the window, explaining that they had come to see the British

High Commissioner. The guard stood up and pressed an intercom beside the lift.

'Tell them who you are,' he said.

Lucy followed her father through a set of wooden doors, through another set of black-framed glass doors, to a spacious modern reception area. The atmosphere was quiet and orderly. To their left they could see through two large glass panels into an office. In front of them, comfortable black leather chairs and sofas were arranged around a coffee table. Lucy gazed out of the window at a tall building that obscured the view towards the ocean. On the right a second reception area behind a glass wall gave a clear view of the high forested hills. The little wall space between floor-to-ceiling windows was painted pale beige.

As Lucy's father stood hesitating in front of the glass panel, a woman emerged through another door, smiling a welcome. Although very young, she looked smart and professional. As she invited them to sit down, Lucy felt unexpectedly reassured. There was more to Mahé than the exotic and the strange. There was also order and common sense. There had to be if they were to find her mother. The woman introduced herself as the Vice Consul, Maggie. She did not look much older than Lucy.

'The job's not as grand as the title sounds,' she added with a short laugh. 'Now, how can I help you?'

As soon as Lucy's father introduced himself and explained the reason for their visit, her demeanour altered. She invited them to accompany her into the office behind the glass wall.

'It's more discreet in here,' she explained as she sat behind a desk in the corner. 'Now,' she went on, her expression solemn, her voice gentle and agreeable. 'Have you told the police that your wife has gone missing, or would you like us to notify them?'

Lucy's father explained that they had been to the local police station in Beau Vallon, and had just come from the Central Police

Station where they had reported the situation in person to Inspector Henri.

'When did you last see your wife?'

The Vice Consul noted everything down as they went through the details of the disappearance once more. Repetition made the account no easier to hear, and the official's expression of concern was alarming as well as comforting.

'Now, feel free to contact us at any time,' Maggie said, when Lucy's father had finished his recitation. 'We have a stand-alone computer which you're welcome to use, and you must let us know if there's anything else we can do to support you until your wife returns. If you extend your stay we can liaise with your insurance company for you. In the meantime, we'll be in daily contact with you. I'll come and see you tomorrow in case you think of anything else we can help you with, and I'll pass all this on to the High Commissioner. She's not here today, but she always takes reports of missing persons very seriously.'

'Do people often go missing?' Lucy asked.

She held her breath. She did not know if white slave traders still existed, but she had heard stories of Somali pirates in the Indian Ocean, although it seemed hard to believe they could have seized her mother at the Garden of Eden Hotel.

'Yes,' Maggie replied, 'but they almost always return after a few days. Coming to the island seems to have that effect on some people, especially women around your mother's age. Sometimes they go off for longer periods. One woman reappeared safe and sound after she had been missing for nearly three weeks. She'd been on Aldabra, communing with the giant tortoises.'

Lucy's father grunted. 'I can't see Angela doing that.'

Listening to her father chatting with the Vice Consul, Lucy felt more worried than ever. There was no way her mother would have run off without telling them. Apart from the fact that she had no reason to do so, she of all people knew that Lucy needed her support right now. She slipped her phone from her pocket and glanced at the screen in case her mother had called. There were no messages.

16

'So what do we do now?' her father asked the Vice Consul, who smiled sympathetically.

'As I said, the High Commissioner is away today, but I'll make sure she's fully apprised of the situation on her return, and the police will be organising a thorough search. I assure you, they take these incidents very seriously, as we do here. Hopefully they'll have some good news for us very soon.'

She smiled at him again.

'And what can we do?' Lucy asked.

'I suggest you go back to your hotel and wait. I know it's hard, but there's really nothing more you can do for now. Let us know if you think of anything else, anywhere she might have gone, anyone she might have been in contact with, and of course we'll be in touch as soon as we have any news. And do let us know straight away as soon as she turns up.'

She stood up and held out her hand.

Neither of them said much on the way back to the hotel. Her father stared at the road ahead. Lucy gazed out of her window at the sea. With nothing more to be done, they shared a sense of misery at the thought of facing the rest of the day without her mother.

'Perhaps we shouldn't go back to the hotel,' Lucy ventured.

She was not sure she could bear to sit by the pool, at the buffet, or in the dining room, or walk on the beach or in the gardens; wherever she went in the hotel she would be expecting to see her mother.

'I'm sorry, Lucy, I'm shattered. We can go out later, eat in Victoria. I know you want to get away from the place, but right now I really need to get back to the room and rest.'

Lucy understood. It had been an exhausting few hours and she was feeling emotionally drained. She could only imagine how worried her father must be.

'That's a good idea,' she said gently.

'And I want to be there when she comes back.'

Adrian was waiting for them in the lobby when they arrived at the hotel, keen to hear what had happened. After they brought him up to speed, her father excused himself, saying he had to rest. He assured Lucy he would keep his phone at his side in case her mother made contact and would call her the minute he heard anything. In the meantime, he suggested Adrian take her out for the rest of the afternoon.

'Out?' Lucy repeated, taken aback at the suggestion.

'It would do her good to get away from here for a few hours,' her father explained.

When Lucy disagreed, her father insisted he was going to sleep and did not need her for a while. The police were conducting a massive search for Angela, and they had to leave it to them to find her. There was nothing else they could do. While they waited, it would serve no purpose for Lucy to upset herself moping about in the hotel.

'Shouldn't we at least be out looking for her?' Lucy asked.

Adrian shook his head. 'We could try, but she might be anywhere. My guess is she took a trip to one of the other islands and got stuck there without a phone signal.'

'But—'

'The police will find her soon enough. She'll probably be here by the time we get back.'

He offered to drive Lucy to a stunning bay nearby, promising they would not stray far from the hotel. If there was any news they could be back at the Garden of Eden in next to no time.

'And we won't go swimming,' he added with a gentle grin that lit up his dark eyes.

Lucy smiled. She could not deny it would be a relief to get away from the hotel for an hour or two. And although she would never have admitted as much out loud, she would welcome a brief respite from the strain of having to hide her distress from her father. He had enough to handle without witnessing her lose control on top of everything else.

Adrian took her to a bay similar to others along the breathtakingly beautiful coastline. Like the first one they had visited together this beach was deserted, and they wandered down to the sea and walked for a while in the shallows, cooling their bare feet in the tepid water. Lost in wonder at the scenery, Lucy could almost forget about her mother for a moment. It was hard to believe anything dreadful could happen on such a lovely island. She felt a sensation of release that was almost spiritual.

'Do you believe in God?' she asked Adrian.

'No, not really. Although it's hard not to, when you see all this.'

After a while they went and sat together on the sand and Adrian questioned her about her life in England. She knew he was trying to distract her from thinking about her mother and was grateful for his consideration.

'I studied English at uni,' she told him. 'It's not a particularly useful subject unless you plan to teach, which I don't, or want to go into publishing which is currently in chaos, or journalism where the future is even more precarious.'

'So what do you do?'

She shrugged. 'Just a job, you know. I work in a café, as a waitress.'

'Isn't that rather a waste of your education?'

She gave a rueful grin. 'It would be if that was all I planned to do for the rest of my life, but I hope I'll find something a bit more challenging to do.'

'Like what?'

She leaned on one elbow and clawed at the sand with her other hand, watching the grains flow through her fingers like water.

'I don't know. That's the problem. If I knew what I wanted to do, I'd get on with it. I met Darren in my first year at uni and I suppose I thought we'd have a family and that seemed to be enough, a future with him. You know how it is.'

He frowned so that she was uncertain if he understood or not. While she hesitated over whether to ask him, he posed another question.

'Do you want children then?'

She shrugged again. 'Oh, I don't know. I just thought it was something we'd do. Get married. Have a family. Isn't that what people do?'

Seeing his anxious expression, she smiled. 'It's OK, I'm over him now. That is, I'm getting over him. At least, I think I am. It's just that I've got to rethink my entire life, sort myself out somehow.'

It was not only her life she had to re-evaluate, but herself. She had always thought of herself as level-headed. She had been shocked at how quickly she had gone to pieces over losing Darren.

'Would you take him back?'

'No.'

'Good. Clearly he didn't care for you as much as he led you to believe. Put it behind you and get on with your life. Life's too short to waste on people who treat you badly.'

He was the first person who had not trotted out platitudes, telling her she was still very young, she had all her whole life in front of her, and the pain would lessen over time.

'I'm sorry if that sounds harsh,' he added.

'No, I appreciate your honesty.'

That was only partly true. It felt liberating, yet at the same time unnerving, to be addressed so bluntly. Unlike Adrian, Darren had always treated her like a child, and naturally her parents did too. Yet her father had turned to her for help now he was in trouble. It was all very confusing. Not wanting to think about herself any more, she turned the focus on Adrian. Although he had enquired about her past, she refrained from probing into his personal life for fear of implying she was interested in him. Instead she focused on his career.

'Did you always know you wanted to be an accountant?'

He laughed. 'It wasn't exactly a Paul on the road to Damascus revelation, more like what the hell am I going to do to earn a living? Then I had the chance to study in England and decided to make the most of the opportunity, make it count for the future, so I plumped for accountancy. It was a hard slog, I can tell you, but I got there in the end so I guess it was worth it.'

'We're totally different, aren't we? I wish I was more like you. Your life sounds so clearly mapped out. You know where you're going.'

'Not really. It's just that accountancy seemed like a sensible idea at the time.'

Lucy nodded. Darren used to scoff at people who were sensible. Playing it safe, he called it, accusing her of being risk averse, as though that was a character flaw.

'Go with the flow,' he would tell her.

In retrospect, their relationship had been immature, based on a fear of the future after the cocoon of university. But while they had both been cowardly in clinging on to a spurious sense of security, at least she had been sincere about her commitment to him. She sat up and brushed sand off her legs.

'How did you get to be studying in England?'

He shrugged. 'I worked damn hard to get there—'

'What?' she interrupted him. 'You wanted to go to England? You're kidding me.'

'No. It wasn't that I wanted to leave Mahé,' he explained, 'but I wanted to escape the shanty town lifestyle and better myself. I thought that if I could study in England, I'd come back and live like a rich man, have a better life.'

'And is it? A better life?'

He gazed out at the ocean. 'I don't know. Sometimes I wonder if I wouldn't have been better off working behind the bar like Eddy, without all the responsibility and stress. I'd have been just as happy, I guess.'

'Is that what it's all about then, being happy?'

'You tell me.'

'You can't regret having studied,' she said after a while. 'And you have bettered yourself. I think that's admirable. Not many people do that.' She did not add that she would have been unable to do what Adrian had done.

Adrian sat up, leaning back on his elbows. 'Thank you. I sometimes think it was all a waste of time, but of course you never know, do you, what your life might have been like if you'd followed a different path.'

'Yes, we all have to live with the consequences of our choices.'

She sighed, thinking about how she had trusted Darren. She was not sure she would ever trust her own judgement again about anything. Adrian lay back on the sand and shut his eyes and Lucy studied him furtively. Tall, bronzed and powerfully built, he was not really her type. Muscular men in England always gave her the impression they must fancy themselves, conscientiously working out to develop their impressive physiques. Yet here on the island it was different. Adrian's physical strength was probably the result of water sports, not narcissism. Opening his eyes he sat up suddenly, aware of her scrutiny, and she turned away, embarrassed. Just then a young couple appeared, walking hand in hand along the edge of the sea. Lucy and Adrian watched them until they disappeared round the edge of the bay.

'It's a romantic setting,' Adrian said.

Lucy nodded dumbly, uncertain how to interpret his comment.

'You know if it wasn't for this – for my mother . . .' she began and stopped, afraid she might be presuming too much from his reference to romance. He was probably just making conversation, prompted by the young couple they had seen walking past.

'Don't worry, I'm not going to jump on you,' he laughed, lying back on the sand again.

'Thank you.'

'I'm not saying that under other circumstances things might not have been different,' he added with a sly grin as he closed his eyes.

She wondered if he really meant that, and how she might feel if he reached out and touched her, but it was not the right moment for such speculation. It was the first time since Darren had dumped her that she had felt even vaguely attracted to another man. Surprised that her thoughts had wandered so far from her mother she gazed at the water, listening to the regular beat of the waves on the shore, but the soft swishing no longer comforted her. The grey clouds suddenly flared with orange light, and the sea shimmered pink and golden beneath the setting sun.

'The sunsets over the sea are spectacular, aren't they?' Adrian murmured.

Lucy nodded. Her mother loved watching the sun set over the water. Unable to speak, she turned her head away so Adrian would not see her tears. Gazing at the vast dark water she wondered if her mother was out there, lost forever in the ocean depths. In a rush of emotion, longing for her mother overwhelmed her. Dropping her head between her knees, she howled. Adrian put his hand on her shoulder and sat beside her in silence.

17

WITHOUT KNOWING WHAT HAD disturbed him, George was convinced there was someone else in the room with him. He lay perfectly still, straining to listen; all he could hear was the gentle roar of waves breaking on the sand. The darkness was almost impenetrable. A cloud floated across the sky, exposing the moon, and he was able to distinguish curtains hanging on either side of his open windows, and the shape of a table at his bedside. Without moving his head he swivelled his eyes round the room and paused at the door to his bathroom. He tried to remember if he had left it open when he went to bed.

Silence.

He decided his imagination was playing tricks on him as he lay there half asleep, distraught about Angela. He turned on his side and lay for a while in a foetal position, one arm reaching out across the empty side of the bed, before he rolled onto his back again, unable to relax in unfamiliar solitude. He had not slept alone for twenty-five years, apart from the one night Angela had spent in hospital when Lucy was born. Even then George had been at her side, only nipping home for a few hours in the morning when Angela was resting and the baby was asleep.

Suddenly he heard it again. This time there was no mistaking the sound of a gentle intake of breath.

His first instinct had been right. He was not alone. A sudden spurt of joy thrilled through him.

'Angela? It's all right, I'm awake.'

No answer.

'Angela?' he called again, his voice barely above a whisper this time. 'Angela? Is that you?'

He fumbled for the bedside light, unable to find the switch in the darkness. Inadvertently, he knocked his mobile phone off the table.

'Who's there? Is it you, Lucy?'

But Lucy did not have a key to his room and she did not stink of stale cigarettes and sweat. His joy turned to fear.

'Who is it? I know you're in here so – I'm calling security.'

He reached for the phone but someone else was there before him, snatching it from the table and yanking the cord out of the socket.

'What the hell are you doing? Who are you? What do you want?'

The questions were inane because he knew what the night prowler was after. He spoke very slowly and clearly so there could be no misunderstanding.

'My wallet is in the safe. My passport is there too and you'll find cash – quite a lot of cash – Seychelles rupees and pounds sterling – and my credit card. It's all there, in the safe. Oh my God, please don't take my phone because my wife's gone missing and she might try to call me.'

There was no answer.

'What are you doing?' George asked again. 'Who are you?'

Suddenly a hand grabbed him by the throat so tightly he thought he would suffocate. A hoarse voice hissed in his ear speaking in a thick Creole accent.

'I could murder you in your bed.'

The grip loosened slightly.

George gagged as he tried to speak. 'Who are you? What do you want?'

The intruder released him. At the same time George heard someone spit and felt a splash of saliva dribble slowly down his cheek towards his mouth. With a cry of disgust, he wiped the spittle away with the back of his hand and rubbed his hand on the bed sheet to clean it.

'Who are you?' he whispered again.

The intruder's silence was more menacing than the threat to kill George.

'Look, just take all my money and go away,' he cried out, with a boldness he did not feel.

'I do not want your money.'

The dry voice grated on George's taut nerves. He rolled over and sat up straining to see the intruder, but clouds had drifted over the moon. All he could discern was a vague hunched shape. In a brief flicker of moonlight between clouds, the whites of two eyes glared wildly at him for an instant before they were swallowed by darkness. After twenty-four hours feeling terrified for his wife, discovering a stranger in his room shattered the last vestiges of George's self-control. His pent-up anguish erupted and, with a sudden howl of fury, he flung himself at his unseen adversary, swiping and punching, frantic with fear and rage.

'Get out! Get out! Get out and leave me alone! Get out of here!'

They tumbled to the floor, wrestling. George felt a wiry arm wind itself around his neck and he hit out blindly. His fist encountered something soft and fleshy and he heard a wheezing groan as the hold on his throat loosened. In a state of near collapse George knelt on the prostrate figure, planting his knees on his assailant's chest as viciously as he could, although it had become a struggle to move, his energy was so depleted by the scuffle.

'I – have not come – to kill – you,' the intruder panted. 'It is – your turn – now.'

'What the fuck is that supposed to mean?' George demanded, pressing down with his knees as hard as he could. His head was throbbing and his nose stung where the intruder had landed a wild punch. He had a feeling it might be broken.

There was a loud knocking at his door and a voice called out. As George was distracted, the intruder threw him off with a loud grunt and fled onto the balcony. One of the long drapes swung violently. With a groan, George clambered to his feet and staggered across the room. He flipped the light switch and opened the door.

'Dad, are you all right? I heard . . .'

Lucy broke off in consternation, staring at his face, then looked past him into the room and gaped.

'Oh my God, what happened?'

'Nothing.'

He stepped back from the doorway as a security guard appeared in the corridor behind Lucy.

'Is everything all right here?' he asked, looking from Lucy to George and back again. 'We had a report of a fracas. Has this guest been bothering you, madam?'

'What? Oh no, this is my father. I heard shouting and banging in his room so I called reception and then came to see what was happening. My room's just next door.'

Meanwhile the security guard had been peering past George into the room, his eyes travelling around with sudden interest. George turned to see his sheets in disarray, a bedside lamp smashed, the hotel phone on the floor, and one of his window drapes hanging loose, all but pulled down from the curtain rail.

'Somebody been having a fight here?' the security guard asked, entering the room.

George nodded and his head began to pound. With a start, he caught sight of his own face in the wardrobe mirror. He had only a vague recollection of being hit in the face but his nose was swollen and one of his eyes was closing, a bruise already forming around it. By morning he would have a black eye. He fingered his nose gently but it seemed intact and when he examined his profile, it looked much the same as before.

'Is it broken?' the security guard asked.

George shook his head then regretted the movement. 'I don't think so.'

'You don't think so?' Lucy repeated, sounding shocked.

'Looks like somebody got hurt,' the security guard said.

He folded his arms and stood gazing at George, waiting for an explanation.

'There was an intruder,' George said.

He frowned, thinking back over the fight. As he did so, a wave of exhaustion hit him and he had to sit down, shaking.

'An intruder?' The security guard sounded incredulous. 'That doesn't seem likely, up here on the second floor. Where did your intruder go?'

He glanced around the room, suddenly wary.

As succinctly as he could, George explained what had taken place. The other man listened sceptically, before stepping onto the balcony to check that no one was concealed outside.

'There's no one out there,' he announced, returning to the room. 'He could've climbed down from the balcony, although it's not clear how he got in.'

Clambering down to the balcony below, it was possible the intruder could have made his way to the ground and escaped.

'I'll file a report, sir, and the manager will want to speak to you in the morning.' The security guard glanced around the room again. 'I'll send the housekeeper along to sort the room out for you. Maybe you'd like another room for tonight?'

George shook his head, too tired now to care about the mess.

Lucy spoke up. 'Can you put another bed next door in my room, just for tonight? I don't want you left alone, Dad.'

'I'll be fine,' he insisted, but the security guard had already gone.

After the guard left, Lucy fussed and sniffled and offered to drive him straight to the hospital. At the very least, she wanted to summon a doctor. Wearily, George insisted he was fine.

'Nothing's broken, Lucy. Don't worry. I didn't hit my head or anything like that. It was just a punch on the nose. I think he came off worse. Now I think we should go to your room and try and get some sleep. It'll be morning soon.'

She smiled weakly and he followed her into her room where the housekeeping staff had acted efficiently. A low cot bed had been erected on one side of the room.

Lucy went to bed at last, ordering him to call her at once if he felt at all ill, or was sick.

'And don't lie on your back.'

'I won't.

'Are you sure you're all right, Dad?'

'I'm fine, really. It's not the first fight I've ever been in. I suffered far worse than this at school, believe me.'

'OK, but I'm here if you need me.'

He was relieved when she finally went to sleep and he was able to mull over what had happened. He had not told her what the intruder had said, for fear of upsetting her even more. He had been told that he would not be killed because it was his turn. Still puzzling over what that meant, he drifted into an uneasy sleep.

18

Lucy awoke to find her father had already left her room. She knocked gently at his door. When there was no answer she went down to the breakfast room, hoping to find him there. Reluctant to spend time in the hotel where everything reminded her of her mother, she walked slowly down the wide stone stairs and through the glass doors into the breakfast room. A waitress nodded sombrely at her, as though letting her know that the staff were all aware her mother was missing. She crossed the tiled floor and glanced briefly at picture windows overlooking the patio and gardens. The pool was out of sight down a short flight of steps. She resisted the impulse to nip down and see if her mother was there, stretched out on a lounger, book in hand, iced drink beside her chair. Instead she took the lift back up to her father's room. Her mother and father's room.

She knocked softly on the door and discerned a faint groan from inside. It sounded as though he was calling her mother's name.

'Dad? Dad? Are you awake? It's only me.'

Not my mother.

'Hang on.'

Her father had never been one to express emotion openly, but he looked as though he had been crying. While his injured eye was too swollen to reveal his feelings, the other was puffy and bloodshot. Sitting on the bed fully dressed, he pulled on his sandals and shuffled over to a seat by the window. Lucy joined him and they sat side by side, staring out across the lush gardens to the sea, sparkling in the sunlight. She wondered if he had sat like this with her mother at his side and, if so, what they had talked about.

After a moment she stood up. 'Now, let's go and get something to eat. Things always seem worse when you're hungry.'

'I don't want anything.'

Hunched in his chair, he looked very old and frail.

'Come on, we've got to stay positive. And in any case, I've got a good feeling about today. I think they're going to find her. The police are on it, and it's not as if the island's a big area to search. How long can it take them to find her, now they've started? Come on, you've got to eat.'

George put on sunglasses to hide his battered eye. With his red and puffy nose still visible, he followed her to the patio where they sat in a secluded corner and ordered from the bar menu. They did their best to put a brave face on it for each other, but anxiety over Angela's disappearance was never out of their minds for long and they barely managed to eat anything.

'I don't think we should say too much in public,' her father muttered, looking around the bar area suspiciously with his one good eye. 'It might not be safe.'

He had attracted a few curious glances. It was obvious he had been in a fight. It made Lucy wince just to look at him.

'What do you mean, it might not be safe?'

He leaned towards her over the table, his eyes flicking nervously at the door as he murmured.

'I think someone's out to get me.'

When she pressed him to say more, he hesitated. Just as he was about to speak again, they caught sight of the Vice Consul crossing the patio.

'May I join you?'

They could hardly refuse when she had come there to speak to them. Lucy's father pulled a chair over for her.

'I just came to check on how you are – oh my goodness, what happened to you?'

George shrugged. 'Nothing, I just sent an intruder packing.'

'An intruder?'

'Yes, he managed to climb into my room during the night.'

'You alerted the security guards?'

'Yes, the hotel know all about it.'

'Well, you need to be careful,' Maggie said. 'And the hotel need to step up their security. We'll speak to them about it. That's one area where the hotels aren't usually slapdash. Have you had a doctor take a look at that?'

'I'm fine,' George assured her.

'Have you heard anything about my mother?' Lucy interrupted impatiently.

She knew the Vice Consul only wanted to be helpful, but she was relieved when she left them alone. There was no news, and Lucy was beginning to find her platitudes irritating. By now the pool and bar areas were busy so her father suggested they go and sit on his balcony.

'I have a feeling the intruder didn't come to my room by chance. He said something about it being my turn.'

Lucy felt a stab of fear. If her father was right, that meant someone was deliberately targeting their family. The other possibility was that her father was cracking under the strain of her mother's disappearance, and becoming paranoid and suspicious. She recalled how quickly she herself had fallen apart when her relationship had foundered. Of course that had been different. Darren had rejected her. But the uncertainty over what had happened to her mother was worse, and her parents had been together for more than twenty-five years.

'That doesn't mean he deliberately came to your room,' she replied, doing her best to speak casually. 'Maybe it just happened to be you he hit on. It was your turn to be robbed.'

Remembering her own encounter with a mysterious fish woman in the sea, and her impression that she had seen someone on the rocks when she thought a boulder had fallen, she tried to remain calm. It was unlikely they would both have imagined being attacked, but the only alternative was to accept that someone was really trying to kill them. Enemy or insanity, Lucy was uncomfortable with either hypothesis.

Her father was already backing down from the misgiving he had voiced. 'Yes, you're right. He probably found my room by chance. And I might have misheard him. I was half asleep at the time, and in a panic. For all I knew at the time, he could have had a gun or a knife on him.'

'What if he really was after you, though?'

'You just said you thought it must have been chance he happened to hit on my room.'

'I did,' Lucy agreed, 'but we need to consider every angle and it's possible someone is out to get us. How did he get in?'

'I'm not sure. If he didn't get in through the door, then the only other possibility is the balcony, although I'm pretty sure I locked the doors.'

'What about the missing key?'

'What missing key? I never said anything about a missing key.'

'I mean mum's key to your room. She didn't leave it behind when she went, so she must have taken it with her. What if she dropped her arm band and someone found it?'

'No one would know which room it came from.'

'They would if they knew whose key it was.'

Her father's good eye opened wide in surprise.

'Your mother would never let a stranger know the number of our room if he had taken her key. You're letting your imagination run away with you again.'

He was tired after his disturbed night, so they arranged to meet at lunchtime and she left him to rest.

'You should try and get some sleep yourself,' he told Lucy before she left. 'You were up half the night too.'

'I'm not really tired. I think I'll just go for a walk down on the beach.'

Her father looked apprehensive. 'Don't go far.'

'Don't worry. I'll stay near the hotel.'

19

Her father was slouched in a chair in the hotel lobby when Lucy returned from the beach. Catching sight of him as he started forward, she felt a flicker of hope that he was waiting to tell her Angela had returned. His face told another story.

'Where have you been? I was worried sick about you. You've been gone all morning.'

'I just went for a walk.'

She did not add that she had been ferreting through the trees and undergrowth along the beach near the hotel, vainly searching for clues to her mother's disappearance. Her father gazed earnestly at her as he asked her to promise she would never disappear like that again without first telling him where she was going. She should have protested but he looked so vulnerable, she felt like crying instead. She gave him her word. More than ever before she was determined to find her mother.

Neither of them wanted to stay at the Garden of Eden so they walked about a quarter of a mile along the beach to the next hotel, and sat on the patio drinking lemonade and beer. They agreed it was lucky her father had woken up and disturbed the intruder before anything had been stolen. Through the mirrored sunglasses he had bought that morning his inflamed eye was invisible even at close quarters, but his bruised face distracted her whenever she looked at him. She tried to focus on his lenses but her attention kept wandering to his bruised and swollen nose, and she felt very protective of him.

'Does it hurt?'

'Not really. Don't fuss, Lucy, it'll be fine.'

As she sipped her lemonade, her father told her he was going to hand in his key for reprogramming before he went to bed that night, just in case someone had found the other key to his room. He drained his beer and went to the bar for another bottle. Lucy sipped her lemonade and waited for him to come back, formulating her plan. By the time he returned she had reached a decision.

'Dad, hang on to your key as is. Don't get it reprogrammed. Not yet.'

'What? Why not? If— when your mother comes back we can sort out her key card at reception.'

'It's not that.'

'What then?'

Frowning with the effort to explain, she urged her father to consider the possibility that the intruder had knowingly taken the key from Angela. At least they should not rule it out.

'Not that again,' he said, rubbing his forehead and frowning. 'I thought we'd agreed it must have been a random burglar.'

'The point is we don't know. All I'm saying is that it's possible, Dad. Unlikely, but possible. We have to at least try. It's our only current lead.'

'Lucy, I've got no idea what you mean.'

She leaned forward trying not to look at his bruised nose as she outlined her idea that the intruder might be in touch with her mother who had sent him to fetch some of her belongings.

'Why would she do that?' her father asked, screwing up his face. 'What the blazes are you talking about?'

She shook her head. The theory made no sense without the suspicion that her mother had left deliberately. Somehow she did not think her father would be receptive to that suggestion.

'OK, forget that. It was a stupid thought. But let's suppose for a moment the intruder kidnapped her for a ransom. It would explain how he got in. He got the key from Mum, then used it to try and rob you.'

'I thought your new theory was that he was going to demand a ransom?'

'Yes, but he might have wanted to get his hands on some cash in the meantime.'

'Lucy, I don't think that sounds very likely—'

'All I'm saying is we should think about it. Because if it's true, then the intruder could lead us to where Mum is. If we can find him, that is.'

When her father replied, she heard her own desperate hope reflected in his voice. 'You really think he might know where she is?'

'I've no idea, but it's worth a shot, isn't it? I mean, what have we got to lose? Apart from another night's sleep.'

Her plan was simple. They would not change the key code. That night they would wait in George's room. If the intruder returned, they would be ready for him. George did not want to involve Lucy in implementing the plan but she insisted on staying with him. He suggested they rope in one of the security guards. It seemed like a sensible idea but they were not sure who to trust. In the end they agreed that Lucy should ask Adrian to pass the night with them in George's room. They had to be sure of overpowering the intruder if he returned. It was not merely a question of their own safety; Angela's life might depend on the success of their night's vigil.

Lucy knew Adrian was likely to go to the bar for a drink after work and waited for him. After about half an hour he appeared. She went up to the bar.

'Let me buy you a drink.'

Something in her manner must have alerted him because he grinned and asked her what she was after.

'Is it that obvious?' she replied, smiling. 'Come and sit down and I'll tell you about it.'

He nearly choked on his beer when she told him she wanted him to spend the night with her. Laughing, she added that her father would be there as well.

'A chaperone? Lucy, what the hell are we talking about here?'

First she swore him to secrecy and only after he had given his word did she explain her request.

'We know it's a long shot,' she concluded, 'but we're desperate, Adrian. We can't ignore any possible lead, and we're going to do this whether you help us or not.'

He looked sceptical. 'Honestly, Lucy, what are the chances that this burglar has got anything to do with your mother? And even if he is implicated in her disappearance, is he likely to come back to your father's room tonight, especially after your father gave him a thrashing last night?' He drained his glass and pulled a face at her. 'Thanks for the beer, but I have to say this all sounds daft to me. If you want my opinion, you should leave this to the police. It's their job to find your mother.'

'I wasn't asking for your opinion,' she snapped, standing up, her face flushed with emotion. 'I was asking for your help.'

She spun on her heel and stalked away.

At ten o'clock, Lucy and her father went to his room and made themselves comfortable. Just after half past ten there was a soft tap at the door. Lucy watched anxiously as her father asked who was there. She struggled to control a wild hope that her mother had returned. If she had not been disappointed, she would have been pleased to hear Adrian's voice. Clutching a carrier bag, he had a blanket over his arm. Her father ushered him in, smiling and thanking him for joining them. Adrian emptied the contents of his bag onto the table: six bottles of beer, a ball of green garden twine and two torches.

'What's the string for?' Lucy asked.

'If anyone breaks in, we'll want to tie him up,' Adrian answered.

They opened three of the bottles and sat, her father on the bed, Lucy and Adrian on chairs by the window, drinking and talking in muted tones. Adrian apologised that he had not brought them a torch each. Her father insisted that Lucy take the second one.

'If you need to, whack him over the head with it,' he said, more animated than she had seen him look since her mother had disappeared.

'We should turn the light out,' her father said at last. 'If he's going to come back, he'll wait until he thinks I'm asleep.'

Adrian wanted to know what time the intruder had broken in the previous night but her father could not remember. Lucy thought it had been about one in the morning when she had overheard the fight. She glanced at her watch and was surprised to see that it was nearly midnight. The time had passed surprisingly quickly since Adrian had arrived. They agreed to take shifts. There was no point in the three of them staying awake all night. Adrian offered to take the first watch. He said he was not tired. He would watch from midnight to two, then wake Lucy who would take the next two hours, waking her father at four.

'If I'm asleep,' he said.

None of them expected to get much sleep but Lucy must have nodded off in her chair because she was fast asleep when Adrian shook her shoulder. Muzzy headed, she peered about her in darkness.

'It's nearly four,' he whispered.

His voice sounded close to her ear and she felt his breath brush her cheek.

'You were supposed to wake me at two.'

'I tried but you were so fast asleep I didn't have the heart to disturb you.'

There had been no sign of anyone trying to enter the room. Charging her to wake him at the first sign of any intrusion, Adrian said he would get some kip. She nodded into the darkness.

At first everything was pitch black but as her eyes grew accustomed to the darkness she made out the shape of the bed, and a faint glow through the curtains that seemed to grow brighter as she watched. The darkness in the room seemed to make the silence more intense, apart from the distant murmur of the ocean, and a creaking in the walls. Somewhere nearby a car door slammed. A long way off, a dog began to bark. Several times she felt her head jerk upright as she stopped herself falling asleep.

When she had conceived her plan to keep watch over night she had been relieved to be doing something, as though just by taking action they would bring her mother back. Now she had nothing to do but listen, and no idea where her mother was, or if she had left them voluntarily. In the darkness, she could no longer distract herself from the fear that she might never see her mother again. All her life she had taken her mother's quiet help for granted. Other than occasional vague anxieties about her parents dying, which she never dwelled on, it had never occurred to her to worry that her mother might suddenly vanish from her life. She promised herself that she would make a conscious effort to express her appreciation of her mother's support in future, if she had the chance.

A noise. In the room. Someone was shuffling across the floor, trying not to make a sound. She reached out and pinched Adrian's arm, surprised to feel the hardness of his muscles even when he was resting. A door opened and closed.

'What?'

'Shh.' She leaned towards him. 'I heard something.'

She blinked at the sudden bright shaft of light from his torch.

'Dad?'

There was no answer. She could barely breathe for fear.

'Come on,' Adrian said, no longer bothering to whisper.

Lucy switched her torch on and they swept the room with beams of bright light. There was no one there.

Lucy and Adrian looked at one another in consternation, and then the toilet flushed. She felt like a fool as her father emerged from the bathroom, blinking in the torchlight.

'Is he here?' he asked, peering around.

Lucy began to giggle uncontrollably as they settled down again. It was nearly five o'clock, so her father took over the watch, but they all knew it was futile. No one was likely to break in now. Other than George's visit to the bathroom, there had been no disturbance during the night.

Lucy woke up with a neck stiff from sleeping in a chair.

'That's that then,' she said wretchedly as her father thanked Adrian again for turning out to help them.

'At least we know who we can trust,' he said.

Lucy nodded. Turning to gaze out of the window at her father's unrestricted view of the sea she wondered whether her father was right, and if they had been wise to share their plan with Adrian. Perhaps the intruder had been warned about their night time vigil. Only Adrian had known about the plan, Adrian who had been present when she had almost drowned. She became aware that her father was calling her.

'Aren't you going to thank Adrian?'

'Yes, sorry, I was half asleep. Thank you very much.'

She smiled weakly at Adrian who bowed his head in acknowledgement.

20

Tired after his disturbed night, George had told Lucy he would not be rising early that morning. They had agreed to meet for breakfast just before ten. Lucy had gone to bed at six but had not been able to sleep. Adrian had gone home at the conclusion of their night's vigil and had probably not yet arrived back at the hotel. Too agitated about her mother to sit around doing nothing while she waited for her father, Lucy decided to go for a walk along the beach. The fishermen were bound to talk to local people as they shared or sold their daily catch. No doubt they enjoyed a gossip. Her father had told her that no one could keep a secret for long on the island. One of the fishermen might have heard a rumour about a fair-haired woman staying on the island by herself.

Lucy refused to believe her mother was lost at sea. She was far too cautious to go out swimming on her own. Her passport and credit cards were in the hotel room. The only plausible conclusion was that she must still be somewhere on the island. Since she had very little money with her, it was reasonable to suppose that someone was helping her. That meant that at least one other person on the island must know where she was. If her mother was determined not to be found, Lucy would have to track down the person sheltering her. Her theory might prove to be completely wrong, but at least it seemed logical. And if there was only the slightest chance she would find her mother, it was still a possibility worth pursuing.

The idea was not as effective in practice as it had initially appeared. For a start, it was almost impossible to make herself understood by the fishermen who spoke little or no English.

'I'm looking for my mother.'

'Ah, mother.'

'She looks like me. Blonde hair.' She pointed at her hair.

The old fisherman gave a tolerant smile. 'You want fish?' he asked with sudden interest.

Lucy shook her head. 'Do you speak English?'

'English. Ah.' The old man beckoned a young boy over. He looked about ten.

'I'm looking for a woman,' Lucy explained.

The boy nodded seriously. 'Woman,' he repeated.

'My mother. She has fair hair, blonde, like me.' Again the pantomime with her hair.

The boy nodded and pointed to his own hair. 'Hair,' he said.

At a signal lost on Lucy, the old man and the boy turned away and hurried to help their companions who were hauling in the net. Under other circumstances, Lucy would have stayed to watch them, intrigued to see what they had caught. A couple of other tourists had gathered, cameras poised.

'They caught a turtle yesterday,' one of them told Lucy. 'We saw it.'

'But they threw it back,' her companion added. 'It's illegal to keep them.'

'It was beautiful. You should have seen the shell.'

Lucy turned away and began making her way back along the beach. It was just past seven o'clock, and relatively cool. Instead of turning into the hotel, she walked on. Adrian had mentioned a number of bays, all quiet. According to him, one in particular was difficult to access and so always deserted. If Lucy had wanted to disappear for a few days, she could not think of a better place to hide out. Equipped with enough provisions and plenty of water, she would not even need to rely on help from anyone else. The more she thought about it the more excited she grew. Her mother could be camping out in a little bay along the coast. The fact that the police or coastguard would probably have spotted her was not conclusive. It must at least be possible for someone to hide among the rocks for a few days without being seen. And in any case, she was not convinced the authorities had searched everywhere.

The bay she had been to with Adrian was further away than she remembered. She was tempted to turn back, but it was still early and not yet blisteringly hot. Besides, she had her phone. If she was late back, she could always call her father and tell him she had gone for a walk and would be there soon. She kept walking. This time instead of clambering over the rocks, she splashed through shallow water to reach the bay she had visited before. It was deserted and just as beautiful as she remembered it. Feeling slightly foolish, she called out quietly, 'Mum! Mum! It's me, Lucy.' The only response was the gentle breaking of waves on the shore. She carried on, searching for the next sheltered spot.

Climbing over wet rocks on the far side of the bay, she nearly lost her footing. Reaching out to steady herself, she dropped her bag. It slipped between the rocks and landed on a narrow strip of sand. She snatched it up before the next wave came in. A few seconds later it would have been drenched in sea water, ruining her phone. Her heart pounded. It was time to turn back. This was not a sensible place to be exploring on her own. Besides, the police and coastguard had made a thorough search of the island. She had been an idiot to think she could find her mother after they had failed. Cursing herself for being stupid and arrogant, she sat on the rocks for a moment and gazed at the ocean stretched out in front of her, endlessly blue.

Looking down from her vantage point on the rocks, something caught her attention up ahead. Craning her neck she stared, hardly able to believe her eyes. The next moment she was climbing over the rocks, careless of her own safety.

'Mum!' she yelled, breathless with disbelief. 'Mum! Is that you? Mum!'

Her foot slipped and she twisted her ankle. Slowing down, she picked her way more carefully over the rocks, glancing up every few seconds to make sure the figure she had seen had not vanished. The woman was still there, lying on the sand, her position unaltered. She looked as though she was asleep. A terrible thought struck Lucy.

'Mum!' she screamed in alarm. 'Mum! Wake up!'

Reaching the sand at last, she scrambled down from the last boulder and raced over to the motionless figure. Wearing the remains of a torn bikini, the body looked barely human. The face was horribly mutilated. The eyelids, ears and tip of the nose were missing, eaten away by fish, and the skin on the bloated body was mottled black and white. Despite her abhorrence, Lucy felt an overriding relief that the drowned woman was not her mother. She studied the misshapen figure, fascinated and repelled in equal measure. Looking more closely she thought the dead woman had probably been quite young, with short blonde hair not unlike her own. Pulling out her phone, she was not sure what number to dial for the emergency services. She did not even have the police inspector's card on her. With trembling fingers, she phoned the hotel and asked for Adrian. She could have cried with relief when his voice came on the line. He undertook to alert the police and speak to her father, and offered to pick her up.

'The police will find the body easily enough, and it might be better for you and your father if we keep you out of it, with everything else that's going on at the moment. Why don't you stay put and let me come and get you? It's not a good idea to go climbing around on the rocks by yourself at the best of times.'

She did not remonstrate at the criticism. He was right. 'I'm fine. I'll wait for you here. I won't go anywhere.'

'Good. And don't worry about your father. I'll look after him. You just stay put.'

Lucy thanked him, and he rang off at once. She went over and leaned against the rocks to wait. Once again Adrian had helped her, but she could hardly accuse him of being involved in this incident. Curiosity overcame her revulsion, and she approached the body to take another look. Caught up in a strand of seaweed, she discerned a charm bracelet wound around the dead girl's wrist. She stared at it in terrible fascination, recognising the letters interspersed with tiny bells. There was no doubt that she was looking at the bracelet that Judy had shown her just a few days earlier. It was horrible to think of that vivacious girl reduced to this hideous mound of dead flesh. Shaken by a sudden wave of nausea, she ran up the beach and vomited under the trees. It should have made no difference to her that she had met the dead girl, talked and laughed with her. Death was appalling, irrespective of the individual's identity. But until she had realised who it was, she had not really registered this misshapen lump had once been a living, breathing human being. Now that she knew who it was, Lucy even recognised Judy's red and blue bikini. Only her poor distorted face was unrecognisable.

Going back to kneel on the sand beside the body, she spoke softly to the dead girl. 'You poor thing, you're never going to find a rich sugar daddy now, are you?' Gently she picked a few small white petals out of Judy's hair and brushed her straggly fringe out of her hideous eye sockets. All of a sudden, she started back as though she had been stung. Right in the centre of Judy's forehead was a small round black hole. She had not drowned. She had been shot. Lucy sprang to her feet and looked around. She had already been attacked in the water and among the rocks. Judy and she looked very similar. It seemed likely that she, not Judy, had been the intended victim of this murder.

21

ADRIAN WAS BETTER THAN his word. Within a few minutes Lucy was relieved to hear a car draw up nearby and the sound of someone crashing through the trees.

'There you are,' he panted. 'Thank goodness. Come on!' Without a word of explanation, he grabbed her by the hand and dragged her up the beach and through densely packed trees to where his car was waiting, with the engine running. As they drove off, they heard sirens approaching.

'I hope I did the right thing,' he said. 'I told your dad you were stranded on rocks and I was coming to show you the way back to the road.'

'But—'

'It was the best I could come up with at the time. Don't panic, I didn't say you'd done anything stupid, or were in any danger. The opposite, in fact. I said you thought you could get back quite easily by yourself, but you didn't want to take any chances so you were playing it safe, calling me.'

'So you could be the hero, and rescue me again?'

'Would you rather I'd told him the truth?' he asked, sounding exasperated. 'Hasn't he got enough to worry about?'

'Yes, I suppose you're right. But he's going to find out I was there, isn't he? I mean, the police will want to know what happened, and what I was doing there, and—' She began to cry at the enormity of what had happened.

'The police don't know you were there. I told them that a passerby had reported seeing a body and that was all I knew. I thought it best to keep you out of it. There's nothing you can say to help the situation. The poor girl's dead, and,' he sighed, 'I'm afraid this happens from time to time. People go swimming where it's not safe, on their own, and sometimes they drown. I just think you've got enough going on right now without getting grilled about some random girl drowning.'

'It wasn't a random girl, and she didn't drown.' Breaking down in tears, Lucy told him about Judy. 'She didn't drown. She was shot.'

'What?' Adrian slammed on the brakes and turned to her. He looked frightened. 'Do you want to tell me what you're talking about? And what the hell I've just lied to the police about?'

With an effort, Lucy pulled herself together. 'I don't suppose you've got any tissues?'

Adrian shook his head. She wiped her dripping nose on her shirt and began. She told him everything, from her abortive encounter with the fishermen, to the moment when she had recognised Judy's bracelet, and seen the bullet hole in her forehead.

'The thing is,' she concluded miserably, 'I think whoever killed her might have thought she was me.'

'Who might have thought who was you? Sorry, but you're not making sense again.'

Lucy took a deep breath and listed the attacks that had taken place on her family. 'Not just me, but there's the intruder in my father's room, and of course my mother—' She broke off and blew her nose on her shirt again. 'So I think whoever shot Judy must have mistaken her for me . . .'

Adrian looked troubled. He spoke gently. 'Lucy, I know it's very hard for you right now, with your mother going missing, but you have to see things in perspective. Not everything that happens is about you and your family. It might seem like it right now, but you've got to get a grip. Terrible things happen, and there's often no reason for it. People go swimming and occasionally they drown.' He smiled anxiously at her. 'You'd better wash your face before your father sees you.'

As he drove off, he asked her quietly if she was sure Judy had been shot. Lucy tried to describe the injury she had seen on Judy's head. Never having seen a real bullet wound, she could not be sure Judy had been shot. She might have drowned after all. The hole in her head could have been made by some sort of fish. Listening to Adrian's calm words, Lucy could not help thinking she must have been mistaken. It seemed impossible to believe Judy had really been shot.

Her father was quiet at breakfast. Dazed and shocked, and tired after their disturbed night, Lucy could not interpret his state of mind. It was difficult to see his expression through his sunglasses. He seemed cheerful enough, although she noticed he only picked at a plate of fruit while she ate.

'Dad,' she began and paused, uncertain how to tell him about her own confusing encounters with an unknown assailant. She resumed, wanting to hear his perspective on what had happened. 'I think I've been targeted too.'

Her father nodded. 'Yes, I know. This affects us all.'

'No, I don't just mean what's going on with you and Mum.' She paused. They had no idea what had happened to her mother. She lowered her voice. 'I think someone's been trying to kill me.'

Her father did not even turn to look at her as she told him how she had almost drowned.

'So you nearly drowned, and Adrian rescued you?' was all her father said when she finished. 'I hope you thanked him.'

'Yes, of course I did. But what I'm saying is that I think someone pulled me under.'

'Did you see who it was?'

'Well, no, I didn't actually see anyone there.'

Her father frowned. 'What did Adrian say about it? He was there.'

Lucy sighed. 'He thought it was the current.'

Her father nodded. 'I'm sure that's what it was. The currents can be very strong round here. You have to be careful, Lucy. Promise me you won't swim too far out. Even if you're not out of your depth a strong undercurrent can sweep you off your feet. Promise me you'll be more careful.'

'I promise.'

She launched into a description of her walk along the beach, and the rock fall, but she could see her father's attention was wandering. There was no point in continuing. Her father was not going to believe that had been a deliberate attempt on her life, any more than he believed she had been attacked by someone swimming beneath her in the ocean. It was time she stopped bothering him with her worries and uncertainties, and began to work out her problems for herself.

When they finished their coffee, her father leaned back in his chair and announced his intention of returning to the police station after breakfast to find out if there had been any progress.

'I know they said they'd let us know if there was any news, but there's nothing like putting in a personal appearance.'

He was pleased when Lucy offered to accompany him. She thought he was becoming more uneasy than ever about letting her out of his sight. After leaving a message that her father was to be contacted if his wife reappeared, they set off. Lucy was relieved that they were driving into the town, away from the coast where every view of the beach reminded her of Judy's body. Somehow the mutilated face seemed more harrowing now than when she had first seen it lying on the sand. Whenever she thought about it, she felt sick. But she said nothing, aware that Adrian had lied to the police because of her. If she told her father, he would only worry more about Angela. Perhaps he would insist she admitted everything to the police, which might get Adrian into trouble. Uneasy about lying to the police, she had gone too far to confess the truth now without stirring up more problems.

The heat of the day was building up. The humidity was oppressive and it was a relief to be bowling along the coastal road with the air conditioning on full blast. As they drove, the sky grew overcast. Lucy's father predicted a storm would hit the island. A few seconds later a bolt of lightning flashed over the ocean, followed by a crash of thunder. Lucy cried out. Then the rain fell. They had to pull over to the side of the road. It was impossible to see through the windscreen, even with the wipers on full speed.

'Is it safe in the car?' Lucy asked, but the lightning did not strike again and the sound of thunder grew fainter.

The road into Victoria wound round several sharp hairpin bends so her father decided to wait until the rain eased off. As they sat in the car watching the rain, he assured Lucy that such violent tropical storms never lasted long, and after a few moments the noise of rain drumming on the roof faded. He turned the wipers on and the windscreen cleared. Only a few stray splashes of rain streaked the glass. Looking round, Lucy was surprised to see that it was still pelting on the other side of the road. An invisible glass wall appeared to cut them off from the downpour a couple of feet away. Her father was amused when she was afraid the engine had caught fire. He pointed out steam rising from the ground all around them.

By the time they reached the police station in Victoria, the clouds had cleared. The sun beat down on them with its customary ferocity, and the ground was dry as they crossed the road to the police station. Her father announced his name at the Enquiries desk and a policeman behind the desk looked up blankly.

'My name is George Hall,' he repeated, sounding slightly put out that the policeman did not appear to recognise his name. 'I'm here about my wife. We reported her missing two days ago. We're English tourists.'

The officer nodded. It was not clear which part of the statement he was acknowledging. Instructing them to wait, he picked up the phone and began to jabber in French. He spoke too quickly for Lucy to pick out more than a few words: '*ici . . . anglais . . . maintenant . . . attend.*'

'Inspector Henri will be here soon,' the policeman told them as he hung up. 'He asks that you take a seat and wait for him. He is very busy.'

The tall inspector arrived shortly afterwards. He led them across the courtyard to his office.

'Mr Hall, we have been conducting an extensive search for your wife,' he began, an anxious smile stamped on his face.

Lucy observed her own disappointment in her father's face before his head drooped forward.

'Conducting a search,' he repeated flatly. 'Have you found anything, Inspector, anything at all?'

The policeman shrugged his shoulders, raising his hands in the air.

'Your wife has been missing for three days.'

'Yes.'

'Although you did not report her absence until two days ago.'

'Well obviously we didn't come here the minute we noticed she'd gone,' Lucy's father snapped.

Lucy could hear the frustration in his voice and glanced at his face, flushed with anger. Ignoring his evident vexation, the policeman smiled at him, perhaps intending to reassure him that everything was under control.

'We are uncovering the moss,' he said cryptically. 'Such investigations take time. It does not help that she is unknown on the island. No one can tell us her movements, who are her friends, where she is likely to go.'

'I would have thought that would make her stand out more, and make her easier to trace,' Lucy said.

The policeman turned to her for an instant, as though uncertain whether she was challenging him, before he turned back to her father. 'We have carried out a massive search, I assure you.'

'What exactly have you done?' Lucy asked. 'Have helicopters been sent to search the coast and inland as well, in case she got lost on the hills? And have you been asking in all the hotels, and questioned everyone in the local community? We'd like to know,' she added quickly, afraid she might antagonise the policeman if she was too outspoken. 'It's just that, like you said, no one here knows my mother except us, and obviously we want to do whatever we can to assist your police investigation.'

The policeman raised his eyebrows. 'Police investigation?' he repeated. 'I am not aware a crime has been committed in this instance.'

'My wife's been abducted and you don't think a crime has been committed!' her father shouted, losing his temper.

The inspector shook his head. Nothing seemed to rattle him. Lucy felt a sudden urge to leap across the room and slap the smile from his smug face.

'We do not know there has been an abduction. Your wife is not a child that we should be so frightened. Mahé is not London.' He leaned forward confidentially. 'It can happen sometimes that a woman likes to take time for herself, to reflect on her life. Here on the island people make many discoveries about themselves. It may be that your wife is – how shall I say it? – discovering herself. I am hopeful your wife will return to you very soon. In the meantime, we will continue to enquire and will inform you if we receive news of her. The case is by no means closed, although the search will diminish now, after seventy-two hours. I assure you we are following the usual protocol in this, but we cannot continue to devote all our resources to this case.'

'However much manpower you are devoting to the search, it's not enough,' Lucy's father replied.

The inspector raised his eyebrows and heaved a loud sigh. 'I assure you we are doing what we can, but we have another case on our hands that I am afraid is taking precedence over everything else.'

'Precedence over my wife going missing? I don't think so.'

The policeman vacillated for a second before leaning forward in his chair. He spoke rapidly in a low voice.

'You may not have yet heard that a body was discovered here on the island only today. You will no doubt read about it in the papers before long, the body of a girl found on the beach early this morning.'

Lucy's father nodded grimly. 'Yes, someone at the hotel told us. It's terrible, of course, but in the meantime, my wife is still missing and possibly in danger. That girl is dead. Unless you want another woman to be killed here, you need to make my wife's disappearance your number one priority.'

The inspector hesitated. He stared hard at Lucy's father and heaved a deep sigh.

'We have reason to suspect the girl died from unnatural causes. I am unable to tell you more. But you understand, we are now most busy investigating this death. We need to catch the killer as a matter of extreme urgency. It may be that more lives are in danger, including that of your wife.'

The words echoed inside Lucy's head. Her mother had gone missing and now a girl had been found, murdered. She bit her lip, wary of letting slip how much she knew about Judy's death.

'We need to catch the killer of this poor girl,' the policeman repeated. 'Like you, she was staying in Beau Vallon. Her identity has not yet been confirmed, but we suspect she was an Australian girl . . .' He hesitated. 'Her family are on their way now to identify the body. She was the same age as Lucy.'

'Oh my God,' Lucy's father burst out.

'Yes, it is a terrible tragedy. And you see, there is much to do. So you must excuse me.'

The inspector rose to his feet, indicating the interview was over. There seemed little more to say beyond thanking him and exhorting him to step up his enquiries into Angela's disappearance. As they were leaving, her father made a final attempt to convince the policeman it was inconceivable his wife would have left voluntarily, without a word of explanation.

'She'd know how worried we'd be,' he insisted.

The policeman shrugged. 'Ah, who can tell what is in the mind of a woman?'

'Another woman,' Lucy suggested sharply.

Still smiling sadly, the inspector ignored her remark.

'Well, he was a fat lot of help,' Lucy grumbled as they reached the street. 'What now?'

Her father suggested they visit the British High Commission. The Vice Consul had been to the hotel to see them every day, but while they were in Victoria it made sense to go and speak to her. As they took the lift to the third floor, Lucy tried to feel pleased that the dead girl had been Australian. At least the British High Commission would not be focusing all their attention on a dead foreigner. But it was a mistake to think about Judy. As the lift doors opened, Lucy wiped away tears for the girl who had been washed up on a deserted beach, far from home, her face eaten away by scavenging fish. Her father assumed she was crying for her mother, and in a way she was.

As usual, Maggie was sympathetic and supportive, and she assured them everything possible was being done to assist the police enquiry into Angela's whereabouts. But when George complained that the police did not appear to be doing very much, Maggie just shrugged. It was all very frustrating.

'I'm sure they're doing everything they can,' she replied. 'The High Commissioner is in regular contact with the station commander, and we have his assurance that the police have by no means closed the case. They've already devoted an unprecedented level of man power to the search. Believe me, everyone is taking this case seriously.'

George nodded. 'Yes, and of course we know about this dead girl who's turned up, but that doesn't make any difference to the fact that my wife has disappeared.'

'It's shocking.' Maggie agreed. 'The victim was the same age as Lucy. I don't know how much you've heard, but it's a very sad case.'

'We heard she was murdered,' Lucy's father said. 'But if anything, knowing there may be a killer around makes it even more important that we find Angela. We need to keep up the pressure on them to look for her.'

'Of course, and I'm sure they're doing everything they can. In the meantime, if you can think of anything that might assist them—'

'We think there's someone out to get us,' Lucy piped up and immediately regretted having spoken.

'What makes you say that?' Maggie asked.

Lucy hesitated. Although Inspector Henri himself had told them the police suspected foul play, Lucy and her father had not yet been told the identity of the dead girl. There was no way either of them could know that she resembled Lucy.

'She's talking about the intruder who broke into my room,' her father interposed.

With a silent sigh of relief, Lucy sat back and listened to her father and Maggie discuss the intruder.

'Do you know yet how he got into your room?'

'Lucy thinks he might have got hold of Angela's key, but the likelihood is he entered the room the same way he left it, up onto the flat roof below my window, and in and out through the balcony. I mean, I keep the balcony doors closed, of course, because of the air conditioning, and I'm pretty sure I would have locked it before I went to bed, but—'

'It's understandable you might have forgotten to lock it, with all the trauma you've been experiencing,' Maggie said.

She went on to express her regret that they were having such a dreadful holiday on Mahé. With a helpless shrug she offered George another biscuit.

22

Having lost all sense of time passing, Angela had no idea if she had been crouching in the dark for hours or days. Either way, it made no difference. She could not make sense of her situation, could not remember where she was, or what she was doing in this rough prison. The wooden slats of the wall pressed against her shoulder bones. From the blackness, a dark angel stared at her. Although it was invisible, she could see it clearly when she shut her eyes. Through closed eyelids she examined its huge dark eyes. It was the only living creature she had seen since she had been blindfolded and imprisoned in the hut. She stared at its lidless black eyes and it gazed solemnly back at her as though it understood her plight, before it dissolved into thousands of tiny dots of light, shimmering against a black sky.

She was dimly aware that she was starving. For a while she had thought of nothing but food: bunches of bananas growing in the shelter of wide leaves, large avocados, giant king prawns, fish curry, and earlier memories of muesli with cold milk, cheese on toast, hot chocolate. But she had stopped fantasising about food. Now, the thought of eating made her nauseous. Her guts were held in the grip of a vice that was squeezing the life out of her. Lightheaded and dizzy, she understood that she was dying. She hoped it would not take long.

Bright sparks of light flashed in her head. There was a crashing in her ears, the sound of a door slamming shut. Knowing Veronique had not come to kill her, she wept. She had given up thinking about George and Lucy. They existed in a world beyond her prison. That life seemed like a distant dream, agonising to recall, knowing it was lost to her. All she wanted was for her degradation to end.

A voice filled her ears. 'Eat.'

Grains of rice in her throat made her retch.

'You have to eat,' the voice said. 'If you do not eat you will die. It is not the time to die now.'

With a spurt of rage she thrust her chin forward and pushed the bowl of rice aside, biting at her tormentor's hand in a frantic attempt to draw blood. She was too weak to pierce the leathery flesh. When the spoon was shoved into her mouth for a second time she could not resist her body's compulsion to survive. Salty tears slithered down her cheeks. The rice tasted good.

'That is better.'

The voice was right. She felt a resurgence of strength coursing through her body, like a rebirth. The pressure in her head lifted. Behind her eyes the bright lights stopped their insane flickering.

'Water,' she murmured.

Her own voice sounded unreal, like an echo in her ears, but there was nothing insubstantial about the cold water splashing against her lips. She drank, cautiously at first, then with greedy gulps. She considered kicking her captor again, but doubted she could lash out with enough force to inflict any pain. In any case, if she succeeded in injuring Veronique, that would not help. No one else knew where she was. Without Veronique to keep her alive, she would certainly perish alone in this dismal place.

She no longer wanted to die. She wanted to live and look up at the sky, breathing in air that was not foul with the stench of excrement and vomit. With a profound ache that was almost physical, she yearned for her husband. She thought of the daughter who still needed her, although she was a grown woman, and felt guilty that she had longed for death.

'You loved George, didn't you?' she cried out in desperation. 'Please try to understand that I love him too, and he loves me. Maybe he loved you in the past, but that was a long time ago. He's been my husband for twenty-five years. If you let me die he'll be devastated. You wouldn't want George to suffer like that, would you? My husband is a good man. He doesn't deserve to suffer.'

There was no answer.

'I have a daughter,' she went on, increasingly frantic. 'You can't take me away from her. She needs me.'

Still there was no response.

She tried again. 'Why do you want me to die? I'm nothing to you. We're just tourists, we came here on holiday. If you don't let me go, you'll be a murderer. You wouldn't want to live with that guilt, would you? And for what? My death won't help you. If it's money you want, my husband will pay you. Just ask him. He'll pay.'

Still Veronique did not speak.

'I can see that you loved him very much. I love him too.'

The door slammed shut. Alone again, she sank to the floor, exhausted. Her pleading had made no difference. All she had achieved was to tire herself out.

'What do you want with me?' she called out. 'What have I ever done to you?'

But she knew the answer. She had married the man for whom Veronique had been waiting for thirty years.

23

After their dispiriting visit to the police, Lucy and her father agreed to stop at the neighbouring hotel for a drink before returning to the Garden of Eden. Neither of them felt inclined to go straight back to their own hotel. With uncharacteristic extravagance, her father came back from the bar with two cocktails the colour of cranberry. He grinned down at her, doing his best to appear cheerful, and she tried to smile back. He sat down with a quiet grunt and held up his glass. She clinked hers against it and they sipped in silence, gazing at the sea.

'Well? What do you think?' he asked, holding up his glass and inspecting the ruby coloured liquid.

'Mmm, it's nice. What is it?'

'Oh hell, the girl did tell me, but I've forgotten. Some local cocktail that was allegedly invented by one of the barmen here, and twice the price of other cocktails as a result.'

She laughed. 'It's nice.'

'It is, isn't it?'

He sounded surprised, as though he no longer believed anything good could happen ever again. Worried about him, Lucy resolved to make more of an effort to appear positive. Tasting like tangy lemonade, the cocktail was deceptively strong and they both relaxed.

'We could have lunch here, if you like,' her father suggested as they finished their drinks.

She nodded gratefully. She had eaten little at breakfast, and her head was spinning.

'That would be great. I'm really hungry.'

She felt better after eating. When they finished they went back to the Garden of Eden where they went straight out onto the patio and sat in a corner beneath a large parasol, with a clear view of the sea.

'Can't hide in bed for ever,' her father said and sighed.

Five minutes later he was fast asleep and snoring softly. Lucy closed her eyes but she was not tired. After fidgeting in her chair for a while, she went for a wander around the gardens. It was too hot to move quickly. She tried to enjoy the delicate scented flowers with their exotic names: frangipani, hibiscus, bougainvillea, while unconsciously scouring the ground for signs of her mother. As she searched, she thought about her father's intruder, wondering if he had used her mother's key and whether she had relinquished it willingly. Once she thought she spotted a pair of sunglasses hidden under a bush, sunlight glinting off the lenses. When she stooped down to take a closer look, she found an empty beer bottle.

It was too hot to go down to the beach so she followed the path to the hotel. In one direction it led to the car park. She turned and followed it the other way round the main hotel block to what looked like the rear of the kitchens. A couple of waiters were standing by the bins, smoking. They glanced at her incuriously as she passed. There was nothing of interest there so she turned and made her way back towards the gardens along the dusty path that ran alongside the hotel.

She was about to turn back when she felt a hand slapped across her mouth. A smell of stale beer wafted past her as a strong arm seized her around the waist, lifting her right off her feet. Recovering from her shock she kicked out in ferocious panic. One of her sandals fell off and she stubbed her toe painfully against the side of a rusty white van, its paintwork pitted and scratched. The door was open. One of her arms was twisted so sharply up behind her back she thought her shoulder would be dislocated. Her shorts ripped and she scraped her knee on a jagged edge of metal as she was propelled forwards.

The floor of the van shook as the door slammed behind her. She was lying on her front, head turned to one side, trembling and groaning. The pain in her toe was excruciating. She was afraid it was broken. For a few seconds she was too stunned to move or cry out. The engine revved noisily and, with a violent jolt, the van began to move. It swung around a corner and she slid across the floor, whacking her head. She felt dizzy. The van gathered speed. She called out as loudly as she could until her throat felt sore, bruising her fist as she punched the side of the van. Her commotion was drowned out by the roar of the engine. Realising she was wasting her energy, she slumped against the side of the van. Doing her best to ignore the throbbing in her head, and the pain in her toe, she tried to think clearly.

It was dark inside the van. The floor was slippery, covered with what felt like petals, and there was an overpowering scent of frangipani. Groping her way around the walls, she felt the crack between the doors, but couldn't find a handle. Fumbling in her pocket she pulled out her phone and shone the screen light around the interior of the van. The door was locked with no means of opening from inside. There were no windows in the back of the van which was blocked off from the driver's cabin. She punched in her father's number but there was no signal. She tried again, and again, but it was no use. Disappointed, she put the phone away in her pocket. She was trapped.

She scrabbled in her pockets and all over the juddering floor for something she could use to try and prise the door open, but drew a blank. There was nothing at all in the back of the van apart from masses of petals covering the floor. Beneath a layer of soft petals her fingers found older ones, brittle and shrivelled. Their scent filled the van. But petals were not going to help her escape. Her only hope was to burst from the van as soon as the door opened and barge the driver out of the way. To succeed, she would have to take him by surprise.

They seemed to travel for miles before the van finally slowed down and came to a halt. Disregarding the pain in her foot as well as she could, she crouched down, poised to leap at the driver when he opened the door. Nothing happened. Minutes passed. Her tensed muscles began to ache. Resigned to the fact that the door was not going to open, she shouted and banged on the partition behind the driver's seat. She was making so much noise that she did not hear the door open behind her. Once again a hand pressed hard against her mouth. Another hand gripped her by the throat and squeezed, dragging her backwards out of the van. Darkness clouded her mind. As she fought to remain conscious, she thought she heard a hoarse whisper: 'Very unique.'

She struggled to ward off the darkness. 'What do you mean?' Her lips struggled to repeat the question. 'What?'

'Tell George she is waiting,' the voice rasped in her ear. 'He knows her. She is very unique.'

The voice echoed in her head, the words reverberating in her mind until 'Very unique' changed to 'On the beach', repeating in her mind like waves breaking on the sand. Her vision clouded over and she felt herself falling into a deep pit of darkness.

24

George opened his eyes and glanced lazily around. There was no sign of Angela or Lucy. With a start he remembered what had happened. He groaned and glanced at his watch. He had been asleep for over an hour. He stood up, stretched and wandered to the edge of the patio to look down at the beach where a few holidaymakers were lying beneath parasols. He could not see Lucy. He pressed her number on his phone.

'Hello, this is Lucy. Please leave your name and number and I'll call you back.'

He knew he was foolish to worry about his daughter. He understood she could not just sit around the hotel, waiting for him. She needed to take her mind off the awful events that had been happening. She was probably with Adrian, who knew all the secluded coves and beauty spots along the coast and obviously enjoyed showing her around. George could hardly blame him. Lucy was a very attractive young woman. In any case, whatever George thought of Adrian, it had been a relief to see Lucy looking cheerful again, until Angela had disappeared.

While he was fretting, Maggie arrived.

'I've just popped in to see if there's anything you need.'

He did not tell her that he needed Angela, and decided not to mention Lucy. She would be back soon. Maggie stayed and chatted for a while. George found her positivity reassuring. After reiterating that the police were continuing to search, and were bound to find his wife soon, Maggie left.

By now over half an hour had passed since George had woken up, and Lucy still had not returned. He fought to quell his anxiety. He closed his eyes, willing himself not to think about anything, but was unable to sit still, not knowing where Lucy was. With a sickening sense of déjà vu he went up to her room and knocked on the door, in case she had returned without him knowing. There was no response. He tried her phone, holding his breath as it rang. It went to voicemail. He showered and changed but she had still not returned to her room by the time he had finished. Telling himself she must have gone out with Adrian, he went to the bar area to sit at a corner table and watch the sunset. Contemplating the natural beauty of the island helped him believe his wife would return to him unharmed. He did not believe in God, but watching the glory of the sun as it set over the ocean gave him a comfort that was almost spiritual.

When Adrian strolled through the door and went to sit at the bar and share a joke with the barman, George felt the ground sway beneath his feet. He stared at their two heads, one blond, the other dark, willing the fair head to be Lucy. It was crazy because, thinking rationally, he knew Adrian was talking to the barman. Adrian looked up and smiled when George greeted him. Struggling to keep his voice steady, George asked if Lucy was with him.

'Are you all right, George?'

'Is Lucy with you?' George repeated.

'No, I haven't seen her all day.'

Adrian glanced around as though checking to see if she was there.

George clutched Adrian's sleeve. 'I don't know where she is. I can't lose her too.' He was nearly in tears.

He was loath to embarrass himself by giving way to his emotions, and was relieved when Adrian slipped off his stool and led him over to a corner table. They sat down together and George was grateful that Adrian waited patiently while he regained his composure. George explained the reason for his anxiety. There was not much to tell. Adrian was reassuring, but he did not know where Lucy was. All he could say was that he was sure she would return soon. He agreed she might have gone to look for her mother without telling anyone where she was going.

'We have to find her, Adrian, we have to find her,' George kept repeating.

They decided they could cover more ground if they split up to search. George had the impression Adrian was not too concerned about Lucy going missing, and only offered his help on account of the stress George was under with Angela's disappearance. They agreed that George would scour the Garden of Eden, while Adrian drove to a nearby hotel. Lucy had struck up a fleeting friendship with the American girls who were staying there and might have gone to visit them. It was difficult to believe she would have gone off without telling him, but it could have been spontaneous, if the Americans had turned up unexpectedly and offered to take her out with them. With no signal on her phone, she might not have been able to contact him straight away. It was unlikely she had forgotten to call, but possible.

Once Adrian had gone, George set about searching the hotel again. He approached the task methodically. Already he felt calmer, embarrassed at having exposed his frailty to a stranger. But this was a time of unprecedented emotional stress. He checked at reception in case Lucy had left a message for him but there had been no communication from her. He asked a security guard if he had seen Lucy that afternoon. The security guard gave him a curious look. It was only a couple of days since George had been asking the exact same questions about his wife. Neither the receptionist nor the security had seen Lucy that afternoon.

'The last time I saw the young lady, she was with you,' the security guard said, his eyes narrowed suspiciously at George.

After asking at the hotel entrance, George went back to search the pool and beach area. He checked the hire car was still in the car park then went back indoors to see if Lucy had returned to her room while he was out. He scribbled a note and slid it under her door, in case she returned without him seeing her.

'Lucy, please call me right now.'

But she did not call.

25

Lucy opened her eyes. She was not sure how long she had been unconscious, or what had woken her. It came again, a surge of cool water caressing her feet, a relief from the stifling heat. She stirred. Her shirt was soaked with sweat. Her head was pounding. No one could survive for long in that heat. Panicking, she knew she had to move, but she was too dazed to stand up. Cool water washed her feet again, creeping up her calves. She realised she was lying on sand at the water's edge. With a start, she remembered the body she had discovered on the beach the previous day. If she did not get up soon, she might be carried out to sea and drown.

She did not know how long she had been lying there, nor how she had arrived there. She knew only that she could not afford to remain exposed to the burning sun. One of her toes hurt. With difficulty she raised her leg and squinted down at it. Her toe looked bruised. She lowered her foot and let her aching head fall back. She was feeling drowsy but, whatever happened, she knew she must not fall asleep. She had to get out of the direct sun as soon as possible. The throbbing in her toe seemed to worsen as she sat up. Frowning, she dragged herself up into a sitting position and looked around. The particular stretch of beach was unfamiliar, but she could see the road on the far side of a row of trees. Somehow she had to hobble up there, and find a bus stop. Maybe a taxi would go by.

Grunting with exertion, she hauled herself to her feet and began limping across the sand towards the road. Reaching the shade of the trees, she sat on a stump to rest for a moment. As she perched there cooling down, a heat haze seemed to lift inside her head. When her mind cleared, she remembered hearing a message that she was to tell George her mother was waiting. A sob bubbled up into her throat. Her mother must have fallen ill, probably from the heat. Perhaps a local woman was tending to her. Her mother was alive. The family would soon be reunited. All they had to do was find her. That could not be difficult, on such a small island. But remembering how she had been pushed into the back of a van and driven away from the hotel, she felt afraid again. She did not understand why she had been given such a cryptic hostile message, when she could simply have been told where her mother was. Still there was no point in worrying about that for now. The pressing need was to find her mother. It was best not to think about what had just happened. The only explanation she could think of was that there was a lunatic on the island. She had a horrible suspicion it might be her.

'Lucy!'

She opened her eyes and saw a worried face staring down at her.

'Adrian! What are you doing here?'

'I was looking for you.'

'But . . .' She frowned. 'How did you know I was here?'

'I didn't. Your dad's been going out of his mind with worry and I offered to take a look around. He said he was going to check the hotel grounds but he thought you might have gone to visit your American friends—' He broke off, with a puzzled expression. 'What are you doing out here on the roadside?'

Lucy looked round but there was no sign of the battered white van. She had not seen the registration number, and there was no way of finding it out now. Clambering to her feet she hobbled towards the place where she thought the van could have been parked. There were tyre marks on the earth, but that meant nothing. They could have been made by another vehicle. Walking gingerly, she examined her injured foot. None of her toes were broken as she could wriggle them without difficulty, although her little toe was bruised. Adrian called out in alarm as she inched her way to the edge of the narrow clearing until she was able to look down the short incline. At the bottom, waves were washing up against the rock face. The water was shallow and clear. She did not know if she should tell him what had happened to her. The sequence of events was so muddled in her memory, she was not even sure she could relate her experience coherently.

Adrian fetched a bottle of cold water from his car and she drank gratefully. When the bottle was almost empty, she poured the remainder over her head, squealing as the chilly water ran down her back.

'Feeling better?' he asked.

She nodded.

'You'd better call your dad and let him know you're OK. He'll still be looking for you.'

'Oh God,' she replied, aghast. 'What on earth am I going to say to him?'

'Good question,' he replied. 'What happened to you? Did you fall asleep in the sun? Are you OK now? You seem so drowsy.'

Lucy tried to explain how she had been pushed into the back of a van, but her account sounded unlikely even to her ears.

Adrian looked sceptical. 'Are you sure you didn't dream all that?'

'There was a van, Adrian. I'm telling you, someone must have carried me down to the beach and left me there unconscious.' She remembered a hoarse voice whispering to her, something about the beach.

'Lucy, don't take this the wrong way, but there's no van here. I think you must have suffered another touch of heat stroke. Think about it, why would someone throw you in the back of a van and then let you go again? It doesn't make sense. You must have fallen asleep in the sun. Don't blame yourself. It's hardly surprising. You're bound to be exhausted, after everything that's happened.'

'It wasn't a dream. Someone pushed me into the back of a van and I stubbed my toe. Look.' She held out her foot, aware that her stubbed toe proved nothing.

'We can get that looked at back at the hotel,' he told her kindly, misunderstanding why she was showing him her injury.

She could tell he did not take her garbled account seriously and decided to drop it. There was no point in her trying to convince him, if he was determined not to listen to her. Now that she had cooled down and was talking to Adrian, soberly and calmly, she was beginning to distrust her memory herself. Too much sun could have a powerful effect on the brain. She might have imagined the whole episode of the cryptic message in the van. If she had not been hallucinating, it might at least have been a dream. In her desperation about her mother, her mind could be playing tricks on her. Yet there was a chance she had just been given a message that would help her find her mother. Listening to Adrian's doubts might lead her astray. Perhaps it was his scepticism that was misguided, and not her recollection of what had happened. She decided to stop trying to convince Adrian she was telling the truth. Instead she determined to rely on herself. Depending on other people had not helped her in her life so far.

'Oh, never mind,' she said crossly. 'I'd better call my dad and let him know I'm OK.' She glanced up at Adrian, without making any move to get her phone out.

'Are you OK?'

'I'm fine now, really. I'm feeling much better.'

'Lucy, I'm not sure you are OK,' Adrian replied hesitantly. 'I don't think you should carry on trying to cope with all this stress on your own. Lots of people need help to sort themselves out, and these hallucinations you've been having must be a cry for help. The point is you don't have to deal with this alone, Lucy. There are – people – who can help you.'

She understood what kind of help he meant. He thought she was losing touch with reality. Worse than that, she was afraid he might be right. With her mother's disappearance coming on top of her distress over Darren, it was possible her mind had become unbalanced.

'I'm not going crazy, Adrian,' she protested vehemently. But she was no longer sure she believed that herself.

Without responding, Adrian stood up and walked slowly to his car. She had two dozen missed calls and several messages on her phone. All of them were from her father. Without stopping to listen to any of them, she called him to reassure him that she was fine and would be back soon. She promised to explain what had happened when she saw him. Then she clambered to her feet and limped over to the car.

'Are you sure you're OK?' Adrian asked as she got in beside him.

'Yes, I'm sorry. Thank you. I really am grateful. God knows how I would have got back if you hadn't come along.'

It would have been churlish to say that she could have phoned her father or called a taxi. Adrian's explanation of his arrival on the scene made perfect sense. They had been spending a lot of time together, so she should probably dismiss it as coincidence, but this was the second time he had been around when her life had been threatened. She wondered if he knew more about the island's secrets than he was letting on.

26

Lucy went straight up to her room to shower and change. She did not want her father to see her filthy and dishevelled, limping in one sandal with her shorts ripped. Uncomfortably self-conscious as she crossed the hotel lobby, she was relieved that no one paid her any attention and thankful when no one joined her in the lift. Unless it had been thrown away, her missing sandal would still be in the car park but she could not be bothered to go and look for it. In any case, her toe was too swollen for her to be comfortable in anything other than flip flops. They could not conceal her injury, but under loose summer trousers the bruising would not be visible. Before she went downstairs, she checked her phone again. Her mother had not been in touch. Disappointed, she slipped her phone in her pocket and went down to the bar to face him. She knew she had to tell him everything that had happened, and share the message she had been given. She hoped her father would take her account seriously. She needed his help to work out exactly what it all meant.

Her father leapt to his feet, eyes shining, waving at her as soon as she walked in. He must have been watching for her to come through the door.

'Adrian told me he found you but he wouldn't say where. How could you go off like that without a word?' he demanded as she sat down, his face wavering between joy and outrage.

Carefully tucking her bruised foot behind her other calf, she said she needed to talk to him. As succinctly as she could, she reminded him how she had almost drowned, pulled under the water by some unidentifiable figure.

'You must have been mistaken, in all the confusion and panic,' he reassured her. 'It's only natural. I thought we decided it was the current.'

'That's what Adrian said.'

Lucy took a deep breath. Her father looked so drawn, his face sunken, his shoulders bowed like an old man. She did not want to carry on, but she knew Adrian was right. It was time to come clean and tell her father everything. It was bound to come out in the end and the longer she delayed, the more hurt he was going to feel when he finally discovered the truth.

'What do you mean, that's not all?'

Her father raised his eyes, searching her face. He listened attentively to her account of the rock that had fallen to the ground right in front of her.

'There was a rock fall?' he repeated, bemused.

'Not a rock fall. It was just one boulder that fell a few inches in front of me.' She paused. 'I know it's a lot to take in.'

It was a relief to tell her father everything, even her suspicion that Judy might have been mistaken for her.

Her father stared at her. He looked shocked. 'But there's no actual evidence for any of this, is there?'

She ploughed on and told him how she had discovered Judy's body that morning, and had been driven off in a van that afternoon after their visit to Victoria.

'And I woke up, having been left, unconscious, in the sun.' She paused. 'I need to ask you something.'

'Well, what is it? Fire away.'

'Do you know anyone here?'

Her father looked bewildered. 'What?'

'One of the local people said something about you knowing someone, someone unique. Does that make any sense to you?' Her voice tailed off as she saw how confused her father looked. He seemed to have no idea what she was talking about.

'What do you mean, someone? Lucy, what have you heard?'

He sounded agitated, but she pressed on. She had to know. 'Do you know anyone who lives here?'

'No.'

Her hopes dashed, Lucy bit her lip, fighting back tears. She had been so desperate to believe that a friend of her father's was looking after her mother. Almost as bitter as the disappointment about her mother, was her growing fear that she was going mad. It was difficult to pinpoint exactly when she realised that her father was not taking her stories seriously. Like Adrian, he suggested she had just fallen asleep in the sun. On the face of it, that was certainly a more likely explanation. If she was to be believed, she had narrowly survived being drowned, crushed by a rock, shot and dumped in the sea, and left unconscious in the sun, all as the intended victim of an unknown enemy. The message she remembered could have been a product of her own feverish imagination.

Adrian might be right when he said she needed help. Her father appeared to feel the same way. His face had gone very pale and he looked at her with a stricken expression. Yet she was not sure why she should trust her father and Adrian more than her own senses. Her memories seemed real. What if she was right, after all? She remembered how Darren had let her down when she had trusted him unquestioningly.

Maybe it was time she took responsibility for her own decisions, and stopped relying on others to tell her what to believe.

'Don't worry,' her father said as they parted for the night. 'I'm going to be keeping a close eye on you from now on.' He gave a tense smile. 'I'll take care of you.'

She did not think he meant that he intended to protect her from real physical danger. He was concerned that she was going insane.

27

After a night's sleep and a good breakfast, Lucy had another idea. The curious message she had been given suggested that her mother might be staying with a local woman who knew her father. She could be someone who had worked at the hotel thirty years ago. There must be a way of accessing records of past employees. Lucy was going to speak to Adrian. It was a long shot but as a local man, working at the hotel, he might be able to shed some light on the identity of the woman. She was not willing to wait until the evening to look for him. This was too important a lead.

'I'm here to see Adrian, the accountant,' she told the girl on the reception desk. 'Where can I find him?'

'Adrian? He'll be at his desk, but—'

The receptionist was chary of giving out the information Lucy wanted. 'Guests don't usually go up there. I can call the manager for you if there's a query with your bill.'

The front of house manager was more helpful when Lucy asked for Adrian by name. He led her outside, past the pool, around the back of the bar and through a door marked 'Staff Only', where he directed her to the far end of the corridor. She walked past several offices, opposite an air-conditioning unit, to the door at the end which was marked Accountant. She knocked and a woman's voice invited her come in.

Four desks were crammed together in an office, surrounded by grey metal filing cabinets. Two women and a man were seated at keyboards, at right angles to the door. They all looked up as she entered. In their thirties and forties, smartly dressed, they turned to gaze incuriously at her with gentle black eyes. To the left of them Adrian was visible sitting at a desk in an inner office, with the door wide open, facing his colleagues. He looked surprised to see her, and half rose to his feet.

'Lucy? What are you doing here?'

She smiled anxiously and said she needed to speak to him. The three accounts clerks watched, their fingers motionless on their keyboards. Adrian glanced at his screen and tapped a few keys before turning back to her.

'What's up?'

His phone rang and he gestured to her to wait while he answered it.

'Sorry, it's work,' he apologised to her, before taking the call. Lucy tried not to eavesdrop on his telephone conversation.

'Yes, I'm aware of the situation but as I explained yesterday, I'm a joint signatory, so there's nothing I can do right now. I'll deal with it as soon as I can, hopefully before the end of the day, but until I speak to the manager my hands are tied.'

Adrian was working on a computer around which his desk was littered with open paper files, brown envelopes, pens, staplers, Sellotape, paper clips and treasury tags. In contrast to the buzz of activity at his work station, an atmosphere of quiet industry pervaded the outer office where the man typed sporadically, while the two women sat chatting in low voices.

As she gazed round the outer office, Lucy noticed a large blue-and-orange canvas bag lying on a pile of clothing in one of three large storage containers. Her breath caught in her throat. Without waiting for permission, she darted forward. Adrian was promising his caller he would resolve the problem as soon as he could. Looking up at her, he drew his phone call to an abrupt end and swivelled his chair around to face her.

'Lucy, what are you doing?'

Lucy seized the bag and rummaged inside it. She pulled out a bottle of sunblock and a silk scarf, brandishing them in the air. The delicate fabric quivered in her hand.

'Where did you get this?' she asked, running into his office and waving the bag in front of his face.

Seething with emotion, she was surprised her voice sounded steady.

'What are you talking about?'

'This bag! Where did you get this bag?'

'I don't know. Why? Is it yours?'

'Where did you find it?'

She raised her voice, dimly aware of the three accounts clerks gaping at her. They dropped their gaze when she glared at them and one of them gabbled rapidly in Creole, repeating the word *bagaz*. Lucy looked away. The whole world could stare at her for all she cared. Nothing mattered except the bag clutched in her hand, with its familiar pattern. She had even detected the scent of her mother's perfume as she drew the scarf out. Adrian reached forward to take the bag from her. She snatched it away from him.

'Where did you find it?' she repeated, the bag was shaking in her outstretched hand.

'Lucy, what's wrong with you?'

'What are you doing with my mother's bag?'

Adrian looked surprised. 'That's your mother's?' he repeated. 'Oh my God. I had no idea—'

'Where did you get it?'

'I don't know where it was found. I'm sorry, but it was just handed in. It would have been picked up somewhere on the hotel premises, or on the beach outside. That's as much as I know.'

'What's it doing here, hidden in your office?'

'It wasn't hidden. Bags left lying around are brought here in case there are any valuables in them that need to go in the safe. Hats, shirts, sunglasses, shoes, and non-valuable items that guests leave lying around are kept behind the desk at reception. Cash and credit cards, and valuables, watches and jewellery or phones, I keep those locked up. Every few weeks we get rid of stuff that hasn't been claimed.'

'Why didn't you tell me?'

'Tell you what? That someone had left a beach bag lying around? How was I supposed to know it was your mother's? You didn't tell me it was missing.'

'I didn't know.'

'Do you want – that is, you can take it, if you're sure it's hers. I think there may have been a purse in it, with local currency. I'll have to check the book. Anything valuable is recorded and kept in the safe.'

Adrian checked and brought Lucy a purse. She nodded in recognition and took it from him without a word. Back in her room, she flung herself on the bed. Clutching the beach bag, she cried for her mother until her head ached. At last, she tipped out the contents of the bag. If her mother's purse had disappeared, there would have been a chance she had gone away deliberately. But the purse was there, stuffed with Seychelles rupees. She had been missing for five days, with no money.

As Lucy returned everything to the bag, she found a crumpled piece of paper. Flattening it out to see what it was, she felt as though she had received an electric shock. The letter, written in her father's neat spidery scrawl, was addressed to Veronique. Lucy read it several times, wondering what it could mean. Undated, the letter had clearly been written after their arrival in the Seychelles. Her father had written that he was 'back on the island, staying at the Garden of Eden'. He referred to his promise to return, and assured Veronique that he had not forgotten her. It was signed with only the letter G. There was no reason why Adrian would have linked it to Angela if he had seen it in the bag. But Lucy knew who had written that letter, and her mother would have known too.

She took a deep breath. The whisper she had heard as 'very unique' in the van had actually been a name, 'Veronique'. Her father's letter proved that the message had been no dream. She was furious that he had lied to her, telling her he did not know anyone living on the island. What was more, the messenger in the van had been right to say her father knew Veronique very well. Taking a deep breath, she tried to work out what must have happened. After reading the letter, her mother must have gone to look for Veronique. Evidently she had found her and had gone to stay with her. Crying with relief, Lucy wiped her eyes. Her mother was alive. She must have insisted Lucy be reassured, in such a way that no one else would believe her. Lucy considered the theory carefully. Everything fitted. Angela and Veronique were keeping the truth hidden from the man who had betrayed them both. They wanted him to suffer. It made Lucy feel sick to know that she could not trust what her father told her. But she was going to uncover the truth for herself. The key to the mystery lay with Veronique.

28

When Maggie left, Lucy invited her father to sit on her balcony with her. She was determined to find out what he knew about the woman called Veronique.

'Dad,' she said, 'you told me you didn't know anyone living here.'

He stared at her but did not answer.

'What about a woman called Veronique?'

Her father turned away. 'I don't know what you've heard but I told you, I don't know anyone living here. It's over thirty years since I was here.'

'Are you sure?'

He shook his head and looked away. 'I told you, I don't know anyone here any more. It was all such a long time ago.'

Trembling with fury, Lucy pulled his letter out of her bag. 'Stop lying!' she cried, brandishing the crumpled sheet of paper in front of his face. 'You wrote this!'

'My letter?' he muttered, baffled. 'What are you doing with that? Where did you find it?'

Lucy had to force herself to speak. She felt as though she was choking. 'Who is this woman you wrote to when we came here? Who is Veronique?'

She waited, deliberately holding back the message that Veronique was taking care of Angela. First she wanted to hear her father confess that he had betrayed her mother, and lied to her, over the mysterious woman in his letter.

'Yes, I knew Veronique,' her father said at last, his voice breaking with emotion.

He did not look at her, so she carried on gazing at the view as she listened, struggling to suppress her anger at his betrayal. Although she had hidden her own youthful secrets from him, perhaps it had been naïve of her to suppose he had kept no secrets of his own. Whenever he spoke, the child in her listened. She had never really regarded him as a man like other men. It touched and disturbed her to learn there was hidden darkness in his life. He seemed to have aged overnight. Her rage was tinged with pity for the man who had always seemed to her to be so capable. It was almost more than she could bear. She fidgeted uneasily at his side, wishing her mother was there.

'I first came here over thirty years ago. I was a young man, newly qualified and inexperienced in – well, in just about everything. To begin with it was really hard. The accounts were in a mess. My predecessor had lost interest and hadn't been keeping the records up-to-date. The management were hounding me constantly for information I didn't have, and people were on at me all the time for payment when I didn't even know what had been paid and what was still outstanding. One of the suppliers came into my office drunk, banging on my desk and threatening to kill me if he didn't get his money. It was a lot to cope with. I knew I'd be able get on top of things eventually, but I wondered if it was worth all the aggravation. I was alone, you see. The ex-pats at the hotel were friendly enough, but I felt completely isolated with the responsibility. After a few weeks of it, I was thinking of handing in my notice, doing some travelling and going home.'

He stopped abruptly, and rubbed his chin with his hand, staring out at the ocean.

'Why didn't you?'

Lost in memories, he did not answer.

'Why didn't you leave?'

'Because I met Veronique.'

'Who's Veronique?'

Turning to confront him, she was shocked to see tears glistening in the stubbled on his cheeks.

'Who is she, Dad?' she insisted.

'Veronique was the maid who came to clean my house – did I ever tell you the hotel supplied me with a maid?' He sighed. 'Veronique was beautiful. She was the most beautiful woman I'd ever seen. Even now there's never been anyone who could hold a candle to her. They called her the dark angel, she was so beautiful.'

Lucy squirmed uncomfortably in her chair. She wondered why her father was telling her this, especially now with her mother missing.

'Are you telling me you had an affair with her?'

George shook his head as though flicking away an annoying insect.

'Don't make it sound sordid, Lucy. We – that is, I – fell in love. I thought she felt the same way about me. But then I had to leave suddenly, due to the political unrest. I begged her to come to England with me, only she couldn't leave the island.'

In spite of her disquiet, Lucy was caught up in her father's story. 'If you were in love, why did you go without her?'

'I had no choice. You don't understand.'

'Tell me.'

'They put me on a plane. Two hours to pack my bag before they threw me in a car and frogmarched me off.'

'Didn't you see it coming?'

'Yes, but when I asked her to leave with me, she couldn't. She didn't have a passport. Can you believe it? I gave her what cash I could get my hands on and sent her more when I reached England. A lot more. I wrote to her every day, but she never answered my letters. Not one.'

'Perhaps she couldn't read.'

'She could read and she could write,' he said sourly. 'Anyway that was it. I never heard from her again. But she took all the money I sent. Out of sight out of mind, I guess. I'd been a fool to trust her, but, like I said, I was young and naïve. I suppose I should have realised it would be complicated, but at the time it all seemed so simple.'

'Does Mum know about this?'

'No. I met meet your mother years after I left the Seychelles, and somehow it never seemed the right time to mention what had happened. It was all such a long time ago, another lifetime. I never told anyone about the affair. I was too ashamed.'

'Ashamed? There's nothing shameful about falling in love with the wrong person, Dad. How many times have you told me that lately?'

'No, that's not what I mean.'

'What then?'

He hung his head. 'I was ashamed that I'd given away so much money to a woman like that.'

'How much?'

He grunted. 'As much as I could afford. Whatever I had.'

Lucy wondered if her father's parsimony stemmed from this bitter experience.

'But I don't understand why you contacted her again, Dad. Why did you write to her?'

He sighed, struggling to express what he felt. 'I don't know. I guess in some way I felt I needed to see her one last time, just to say goodbye. When I left, the island was a dangerous place. I suppose I wanted to know she was all right.' He paused. 'I'm not superstitious, but I feel as though the island has taken Angela away from me. Does that make any kind of sense to you?'

Lucy only hesitated for an instant. She had decided what to do, and her plans did not involve her father. She was not even going to tell him what was in her mind. It was a hard truth to acknowledge that, like Darren, her father was not to be trusted. Knowing he had lied so readily to her she was burning with fury, although outwardly she remained calm.

'Look, you had an affair with a woman more than thirty years ago. It's history, Dad. With everything that's been going on, you're not thinking clearly. But don't worry. I'm going to find her.'

She was no longer sure whether she was talking about her mother or Veronique. The fate of the two women had become inextricably linked by their love of one man.

He shook his head helplessly. 'Where did you find that letter?'

Her father had lied. She could too. She was going to find her mother without his help. The less he knew about her plans the less he could meddle and mess things up for her mother again.

'I found it on the beach.' It sounded unlikely, but she did not care if he believed her or not. She had been lied to so often, she could hardly be blamed for doing the same. 'When did you tell Mum about Veronique?' She waved the letter at him.

'I didn't.'

'You kept it all a secret from her?'

'It wasn't like that.'

'Why didn't you tell her?' Lucy persisted.

'Because there was nothing to tell. Veronique never replied to any of my letters. There was no point in raking up old history. I haven't seen the woman for thirty years, haven't heard a word from her in all that time. She probably doesn't remember who I am.'

'You had an affair.'

'A long time ago. Women like that,' he shrugged. 'She was beautiful. She probably had a lot of affairs. Why would she remember me?' He sighed. 'I think I'll go to my room now.'

'But I still don't understand why you never said anything to Mum.'

Her father stood up. 'Lucy, I'm going to my room. I just want to be alone.'

In spite of her righteous anger, Lucy felt a stabbing pity for her father. She watched him walk slowly away, his head bowed. Staring out at the sea beyond the gardens, she imagined her mother stumbling on the letter. It was understandable that she wanted to spend some time on her own. George's conduct could hardly be called infidelity, the affair had ended so long ago, but her mother must have been incandescent with rage. Not only had he said nothing about his affair, but he had written to Veronique in secret. Lucy hoped it was merely curiosity that had driven him to write to her. Relief at discovering what had happened to her mother made her forgiving of her father. But she would not let him off completely.

At least now Lucy had a way forward. She was going to trace Veronique, and so find her mother. Once they left the island, she would never have another chance to seek out the woman who had hurt her father so badly when he had been about her own age. She wondered if a similar curiosity had inspired her mother to seek out Veronique, and whether the two women had struck up a friendship. She relished the idea of confronting Veronique and telling her to her face how devastated young George had been all those years ago. Plus, she was curious to meet the woman her father still described as the most beautiful woman he had ever met, in spite of the way she had treated him. Lucy could not imagine ever having a good word to say about Darren. She wondered how her father was going to react when he discovered that his wife had gone to stay with his former lover. It would serve him right if they both sent him packing. It had taken Lucy a long time to get past wanting to punish Darren. She could understand her mother's feelings very well.

Her mind began racing. She pictured a meeting between her mother and a Seychellois woman, wrinkled and skinny, vestiges of former beauty still evident in her high cheekbones and beautiful eyes. Anything seemed possible on this exotic island. She imagined a dramatic conversation between the two women, one fair, the other dark-skinned, her mother's eyes wide with astonishment.

'I hope George is well. You know, he loved me once,' the beautiful old woman would sigh. 'Many men loved me then.'

No one on the island had spotted Angela leaving the hotel or seen her since she had gone missing, but if Lucy did not yet know where she was, at least she now knew who she was with. Her father was in his room. Adrian was working. It was time to look for Veronique herself. She was convinced that Veronique was the key to finding her mother. At the same time Lucy would relish unmasking her father's lies. She had been blind to Darren's betrayal. She would never be taken in like that again. She was going to make sure her father did not get away with his deception, and this time the revelation would be on her terms.

29

Researching Mahé on her iPhone, Lucy found some out-of-date figures suggesting roughly seven per cent of the population were over sixty. That meant that of around seventy thousand people about five thousand might be in their sixties. With more women than men in that age group she estimated there were maybe three thousand women. How many of them would be called Veronique? Her father's maid had probably lived in one of the shanty houses around Beau Vallon. All she had to do was ask the older Seychellois people and there was a good chance she would come across someone who knew Veronique. She was intrigued by the prospect of meeting the woman her father had loved with a passion she could not have imagined him capable of feeling. She was sure she would not still be pining for Darren when she was sixty.

Coming across a group of Seychellois men sitting in the shade of a palm tree a short distance from the hotel, she asked the oldest man if he could help her. He shook his head, mumbling incoherently in Creole. A second man smiled up at her toothlessly without answering. She wondered if she was talking to people who were too old to remember Veronique, and approached a man who looked closer to her father's age.

'Ah, Veronique,' he answered. A dreamy look crossed his face.

He turned and jabbered to his friends in Creole. They all nodded and shrugged their shoulders.

'Do you know where I can find her?' Lucy asked. 'Where is Veronique?'

'Ah, where she go?' he repeated.

'Yes, where is she?'

'Where Veronique?'

Lucy despaired of getting any sensible response from him, but as she turned away, he called out to her. 'You want Veronique?'

'Yes.'

'Ask Maria,' he suggested, gesturing towards a track leading between the trees. 'She live there. She friend of Veronique.'

'She know all people's business,' another old man added.

The other men grinned and muttered to one another, nodding their heads. Lucy thanked him and started along the narrow path with a flicker of anxiety. He might be sending her off the road so he could mug her. It was hardly a city, but no doubt people were robbed on Mahé the same as anywhere else. As she was considering turning back, a rusty sloping corrugated roof came into view through the bushes. Rounding a bend in the path she saw a ramshackle one-storey house, the paintwork on its blue walls faded and peeling. An old woman was squatting on the doorstep in the dappled shade, clutching a bag of breadfruit chips. Her face was hidden beneath a mess of frizzy white hair. Fragments of breadfruit were scattered on dark flowery fabric stretched taut across her ample thighs. As she picked up the bag of chips and brushed crumbs from her lap with the back of her hand, a scraggy chicken darted forward to peck eagerly at the morsels of food.

'Maria?'

The woman squinted up from her perch, black eyes glinting in a wrinkled brown face, before she turned her attention back to her bag of breadfruit chips.

'Maria? Can you help me?'

'I help you?' the woman repeated, staring up at Lucy with a shrewd look in her slanting eyes.

Lucy crouched down beside her and held up a note. Swiftly the woman seized the money, nodding and grinning, displaying a few yellowing teeth.

'What you want?'

'I'm looking for a woman.'

'You found one, sweetheart.' Maria cackled, slapping a brown knee with the flat of her hand. 'I'm all woman.'

'I'm looking for a particular woman who was living here over thirty years ago. She was employed by the Garden of Eden Hotel to clean the house of the accountant working there. Her name is Veronique. Do you know where I can find her?'

Maria gazed past Lucy at the chicken pecking at the dry earth.

'Find Veronique? Ay!'

She heaved a deep sigh. Turning her attention to Lucy she stared at her blonde hair and reached out to touch her arm.

'I would like to find her and kiss her hand. Tell her we were wrong to hate her.'

'Who hated her?'

'All of us.'

'Why did you hate her?'

'Eh, we were young. We wanted our share of attention.'

She glanced over in the direction of the road where the group of men had gathered beneath the tree near the hotel.

'Was she beautiful?' Lucy asked.

'Oh yes, Veronique was beautiful. So beautiful. We called her the dark angel. So beautiful.'

'Tell me about her.'

The woman's eyes glazed over as though she was looking straight through Lucy.

'Maria, I need to speak to Veronique. I think she might be able to tell me where my mother is. Where can I find her?'

The woman shook her head. 'She went away.'

'Went where?'

A wild hope struck Lucy that Veronique and her mother had gone off somewhere together. Maria raised her hands from her lap, palms upward.

'She went away many years ago. They said Mancham took her with him when he went into exile, but I never believed it. He was gone long before she disappeared. The men were all wild at that time, everyone saying life will be better, life will be better. But nothing changed. And that is when Veronique left us.'

'Where did she go?'

Maria shrugged. 'Who knows? We never saw her again. At the time none of us were sorry she went away, except her man.'

'Her man? What happened to him?'

'Some say he threw himself off the mountain. They say he did not die, only broke his back.' Looking down in her lap, she picked out a large piece of breadfruit. 'Others say the dark angel went mad and shot him, right here between his eyes.' Pointing at her forehead, she munched on her chip. 'They say she hid away on the mountain to escape punishment.'

'How terrible!'

The old woman looked up at Lucy with shrewd dark eyes, scrutinising her hair, her figure, right down to her feet. Then she turned her head away and spat. 'Terrible? You know nothing of life.' She stared into the distance. 'Veronique went away, a long time ago.'

Taking my father's money with her, Lucy thought crossly. She felt sorry for her poor father. It seemed that everyone had fallen under Veronique's spell. The old woman closed her eyes.

'Where did she live? Before she disappeared?'

Maria waved her hand vaguely. 'She lived, like we all do.' She leaned back against the wall of her house and closed her eyes.

'Maria, one more question,' Lucy said urgently. 'Has anyone else been here recently asking about Veronique?'

'Many searched for Veronique.'

'I meant just a couple of days ago. Have you seen a blonde English woman, in her fifties, in the past few days?'

Maria shook her head, eyes still closed. Murmuring her thanks, Lucy stood up and walked away. Veronique had gone into hiding on the island years ago. If her mother had been able to track her down, then so could Lucy. With the police unable to find her, Lucy was going to take matters into her own hands. She could not just sit around any longer doing nothing. She cursed herself for failing to notice the registration number of the van. It would have been a start. She needed to find out who had given her the message about Veronique.

The local police station was not far from the hotel. It took her a while to walk there, with her painful toe, but she persevered.

'Yes, madam?'

'I'm looking for a white van.'

The policeman looked puzzled. 'A white van?'

'Yes.'

'You wish to report a theft?'

'No. The thing is . . .' She hesitated to launch into an account of her abduction. 'I want to speak to the driver. He has a white van and it's often parked near the Garden of Eden Hotel.'

'You may find it helpful to ask the security guard at the hotel entrance.'

Lucy nodded. She should have thought of that herself. 'Yes, thank you. I'll do that.'

She limped back to the hotel as quickly as she could, concerned that her father would be worried by her absence. She had not intended to be out for so long. The khaki-clad security guard was polite but unable to help her.

'We see many vans pass by,' he told her.

'If you see a white one, old and battered, can you note down the registration number for me, please?'

'Is there a problem?'

'No, no problem. Actually, don't worry about it. Forget I said anything.'

She would keep a look out herself. It might be best not to alert the driver of the van to her interest.

30

Returning to the hotel, Lucy went straight to her father's room to reassure him she was fine. She did not want to worry him and cause him to keep a closer eye on her, as she tried to track down Veronique. As she had expected, he was anxious about her. She thought he had been crying. What made it painful was his insistence that he was fine when she could see his one good eye was still bloodshot and puffy. It was hardly surprising. Her father attempted to start a conversation about the weather as though nothing was wrong, but he floundered at the first sentence. With her mother still missing, they were both beginning to crack under the strain. Looking nervous, her father tackled the subject of the attacks she had experienced. Gently he suggested she was displacing her anxiety about her mother on to herself. By imagining threats to her own life, he told her she might be unconsciously seeking to distract herself from the real worry that was too painful to think about. When Lucy protested, he merely shrugged and seemed to draw back into the shell he had begun to develop.

'Lucy, I'm going to have a nap. Do you mind? I'll see you later.'

Since her mother's disappearance, he seemed to be sleeping a lot. As she walked along the corridor away from his room, stepping awkwardly on her bruised toe, Lucy wondered if he had been drinking. That might explain why he was so sleepy. Now that she had proof her father had known someone called Veronique, she was convinced that she would be able to find her mother. But she was not going to tell her father yet. Unlike him, she had never lied to her family. He should have trusted her. She did her best to feel positive about the idea that he had wanted to avoid upsetting her, but there was no glossing over the fact that he had deceived her mother. The most difficult part of it all was coping with her father without her mother's calming presence. When Lucy's relationship had come to its catastrophic end, her mother had been there to support her. Now Lucy was afraid she was falling apart, and there was nothing she could do to stop her thoughts from spiralling wildly out of control. She could not talk to her father. Her mother would have known what to say, but she was not there.

She lay on her bed, allowing the air conditioning to cool her, and tried to think through her immediate problems. At all costs, she had to hide her confusion from her father. His worry about her mental state, and his frustration at being unable to help her would be distressing for them both and would help neither of them. For the first time, Lucy glimpsed past her own anger to consider what kind of personal hell her father must be enduring. He had told her everything was his fault. That was more true than he realised. If Lucy could persuade him to talk to her again about Veronique, he might shed some light on where she was now living. One way or another, Lucy was going to find her, and when she did the truth would come out. His wife and daughter might forgive him his indiscretion. However this ended, she realised he would never forgive himself. Despite her anger, she could not help feeling sorry for him.

Without a clue what she was going to say to him, she went up to her father's room and knocked on the door. There was no answer. She tried again. Awful possibilities flooded her mind: her father had taken an overdose; he had suffered a worse injury than anyone had realised and had succumbed to delayed concussion; unable to see properly, he had slipped and knocked himself out and was lying on the floor bleeding to death as she stood in the corridor outside his room, paralysed with indecisiveness. It was not in her nature to be so fearful. A wave of exhaustion overwhelmed her. Leaning forward, she rested her head against her door pleading with him to open it. She did not realise she was talking out loud until someone called to her.

'You are all right, madam?'

She spun round, mortified. A young chambermaid had stopped pushing her trolley along the corridor and was staring at her curiously.

'I'm fine, I'm fine,' she stammered, aware that she must look dreadful, with tearstained eyes and sunburned face, and her hair a complete mess.

'Too much?' the chambermaid asked, smiling and miming a drinking motion.

Lucy nodded gratefully and scurried back to her own room where she flung herself down on the bed. Lying prostrate with one arm across her face she lay inert with grief, unable even to cry. She was afraid she was going to snap again, as she had done when she had discovered Darren had been two-timing her. Distraught over her mother's disappearance, her father would be unable to help her. Where the hell was her mother? Lucy needed her. They both did. She opened the drawer in her bedside table as though it held some clue to her whereabouts. There was nothing in it apart from the ubiquitous hotel Bible.

Someone tapped at her door. Assuming it was the maid coming to do the room, she was on the point of calling out and telling her to come back later when her father called out.

'Lucy, Lucy, are you in there?'

She sat up so quickly her head spun. She felt her heart pounding, and blood pulsing behind her eyes. She realised it was past lunchtime and she was hungry. As soon as her father went for a rest, she would begin her hunt for Veronique.

'I'm coming,' she called back. 'Hang on.'

Hurrying to the bathroom, she splashed cold water on her face and studied herself, blinking. She did not look too bad, considering. Her hair needed a wash, but there was nothing she could do about that now. She slipped on her sunglasses and opened the door.

After a late lunch her father suggested they go for a stroll. Their attempts at conversation over lunch had been stilted and neither of them spoke as they made their way down to the beach. Her father was preoccupied. Looking out at the sea, he spoke hesitantly.

'Lucy, we need to talk.'

She waited. Instead of broaching the subject of Veronique, as she expected, he took her hand and told her he was worried about her.

'About me?'

'Yes.' He paused.

'It's OK, Dad. You can tell me.' When he did not answer, she went on. 'Are you all right? I mean, apart from, you know—'

'Yes. That is, I think so. As far as I can be. How about you?'

'I'm fine.' It seemed they could not help lying to one another.

They looked at the ocean in silence for a moment.

'I think I'll go up and have a rest,' her father said at last.

Lucy nodded. Clearly her father did not feel able to talk to her. As soon as he had gone, she put her latest plan into action. First she borrowed some A4 paper, a box of pins and a thick black marker pen from the hotel reception. In the privacy of her room, she wrote a dozen signs in capital letters, going over the words until they were bold and dark enough to be seen from a distance: 'Missing, blonde English woman, 53. Contact Mr Hall at Garden of Eden Hotel.'

Rolling up the sheets of paper, she made her way downstairs and out of the hotel. A broad walkway ran alongside the beach for a few hundred yards until it joined the road. Lucy walked down the path, stopping at intervals to pin a sign to a tree. No one took any notice of her. By the time she reached the road, she had displayed four of them. She walked along the road, fixing more notices to trees, until she ran out of them. Returning to the hotel, she saw that one of her notices had been torn down. The rest remained. Perhaps a local resident would come forward with information that would lead them to her mother.

31

When her father woke up, he came downstairs and found her in the pool area, lying on a sun lounger as though she had been there all afternoon. Sipping a cocktail, Lucy tried to pretend that life was normal. That everything was far from all right was evident in the way their eyes shied away from contact with each other. Her father was tense. They sat in an awkward silence, facing the ocean. Still the waves washed lightly against the shore, trees rustled softly in the sea breeze, and the delicate scent of flowering shrubs mingled with a sharp salt tang of the sea. They watched the sunset flare across the ocean. Directly in front of them, Silhouette Island rose out of the rippling waters, its peak shrouded in clouds. Although she knew it was over twelve miles away, she had the illusion it was close enough for her to reach out and touch. As the sun set behind it, the island shimmered in hazy light before fading into the gathering darkness.

They made their way down to the beach for a short stroll before going back inside, falling into step as they walked. Drawing level with their hotel they paused, as though the same thought had struck them both.

'Come on, then,' George said, with a brightness he did not feel, and they returned to the hotel where the woman they both loved had disappeared.

'George! George! There you are!' a voice rang out across the patio.

At her side, Lucy heard her father groan. Resplendent in lime green, Gloria strode towards them like an elephantine gecko. Billy followed her, looking around appraisingly as he crossed the patio.

'You poor dears! We came as soon as we heard.'

'As soon as we heard,' Billy echoed, seizing George's hand and shaking it vigorously.

'We are all so upset.' Gloria turned to Lucy. 'The girls feel just terrible. They so wanted to be with you, but they already had plans. They both send you their love. You know their thoughts are with you.'

Bangles jangling, she held out her arms to Lucy who submitted to a hug, rolling her eyes at her father over Gloria's shoulder.

'That's Gloria all over,' Billy confided loudly to George. 'Whenever anyone's in trouble, she's right there.' He smiled complacently at his wife. 'Ain't she something!'

Gloria released Lucy and smiled at George with tears in her eyes. Although she was not in the mood for society, Lucy did not want to appear rude. She had already drunk one cocktail too many and was desperate to be rid of the overpowering American couple, but she understood her father felt obliged to offer their new friends a drink, since they had made the effort to come and offer their support. Sitting in the lobby, they sipped beer. Lucy was relieved to hear that the American family were leaving the island the following day.

'We hate to think we're abandoning you—'

'Nonsense,' her father replied firmly. 'It's not as if there's anything anyone can do. The police are searching and they're sure to find her soon.'

'Sure to,' Lucy echoed.

'But how did you know?' her father asked.

'Did you hear that, Billy? Oh my goodness, George, don't you ever listen to the radio or read the local paper? The Brits at our hotel are positively buzzing with the story. Some of them think it's another shark attack, but Billy and I don't think it's possible a shark could have attacked your wife without anyone knowing anything about it.'

'No,' Billy agreed, 'we don't think that's possible.'

'There's no way George's wife would have taken herself off out into the deep water all alone, we said, didn't we, Billy? She's not a professional diver, or a reckless kid.'

She paused as though waiting for an answer.

'Now, if there's anything we can do to help,' Billy broke the silence, 'anything at all, you just give us a call. You've got my number, haven't you?'

Lucy had been sitting quietly through the conversation. Finally she spoke up. 'We're sorry to hear you're leaving, but shouldn't you be packing?' She glanced at her father, slightly embarrassed. 'We'd hate you to have to rush on our account. It's always better to take your time packing. That way you're less likely to forget anything.'

With further protestations of support, and offers of help, Gloria finally said they would have to go. Lucy's father thanked them, shook Billy by the hand, allowed Gloria to dispense the comfort of her hug, and walked them to the door.

'Don't forget,' Billy said, hovering at the entrance, 'any time.'

'Well, it was nice of them to come over,' Lucy's father said as he and Lucy made their way back to the patio.

'And nice when they left,' she added. 'Sorry, I hope I wasn't rude, but I just wasn't up for listening to them right now.'

'We're neither of us in the mood for socialising,' her father agreed.

Nevertheless, he responded with alacrity when Adrian hailed them across the pool.

'Mind if we join you?'

For answer, Adrian pulled a couple of chairs over to his table.

'How's your face, George?'

'I'm fine, just fine. It's good of you to ask. But I want to thank you.' Her father leaned forward and gazed earnestly at Adrian. 'I've been hearing more about what happened when you helped Lucy in the sea the other day, as well as what you did for her yesterday. We owe you a great deal. More than I can possibly say.'

Adrian shrugged and looked away, embarrassed.

'We can't thank you enough,' her father's voice broke and he covered his mouth with a hand that trembled.

Adrian stared at his glass of beer as though it suddenly fascinated him.

'It was nothing,' he mumbled. 'It was no more than anyone else would have done.'

'Don't make light of what you did,' her father insisted. 'Lucy and I are forever in your debt. Aren't we, Lucy?'

She nodded automatically but she was no longer listening to her father. Her attention had been caught by the old sweeper. His back bent, he was slowly dragging his broom across the path between the bar and the pool.

'Lucy,' her father prompted her.

She was barely aware of Adrian clearing his throat, and her father calling her name. Sitting facing half away from them, she was absorbed in watching the old man sweeping right to the edge of the patio, underneath a flowering white frangipani bush. At one point, he leaned down and fastidiously picked something out of the pile of petals he had swept into a neat pile. Feeling her arm jostled, she turned to her father, startled.

'What?'

'Are you all right?'

'Sorry, Dad, I was miles away.' She struggled to recall what she had been thinking about. 'There was something – I just thought of something – no, sorry, it's gone. I can't remember what it was.' Frustrated, she knew only that it had been important.

'I was thanking Adrian for saving your life,' her father told her, with an edge of reproach in his voice.

Worried that she had been rude to Adrian again, Lucy turned to him. 'Oh yes, of course, sorry.' There was an awkward pause. 'How do you thank someone for saving your life twice?' She shrugged, and Adrian smiled uneasily. 'How about a drink?'

'What would you like?'

She shook her head. 'No, I mean, I'm offering you a drink. I know it's not much of a thank you, under the circumstances. I mean, a drink for saving my life isn't much of a return, is it? And I suppose it should be two drinks, shouldn't it, seeing as you saved my life twice. It's not much, but I don't know what else to say. I owe you big time. I want to thank you. Sorry,' she added, flustered, 'I'm rambling, aren't I?'

Only half listening to Adrian's response, she turned away to watch the old sweeper.

'We had a cocktail earlier on,' her father told Adrian with a forced laugh. 'I think it's gone to her head.'

'No, no, I'm fine, really,' she protested. 'I was just—'

She glanced at white flowering frangipani bushes growing at the edge of the patio, trying to remember what they reminded her of. With all the stress of her mother's disappearance, it was disconcerting that she seemed to be forgetting a lot. When she looked round again, the old sweeper had gone. Instantly her mind felt clearer and she turned back to her companions.

'Come on, let me get you a drink, Adrian.'

'It's time I went to bed,' her father said. 'I know Lucy will be in safe hands.'

Adrian smiled. 'I'm not Superman. I can't tell you how thankful I am that I was able to help Lucy, but I really just happened to be there in the right place at the right time. What I did was nothing special, really. But I'm off too. I've got an early meeting tomorrow and I'm off home.' He stood up. 'I'll see you both tomorrow.'

Lucy said she would stay for a while, watching the ocean. She sat by herself, listening to the gentle swish of waves hitting the shore. It did not help to dull the ache she felt, missing her mother.

32

'PLEASE, WHY ARE YOU doing this to me? You have nothing to gain by keeping me here. I'm begging you: let me go. You can end this now. Please.'

Speech was difficult. Her voice sounded thick and slurred. Her lips were so cracked it hurt to move them. She made a desperate attempt to articulate the words.

'I know you're going to kill me, so why don't you do it? Please, just kill me now.'

Worse than the sickness, the filth and degradation, was the mental torment of waiting, not knowing from one minute to the next when her final moment would come. Far better to get it over with quickly. Life had lost any power it once had over her. She only wanted this foulness to stop.

'Not yet,' the voice said.

'What are you waiting for?' she asked, sobbing because she was not going to be released.

She resisted eating the rice. Squirming, she turned her head away but the spoon forced more of it between her teeth. Fingers poked it along her tongue until she swallowed just so that she could open her mouth and not inhale the stench with every breath she took.

'Get – off – me!'

The spoon shoved another dollop between her lips making her splutter and choke. It was always the same repulsive rice. Sometimes the fingers rammed it too far, making her gag. Once she had closed her mouth, clamping her teeth together on the finger, pressing as hard as she could. A fist had clouted her. She had released her grip on the finger as she fell to the ground.

'Drink,' the voice ordered, slopping water into her mouth.

'Why are you doing this? Why don't you just kill me? Please, end it now, I'm begging you.'

'Like this?'

A deafening shot rang out. It sounded as though the whole mountain had exploded. There was a very slight whiff of burning sulphur, so faint she might have imagined it. The noise of the gun going off seemed to split her head open, before the barrel of the gun was pressed against her temple, taunting her. In her debilitated state, resistance had seemed unthinkable. But the gun changed everything. If she could wrench it from Veronique's grasp, she would not hesitate to shoot, hoping to put a bullet in her tormentor's head. With a sudden jolt of exhilaration she resolved to make the attempt. Even though she could not see where Veronique was standing, there was a slim chance she might shoot and hit her. In any case, whether she failed or succeeded, it made no difference. She could shoot Veronique and then herself, or provoke Veronique into killing her. Death would come either way, and would be welcome. Twisting round, she heard her chains rattle as she raised her arms but she could not lift them high enough to reach the gun.

She moaned, her flash of hope confounded. Through the ringing in her ears she heard hoarse laughter at her humiliation. Bracing herself, she threw her shoulders back and closed her eyes behind the blindfold that prevented her from seeing anything at all.

'Go on,' she urged. 'Pull the trigger again. Do it.'

Adrenaline rushed to her head. Her legs would barely hold her. Her body was in a state of shock, her ears ringing from the noise, but she was prepared. With a final effort she held her head upright, standing as tall as she could, her eyes pressed shut. She would not crumble.

'Go on,' she repeated. 'Do it.'

'I am doing nothing.'

'But – the gun . . .' she stammered. 'You've got a gun. Shoot me.'

'No. There is a better way. That is why we preserved your daughter.'

Fear ran through Angela like a bolt of adrenaline, making her tremble. 'Not Lucy,' she cried out in a voice that tore at her dry throat. 'Please, just finish this now. Shoot me. You don't want my daughter involved in this. It's between you and me. We're the ones who should be fighting over George. It has nothing to do with Lucy.'

'I will not fight for George,' the voice rasped. 'I hate him.'

'Why?'

'You will hate him too, when he abandons you to die, as he abandoned me.'

'What do you mean?'

'You will find out. But not yet.'

'You're not going to shoot me?'

'No. But you will wish I had. You will wish you had died, right here, right now.' She felt the gun tap against the side of her head, mocking her. 'This is for your husband. He is the one who will kill you. And it will be done soon. You are not strong. You must not die before he comes to you.'

The words were completely insane.

'I don't know what you're talking about,' she mumbled. 'My husband isn't going to kill me.'

An angel appeared in front of her, glowing in the darkness. She shivered. The angel had that effect on people. It drove them mad. She had felt its power. In the darkness it shone with an impossible brilliance. Addressing her in seductive tones, it had called to her in the darkness. She had heard its voice, witnessed its power in her waking dreams. Strange thoughts whirled around inside her skull. Her mind was spinning out of control. If she was not mad yet, she soon would be, locked up in this stinking pit. She sank to her knees, unable to stand upright any longer. In spite of her desperation she felt a flutter of relief. She was still alive. She had faced a maniac waving a gun at her head and she was still alive. It was a sign. She was not going to die. A thrill of joy shook her as she lay on the soiled ground. The hut vibrated as the door slammed shut. As she sank into unconsciousness, her last thought was that she was still alive.

The angel was shining at her, its eyes gaping pools of black light.

'Come,' it whispered. 'I have been waiting for you.'

'Not yet,' she replied in her dream that was not a dream. 'It is not yet time.'

The angel's lips twisted in a grin. Its laughter echoed around her prison walls and she felt herself falling. She woke with a jolt, shivering and sweating. But she was alive.

33

While Lucy's father was comforted by the Vice Consul's daily visits to the hotel, Lucy was feeling increasingly impatient with the authorities.

'You can't accuse them of forgetting about us,' her father said. 'Maggie's been to see us every day. She'll be here again this afternoon.'

All the same, he was happy to pay another visit to the town. If nothing else, it gave them something to do. They had driven round the coastal road several times every day, and scoured the streets of the capital, in case Angela was wandering about the island suffering from amnesia. It was unlikely, but at least they felt they were doing something. Spending the whole day in idleness was impossible.

They had been calling in at the Central Police Station every day, and Inspector Henri greeted them like old friends. But although he continually assured them the authorities were doing everything in their power to find the missing woman, he had to report that they had made no progress with their enquiries.

'As you know, we have alerted every police station on the islands,' he said, drumming his fingers on the table and sighing. 'Your wife's picture has been circulated to all the coastguards, hospitals, doctors, hotels and guest houses, and published in all the papers. And the local radio has been most helpful. We have contacted every ship that has been in the area, in case she was picked up out at sea.'

He sighed and shrugged to indicate that they had so far drawn a blank, and repeated that the police were doing what they could. Although he seemed attentive, Lucy could not help feeling he regarded her mother's disappearance as a bit of a nuisance.

'So what you're telling us is that you've done everything you can,' Lucy said.

He inclined his head.

'Then maybe it's time to call in Scotland Yard,' she went on.

The inspector raised his eyebrows. 'Scotland Yard?' he repeated.

'Well, you've done all you can and you haven't found her, so maybe we should try the British police. They're probably more geared up to finding missing persons, aren't they? And my mother's English.'

The inspector explained that a missing person on the island fell under the jurisdiction of the local police. A foreign force could certainly be invited to intervene, but only if that was considered necessary.

'Necessary? Of course it's necessary,' Lucy's father took up the argument.

'Please listen to me,' the inspector said firmly. 'We are very flexible about requesting outside help. Any time there's evidence of a serious crime on the island, we ask for support. We know our limitations. If there's forensic evidence to be examined, we call in foreign experts straight away. But as far as we are aware, no crime has been committed. The case is being treated with the utmost seriousness, but there's not a lot more to be done, as things stand. The responsibility for conducting a local search rests with us. We know the terrain and the people. It's a small island. We know where to look and who to ask. Believe me, we are best placed to do this job.

We would have to direct police coming here from the UK to do the job we're already doing ourselves. I assure you we're doing everything possible to find your wife.'

Lucy appreciated he was dealing with them sympathetically, but at the same time realised that tourists going missing was bad for the island's image. The death of the Australian girl was hardly helping. According to Eddy, the local papers were attributing her murder to a jealous boyfriend.

'Which is piffle,' he had confided in Lucy. 'She didn't come here looking for a boyfriend. Between you and me, she was only interested in money. They're just trying to make up some reason for it so people don't start speculating about a killer on the loose on the island, that sort of thing, you know. It's not good for business. Also, I don't know if you heard, but a lad drowned yesterday. Between you and me, it's not unheard of, but they try not to make a big fuss about it in public. It's the undercurrent that gets them. If you ask me, tourists aren't given enough advice about the dangers of swimming around here, but none of the hotels want to put warning signs on the beaches. It's relatively safe in Beau Vallon. It's probably the best place to swim. But some stretches can be dangerous.'

Lucy could imagine her father's distress if she raised the possibility that her mother might have been swept out to sea by the current. It sounded so final. After ten minutes at the police station, they left. They were both silent on the way to the consulate. The impotence of the authorities only seemed to highlight the futility of their own efforts. Maggie was not available. She sent a message that she was in a meeting all morning and would come over to see them at three that afternoon. There was nothing more to do in town so they returned to the hotel for an early lunch after which Lucy's father said he was going up to his room for a rest before Maggie arrived. Lucy wanted to take the hire car for a spin while he was asleep. He made her promise she would take her mobile phone with her in case she had any trouble.

'Don't worry,' she told him, 'I'll stay on the coastal road and I'll be careful. I won't go far, and I won't get out of the car. I'll just go for a little drive along the coastal road and back. I won't be long.'

She looked away, afraid that her face might betray her guilt, because she knew exactly where she was going that afternoon. To begin with it felt strange to be changing gears manually, as she was used to driving an automatic car, but she soon slipped back into it and although the gears were stiff, she managed to drive without wrecking the clutch. Leaving the grounds of the hotel, she set off towards the house where her father had once lived. He had loved the view from his verandah. Since he had taken them there on their first day, it had occurred to Lucy that her mother might have returned there. Perhaps Veronique now lived in the house she had once cleaned for George, the house where they had fallen in love. It was one of the few places Lucy knew her mother had visited, so it was at least worth going there to have a look.

Parking the car off the road, she walked the last few hundred yards past the clearing where they had stopped on their first visit, and on down towards the house. As she passed a gigantic frangipani bush where her father had paused to smell the flowers, his verandah appeared around the corner of the house, with its unrestricted view of the ocean. Opening a small wooden gate, she went through into a garden of flowering bushes. Her heart began to pound with excitement as she imagined knocking on the front door and seeing her mother's face.

Veronique herself might open the door, her once beautiful features lit up by a welcoming smile. 'You must be Lucy. Come in. We hoped you would find us. Come, your mother's waiting for you on the verandah upstairs.'

Her pleasant reverie was interrupted by a huge Alsatian that bounded onto the path in front of her. Slavering and growling, it glared at her, its legs slightly bent as though it was crouching to pounce. Lucy let out a scream and spun round. A man was standing behind her, blocking the path. Trapped between the snarling dog and the man, she trembled with fear. The man began shouting at her. She did not need to understand a word he was yelling. His red face and bulging eyes conveyed his meaning well enough.

'I'm sorry,' she gasped. 'I didn't mean to trespass. I was – I'm looking for Veronique. *Veronique est ici?*'

The man shouted at her, waving his arms in the air.

'There is no one of that name here. You go away from my house.'

Lucy took a step towards him, and the dog let out a deep-throated bark. With a final bellow, the man whirled round and flung the gate open. Lucy took a tentative step towards it. The man stepped aside. Not daring to glance behind her at the dog, Lucy raced back out through the gate and slammed it behind her. A series of rapid barks from the dog rang in her ears as she sprinted to the car. Seated at the wheel, with the doors and windows closed, she struggled to regain her breath. Her outing to the house where her father had once lived had been a waste of time. The man had not recognised Veronique's name. All Lucy had succeeded in doing was give herself a fright.

34

For the first time, Adrian joined them at breakfast. Lucy shifted her chair to allow him to share the view towards the gardens and he grinned at her.

'Good morning.'

George nodded, his mouth full of papaya. He seemed to welcome Adrian's company. Lucy was pleased too. It was difficult to avoid sliding into despair over her mother's disappearance when she was alone with her father. Their conversations had become uncomfortably tense. He was obviously being careful not to say anything that might upset her, and she was on tenterhooks in case she let slip her suspicion that her mother might be staying with Veronique. It was no more than a hunch and, as far as her father was aware, she knew nothing about the woman he had met on the island all those years ago. She was becoming quite inured to lying, she thought, with a wretched kind of satisfaction.

Adrian's presence lightened the intensity of the atmosphere between them, even if he did not believe Lucy's claims that she had been attacked. She tried not to look too pleased, in case he interpreted her enthusiasm as flirting, but that was far easier to manage than strained relations with her father. He finished his mouthful, wiped his chin on his serviette and looked at Adrian.

'How are you this morning?'

'I'm good, thanks. I've got the day off today so I thought maybe—' He turned to Lucy. 'I wondered if you'd like to do something today?'

She glanced across at her father.

'Both of you, that is,' Adrian added quickly, smiling at her father.

'Day off?' Lucy's father joked. 'Wouldn't have happened in my day.'

They resumed their customary banter, her father joshing Adrian about how easy it was in Accounts these days, compared to the workload of thirty years ago. He reminded his young counterpart yet again that he had not even had a computer when he had worked at the Garden of Eden. After breakfast they made their way down to the beach before it grew too hot and found a pleasant spot under a parasol. Lucy's father lay back in a recliner, Adrian stretched out on the sand, and she sat up, clutching her knees to her chest, staring out at the sea. On the surface the scene was idyllic, but before long before the conversation moved back to Angela.

Lucy wondered how she was going to manage to continue her search for Veronique, with her father constantly watching her. She had no idea where to even begin looking for a woman who by all accounts had disappeared decades ago. It turned out she was not alone in suspecting a past enemy was targeting her father. Adrian also raised the possibility that someone on the island resented him coming back.

'Someone you knew when you lived here. I know it seems unlikely, given that it was such a long time ago.'

Lucy held her breath but her father merely shrugged off the suggestion. 'To be honest, the thought did cross my mind, but it's just too ludicrous to even contemplate. As far as I know, I didn't make a single enemy in all the time I spent here, nothing personal anyway.'

Lucy jumped on his remark. 'What do you mean, nothing personal? What else was going on?'

'I was referring to the political situation. You know I was sent home, but that was only because I was British, and spoke out of turn. No one could possibly even remember that now, apart from me.' He turned to Adrian. 'I'm just not the kind of person to go around pissing people off. I never have been.'

Adrian inclined his head. 'Yes, I can see that.'

'And even if I did antagonise someone without realising it, after an absence of more than thirty years it's ridiculous to suppose that anyone might still be nursing a grudge vicious enough to result in attacks on my family.'

He and Adrian agreed the theory was untenable.

'But it's not impossible,' Lucy said. 'And when you eliminate the impossible, the improbable is . . . possible – no, that's not right. When you eliminate the impossible, what you're left with is the truth, however improbable. Something like that anyway. According to Sherlock Holmes,' she added, seeing Adrian's blank expression. 'That's what comes of studying English at university.'

'Hmm. That must make it seem worthwhile,' he replied sardonically. 'There's nothing like misquoting to show how well educated you are.'

Lucy shrugged. 'Well, we can't just sit around doing nothing.'

'If you ask me, I'd say leave it to the police,' Adrian said. 'They'll find her, if . . .' He did not finish his sentence but they all knew what he meant.

Her father leaned back in his chair and sighed. 'Adrian's right. We have to leave this to the police.'

'But the police aren't doing anything,' Lucy protested. 'They've as good as told us they've given up.'

Her father closed his eyes. 'All we can do is be patient, and start to prepare ourselves, just in case.'

Lucy was shocked. 'You've given up? You think she's never coming back?'

'No. That's not what I'm saying. But we have to face up to the bleak reality of the situation. It's possible she drowned, or had some sort of accident, probably at sea. The worst part of it is that we might never know what happened to her, but we have to be prepared for the worst. She could be—' He broke off and cleared his throat. Lucy suspected he found it easier to talk like this with Adrian present. 'Two people died last year in shark attacks and all I'm saying is that it's just possible . . .' His voice cracked and he looked away. When he resumed, his voice was stronger. 'We have to hope that she has gone away for a while – for some reason – but in the meantime, I find it somehow easier to think of her as dead than still alive and suffering somewhere beyond our reach.' He sighed. 'I'm sorry, Lucy, but I'm too tired to feel guilty any more. All I want to do is sleep and shut out this nightmare.' He broke down and hid his bruised face in his hands. His shoulders shook. 'I just don't know how I'm going to cope without her.' He mumbled something about twenty-five years.

'It's OK, Dad.' Lucy reached across and patted his hand. 'We're going to find her. Everything's going to be all right.'

It felt strange, comforting her father as though he was a child, but she did not know what else to say. In spite of his lying to her, he was still her father, and he had assured her his letter had been perfectly innocent. She could be jumping to conclusions. It was only her supposition that her father had intended to cheat on her mother. Looking at him now, white-haired and slightly corpulent, it hardly seemed likely.

Adrian stared out at the sea, waiting, and she was grateful for his stillness. After a moment, her father dropped his hands with a mortified smile.

'For God's sake, don't apologise for having feelings,' Adrian said, before her father could speak.

'Why don't we try to find the van driver,' Lucy said, trying to sound as though it was a casual suggestion. 'He might know where Mum is.'

She pretended to stare at the table as her father glanced at Adrian who raised his eyebrows.

'Lucy, try to forget about the van,' her father said gently. 'Too much sun can make anyone confused. It happens. Isn't that right, Adrian?'

She shook her head. 'I didn't imagine it,' she muttered.

Disregarding her father's anxious expression, she appealed to Adrian. 'If we did want to trace the van, how would we do it?'

'Do you really want to go out looking for a van?'

'Well, at least we'd be doing something. Couldn't the police help us?'

'Let's say there was a van, there's no reason to suppose the driver owned it necessarily,' Adrian pointed out.

'You mean it could have been stolen?' Lucy asked.

'Yes, stolen or borrowed, or just untraceable,' he replied. 'This isn't England. Documents here aren't always up-to-date. Used vehicles get passed around the Seychellois community, especially old ones, even if they're not actually stolen. The hotel takes deliveries from all sorts of places. It's just not that simple. And would you recognise the driver again?'

'No. I never saw him. He came up behind me, picked me up and threw me in the back of the van. And, stupidly, I didn't look at the registration number.'

'Can you remember anything about him at all?' Adrian asked.

'He stank of beer.'

'That hardly narrows it down. Forget it, Lucy, let the police deal with it.'

Lucy did not answer. She was convinced the van driver would lead them to Veronique, if they could only find him and follow him for long enough. There was no other reason for him to have been sent with that message for her father. Veronique wanted George to find her, and she was using Angela as bait. If it was improbable her mother was still alive, it was not impossible. The only piece of the puzzle Lucy could not figure out was what Veronique was going to do to Lucy's father when he turned up. She seemed set on keeping herself hidden from everyone. Like Maria, who knew all the local gossip, no one Lucy had asked had any idea where Veronique was.

Adrian left for work and her father went up to his room to cool off. Lucy found a seat with a view of the ocean, in the shade of a flowering bush. She reached out and touched a delicate white blossom with the tip of one finger. 'Frangipani,' she whispered. Her father had told her the white flowers gave off the strongest scent.

'It's hard to believe the colour makes a difference,' he had added. 'Some people say they're all the same, but—' He had broken off, a distant look in his eyes. 'She used to love frangipani.'

Lucy knew he had been talking about Veronique. All at once, she felt as though she could see clearly after stumbling around in a fog for days. The floor of the van that had taken her away had been covered in a thick layer of frangipani petals. She recognised the scent. There had been a lot of them, and the strange thing was that there had been no twigs at all, just petals. If she closed her eyes she could still remember the feel of them beneath her, slippery and soft, protecting her from the hard metal floor of the van. She plucked a flower from the frangipani bush and rubbed it between her fingers, crushing it to release the scent. Everything seemed obvious now. She glanced around the patio but there was no sign of the old Seychellois man she had seen sweeping petals from the edge of the patio. Every once in a while he had carefully bent down to pick out the bits of twig and other detritus that he had swept up along with the petals. She was convinced he had been driving the van. He must be working for Veronique. He would know where her mother was being kept.

It made sense. According to Maria, Veronique had gone into hiding when she shot her husband. Someone must have been delivering supplies to her ever since. Who better than a man with a van? The pieces of the jigsaw all fitted. When Adrian joined them for a drink after lunch, she asked him about the old man.

Adrian shook his head. 'There was some tragedy in his life, I don't know what exactly, but I remember my grandmother telling me he was a sad case. I wish I could tell you what happened to him. All I can remember is that it was something to do with a woman.'

'Isn't it always?' Lucy's father said.

'Why do you want to know about him?' Adrian asked.

'Oh, nothing. I just wondered,' she answered vaguely.

The two men began discussing the state of the gardens. Lucy sat quietly, planning. One way or another, she was going to persuade Baptiste to help her. She was looking forward to seeing her father's face when he discovered who had been looking after Angela.

35

THAT AFTERNOON, LUCY KEPT a look out for the old man. Excited but scared, she was sure she was getting close to finding Veronique, and her mother. By early evening she had not spotted the sweeper. At her suggestion she and her father sat outside on the patio. Baptiste usually turned up there at some point in the evening. Once she saw him she would not let him out of her sight. When he left the hotel, she would follow him. Sooner or later he would lead her to where Veronique was living. While she had determined to do this alone, she did not intend to take any risks. The attacks against her had made her wary. But all she was going to do was discover where Veronique was living, and find her mother. She could not see how she could go wrong with that plan. The worst that might happen was that Baptiste would simply go home, in which case she would have followed him for nothing and would have to try again the next day.

During a break, Adrian joined them on the patio. Struggling against the temptation to look around, Lucy pretended to follow the strained conversation between her father and Adrian. After about ten minutes, Adrian made his excuses and returned to work. Lucy and her father finished their drinks in silence. After a while, he stirred in his seat and said he was going upstairs for a rest.

'I'm really tired. I'm going up to my room. I'll see you in an hour or so. Why don't you have a rest yourself this afternoon?'

She nodded and he disappeared into the hotel. As soon as he had gone, Baptiste arrived, as though on cue, flat broom in hand. He looked innocuous enough in his battered straw hat and tattered shirt, sweeping leaves and petals from the patio. A cigarette hung from the corner of his mouth, a thin trail of smoke rising from it, but he never removed it from his lips and did not appear to be smoking it. He gave the impression of being very old, with his bent figure and wizened face, frail compared to the robust figure of her father. Lucy doubted if he possessed the power to have captured her, or to have fought with her father, giving him a black eye. She did not believe the old man could have been involved in the attacks on her and her parents.

But as she continued observing him out of the corner of her eye, she was surprised at how agile he seemed when he bent down to poke around in the sweepings. She watched, mesmerised by the regular motion of his broom only interrupted when he bent down to separate the petals from the leaves. It appeared he might indeed be strong enough to have subdued her, and even her father.

After a while, he picked up his bag stuffed with petals, rested his broom against his shoulder, and crossed the patio. Suddenly nervous, Lucy turned to beckon Adrian, but he had gone. She only hesitated for a second. She could not afford to lose sight of Baptiste. For all she knew, with every passing day her mother's situation might be deteriorating. She had no choice but to follow him while she had the chance. Trembling, she hurried after Baptiste to find out where he was going.

He led her along a path through the garden. She kept several paces behind him, stepping silently on the earth. If he turned, she hoped the bushes would conceal her, but he did not look back. She watched him make his way to the side of the hotel. When he turned the corner of the building, she darted forward and pressed herself against the wall. Hurrying to the corner, she peered round just in time to see his figure disappear around next corner. She ran after him. There were a few people loitering near the front of the building which made it easier for her to observe Baptiste without attracting attention. Meanwhile, he was easy to spot, with his bent back and straw hat. As she watched, he climbed onto a bright red moped and sped away.

Cursing, she ran to the hire car, scrabbling in her pocket for the key. Leaping in, she put her foot down and shot out of the car park in first gear. The engine whined and creaked but she took no notice, more concerned that she had lost Baptiste than that she might be ruining the engine. Struggling to change up a gear, she reached the T-junction at the end of the road. There was no sign of the red moped. She could not afford to waste any time and spun the wheel, barely halting at the intersection. If she did not catch up with Baptiste soon, she would try the other direction.

After driving for about half a mile, she caught sight of him up ahead and slowed down. Relieved that she had not lost him, she watched the moped bumping along the empty road, the old man's hat flapping up and down. With difficulty she manoeuvred her phone out of her pocket and hesitated over who to call. Her father would only insist she return to the hotel. She could not even tell him exactly where she was, although she would be able to find the road again. Her best option remained to mark where Baptiste went without him spotting her. If her suspicions of him were mistaken, no one need ever know she had followed him. Her father might wonder how they had used up more petrol than he expected, but they had been driving around so much, he was unlikely to notice.

'Oh, shit,' she said suddenly.

The moped had taken a sharp turn off the road to disappear up a narrow lane ascending a steep hillside. Tall trees grew in neat lines on either side of the track. Lucy remembered Maria telling her that Veronique had disappeared up the mountain. She slowed down to avoid being spotted. Still Baptiste did not look round. Evidently he could not hear the noise of the car engine above the clunking of his moped as it laboured uphill. She realised he was taking her into Morne Seychellois National Park, a large area of natural forest growing up the mountains, stretching for miles. There was a network of trails for hikers, but most of it was wild territory. Someone could easily be hidden here and avoid discovery, even by police conducting an extensive search. Lucy looked around nervously. Scattered trees had given way to denser forest, dark and sinister.

'There are no wild animals or poisonous snakes in the forests,' her father had told her.

'Just some crazy woman who comes down the mountain and attacks people,' she muttered to herself.

They drove slowly up the hill, turning off the main track onto a narrower path. Lucy winced as protruding twigs and branches scraped along the side of the car. She hoped she was not damaging the vehicle to no purpose. The scratches were bound to be visible. As she wondered whether it might be better to get out and walk, she remembered the side of Baptiste's van had been badly scratched. She pressed on. The path rose steeply. She pushed her way further through shrubbery that seemed to close in around her. Ahead, the path disappeared in overhanging branches and bushes. Although it was still daylight, the gathering mist was too thick to see more than a short distance in any direction. Lucy glanced at her phone. The sun would set soon and she wondered how she would ever find her way out of the forest in complete darkness. It was an effort to keep the car on the track. The engine whined as they carried on climbing.

The moped appeared out of the mist, propped against a tree at the side of the path, almost completely concealed in leaves. Slamming on the brakes, she shivered, wondering what would have happened if she had missed it and kept going. It would be difficult enough to turn the car around where she was. If the path grew any narrower, it might be impossible, and she could not imagine reversing back along that path in daylight, let alone at night.

Closing the car door softly, she trembled as she set off to look for her mother. She needed to be careful to avoid being seen, now that Baptiste had led her close to Veronique's hideout. It was almost impossible to believe that anyone could harbour a grudge for over thirty years, but after everything that had happened, that seemed to be the only explanation for the note her mother had received, and her subsequent disappearance. Veronique's hatred of George had intensified into a dangerous mania.

Without any clear idea where she was going, Lucy made her way slowly forwards. As long as she kept going upwards in a straight line, she should be able to turn back and find the car again. Whatever happened, she would return to the car before darkness fell. With the help of the headlights, she could find her way back down the mountain track. If necessary, she would return the next day, hopefully not on her own. Nervously, she felt in her pocket for her phone, but she had no signal.

The trees were overgrown, the bushes so dense she had to fight her way through them. Very little light penetrated the canopy overhead. It was hard going over ground covered in a criss-crossing maze of creepers and tree roots, interspersed with granite boulders. A few times she almost lost her footing. She had to step carefully, keeping her eyes fixed on ground increasingly difficult to see in the fading light. Pausing to catch her breath, she looked up. She could not see far ahead in the misty bushes ahead of her. It would soon be dark and she was lost, alone in the cloud forest of Morne Seychellois. A series of shrill whistles pierced the air, ringing eerily through the trees, startling her. It sounded like a bird call. It was time to return to the car before Baptiste could tell Veronique she was there.

Pausing in a small clearing, she heard a tall clump of ferns rustle nearby and froze. A heavy animal was moving around in the bushes. Her father may have told her there were no wild beasts on the island, but she remembered his story about being chased by a pack of stray dogs. She stood perfectly still, trying not to show her fear, telling herself the creature was probably tame. This was a national park where tourists went hiking.

Then she heard a hoarse voice.

'Those who come to the mountain, die on the mountain.'

36

Lucy screamed in panic. She had not come here to die. Shocked by her own involuntary shriek, she summoned a fictitious team of police officers to come to her aid. 'Bring the police dogs here!' she shouted. 'Over here! All of you!'

It did not help her now, to be certain of her enemy's identity. Lucy was alone on the mountain with a woman who harboured an insane grudge against her family. All she could think of was to try and scare Veronique away. She hardly dared hope her mother was still alive, but there was no time to dwell on that.

Tripping over creepers and tree roots, she charged up a narrow path and darted in among the ferns to hide. Crouching down, she heard a twig break behind her. A shuffling footstep. Through the fronds she caught a glimpse of outstretched arms, and gnarled hands reaching out. Lucy threw herself headlong into bushes that caught at her hair and clothes, whipping at her face. Closing her eyes against the vicious bushes, she forced her way forward, feeling her way along the uneven ground. Gasping, she pressed on through tangled roots and plants. Stumbling on a rough track, she paused to consider which way to go. If she made her way back downhill she ought to be able to find the car. But Veronique might be there, waiting to intercept her.

More afraid of her pursuer than of the hostile environment, she continued climbing the track through the wild beauty of the forest. Low overhanging trees and thick bushes seemed to close in on her in the misty air as she fought her way along the narrow track, looking for somewhere to hide. Veronique could be anywhere out there, watching her. Baptiste was probably with her. They knew the terrain, while Lucy was stumbling around blindly, slipping on the leafy ground. Once in a while she spun round and waited, but there was no sound of pursuit. She began to hope she was no longer being followed.

Unexpectedly she came across deep ruts in the earth that could only have been made by tyres. Higher up, a few broken branches indicated where someone might have crashed their way through the bushes. With a shudder of excitement, she followed the tracks. They soon petered out in the dense vegetation but she pressed on, convinced she had found the right trail. It was slow going, forcing her way between the branches, but she refused to give up. She was going to find her mother. Together they would subdue Veronique, and Baptiste too, if necessary, and escape. It was like a dream. She was not even surprised when a hut appeared up ahead, shrouded in mist. Almost completely concealed by the forest, it had been constructed in the shadow of a huge granite peak that loomed above it, making it virtually impossible to spot from the air, its corrugated roof covered in thick ivy. It was the perfect place to hide a captive – or a body.

For a moment she hid in the bushes a few yards from the hut. Veronique might be waiting for her, inside. Very little light penetrated the dense canopy overhead. Catching her breath, she hurried across a clearing between the trees and tall ferns, stepping carefully over tree roots. Tense with apprehension, she slowed down as she reached the door and saw that it was bolted on the outside.

Veronique could not be waiting for her in the hut. But if her mother was inside, she was a prisoner.

Lucy almost collapsed. Her legs felt weak. If she did not make her move soon, it would be too dark to see inside the hut. And at some point, Veronique would return. She might bring Baptiste with her. He was paid to do Veronique's bidding. With a sickening lurch she realised that Veronique must be using the money George had sent her, to buy the old man's services. If it came to it, Lucy would use her father's money too, and she could offer to pay more than Veronique. She might be able to buy Baptiste's loyalty, but it was a precarious hope. Her best chance of saving her mother, and herself, was by stealth. She reminded herself that Veronique was no longer young. If her mother was there, the two of them should be able to overpower her, even if Baptiste came to her aid. He was old too.

She glanced around. All was still. Veronique could have followed her, and be waiting to slam the door as soon as Lucy went in. She had to take that chance. Her mother might be sick, locked in the hut. She might already be dead. Lucy could feel her heart palpitating as she reached out to slide the rusty bolt across, as quietly as she could. The door creaked open. She paused and held her breath, listening. There was no sound of pursuit. She stood for a second on the threshold before she went in, steeling herself to confront the nightmare.

The hut was not what she had been expecting. Dilapidated and inaccessible, no one could be living in there. Her visions of Veronique's hospitality vanished at once. She had been an idiot to have considered that was a possibility. Peering into the darkness of the hut, she wished her father and Adrian were with her. This was not a task anyone should face alone. She was more frightened now than she had ever been, terrified of discovering her mother's dead body. Halting just inside the low doorway, she reeled from the stench, fighting the nausea rising in her gullet. Taking shallow breaths, she looked around.

In the shadows she could see the hut was empty, apart from a crude construction in the corner: a wooden box on a plinth, covered by a white curtain. It looked like some sort of shrine. The afternoon's trauma had achieved nothing. Her mother was not there. She had merely stumbled on a disused hut with a neglected shrine that no one visited any more. The interior of the hut was gloomy, only one corner lit by a shaft of light that streamed in through a square hole covered by a metal grid. As her eyes grew accustomed to the darkness, she frowned. The floor of the hut was covered in a carpet of shrivelled petals. Sick with disappointment, she turned back towards the door.

Something stirred. Swinging around, Lucy saw a heap of rags on the ground. Moving, crawling, it rose slowly into an upright position. The face had no eyes, only an open mouth, startlingly red against the white face. The ghastly effigy tottered to its feet and she saw it was human.

'Veronique? Are you there?'

The voice was almost unrecognisable.

Lucy let out a cry of horror. 'Mum?'

'Lucy? Is that you?'

Lucy ran to her mother and flung her arms around her. Always slight, her mother felt like a bundle of rags and bones. Lucy recoiled at the stench. Gently she removed her mother's blindfold, and studied her face in the faint light from the door. Her lips were cracked, her hair dry, and she was filthy. Even her eyes looked different, swollen and filmy with tears. It was hardly the joyful reunion Lucy had anticipated, but the stinking bundle of flesh and bones crawling in the dirt was her mother just the same. She was alive. They would get through this.

'Don't come near me, Lucy, I'm filthy,' her mother rasped in a dry voice.

Delicately, Lucy touched her dry lips, her inflamed eyelids, her dirty neck. She was almost unrecognisable. As Lucy carried her towards the door, their slow progress was halted abruptly. Her mother was chained to the wall.

'Water,' her mother whispered. 'Water.'

Blinking away her tears, Lucy stared at her mother's haggard face. 'Don't worry,' she said stupidly. 'Everything's going to be all right. Thank God I found you in time.'

'You have to get out of here before she comes back,' her mother whispered. 'She'll bolt the door and you'll be trapped. Run!'

Lucy shuddered. Now she had found her mother, she was not going to abandon her to Veronique's insane quest for revenge. Somehow she would save her mother. But first, she needed to wedge the door open so they could not be locked in. After looking around, she ran over to the wooden shrine in the corner of the hut and began rocking the plinth with all her might. At first her effort seemed futile, but soon the massive wooden post began to shift. Standing behind it, she braced herself and pushed as hard as she could, in short strong bursts. With a loud creak, the plinth suddenly toppled over. The curtain over the box fluttered but remained in place as Lucy fell forwards. Her arm hit the edge of the wooden post but she barely noticed the pain. Only the tip of the lid of the wooden box reached the doorway. It was enough. The shrine was too heavy to be lifted easily. The door to the hut could not be closed.

Returning to her mother, she examined her shackles. A large staple was nailed firmly to the wall, holding the chain. With no tools to pick the lock open, the only way to remove it would be to smash the wood, but that would need a large hammer and an axe. All she had was her phone and car key. Lucy groaned. In the dim light, she could see a raw weal on her mother's wrist where the metal had chafed.

Hating herself for saying it, she told her mother she might have to leave her while she went to fetch help.

'Don't worry, I'll be back as soon as I can.'

As she spoke, she heard the shuffle of footsteps. It was too late. She spun round and breathed a sigh of relief on seeing Baptiste. He might be batty, but he was innocuous, and he was poor. Lucy only had to offer him enough money, and he would help release her mother from her chains.

'What have you done?' he demanded, looking down at the fallen shrine.

Lucy took a step forward. In as reasonable a tone as she could muster, she explained that she had wanted to make sure the door stayed open.

'I didn't intend any disrespect to the shrine. We just don't want to be locked in, and there was nothing else in here I could use. You understand that, don't you? We were worried Veronique would lock us both in. But now you're here, you can help us. We can pay you well. I'm sure you don't know how my mother's been abused. Veronique shackled her to the wall. Look!' The chain rattled as she shook her mother's elbow. 'This isn't your fight. Whatever Veronique's playing at, she's not thinking about you, or anyone else. Look what she did to my mother. She might just as easily turn on you. She's crazy. But you can help us, and we'll help you in return. We'll pay you more money than you can imagine, as much as you want. But you have to help us get away—'

He raised his finger to his lips. 'I will help you, if that is what she wants.'

'Of course it's what she wants,' Lucy replied impatiently. 'I mean, look at her. She's been chained up in here for days.'

Again the old man put his finger to his lips to silence her. 'I do my wife's bidding.'

'Your wife?'

He nodded. 'She will be pleased to meet you.'

It had never occurred to Lucy that the old man was married. He had always struck her as a solitary figure.

'Well, all right then,' she agreed. 'Why not? But is she nearby? Only my mother needs to be released as soon as possible. You do understand that, don't you?'

The old man nodded his head. 'My wife understands everything.'

In silence Lucy watched him kneel by the fallen shrine. Muttering to himself, he pulled back the curtain.

'I have a surprise for you,' he crooned softly, taking something out of the wooden casket. 'The daughter has come here to see you.' He paused as though listening. 'Yes, they are both here.'

Lucy could not see what he was holding until he turned and rose to his feet. She barely registered the gun in his right hand.

'Meet my wife,' he said, with a smile. 'This is Veronique.'

Resting in the old man's left hand, a human skull grinned at Lucy in the fading light.

37

Baptiste moved his arm until the light from the doorway fell on the skull. The shiny white surface shone brightly. He must have polished it, or perhaps he had caressed the bone for hours with his fingers, until it seemed to glow with an inner light. Lucy trembled and nearly lost her footing. The room was spinning. She thought she was going to be sick. With his back to the door, Baptiste's face was concealed in shadows. He took a step forward. Quivering with the movement, the skull seemed to be talking to her. She stood perfectly still, staring at it. Above the glaring empty eye sockets there was a circular aperture, less than a centimetre in diameter, its edges sharply defined. Five short cracks in the bone radiated outwards from the round hole, so that it resembled a small black sun in a child's drawing. She gazed, spellbound by gaping holes in a skull that had once been concealed beneath living flesh, a network of soft tissues forming the face of a woman so beautiful people had called her a dark angel. The small spherical hole above the eye sockets could only have been made by a bullet. She shuddered, wondering whether there was an exit hole at the back of the skull, or if the bullet had lodged somewhere inside the brain until the soft tissue decayed.

Rigid with fear, Lucy stared at the eye sockets. It was not Veronique but Baptiste who had brought Lucy's mother to the hut on the mountain. The whole ordeal had been Baptiste's vendetta against her father. There was no one else involved. It was obvious now what had provoked the attacks on Lucy, on her father, and most dreadfully on her mother. A man who kept a skull for decades, treating it as a holy relic, was mad. That much was clear. What was also clear was that, like Lucy's father, and perhaps many others, Baptiste had loved Veronique. Lucy tried to imagine the bowed old man in his youth, capable of a devotion that bordered on insanity. Veronique had vanished, just as Maria had told Lucy, but the rumours surrounding her disappearance had been false. She had never left the island. And she had not shot her husband. Instead, she was the one who had been shot in the head by the man who had kept her skull to himself all these years, the treasured skull he called Veronique.

The pieces of the puzzle were starting to make sense. Veronique had never replied to her father's letters because she had been murdered by her jealous husband, years ago. Killing her had driven him mad, if he had not been completely insane already. Now Baptiste was determined to kill Lucy and her mother in some crazy revenge attack against her father. This was what he had been waiting for. Lucy had walked right into his trap. She swore aloud in fright as he glared at her, his eyes burning with fury. Slowly he raised his gun.

His whisper carried on the still air. 'A life for a life. He stole my wife. Now it is his turn.'

'No!' Lucy cried out, aghast. Her mother's life could not end like this, in a stinking hut on the mountain, chained by a madman. 'Not my mother. She has done nothing to deserve this. Let her go. She's a good person.'

'So was I, once,' he answered quietly.

Somehow Lucy did not believe him, but this was not the time to voice her doubts. With no idea what to do, she played for time. Staring levelly at Baptiste, she did her best to engage him in conversation while her mind whirled, trying to think of a means to escape. It seemed hopeless.

'What has my mother ever done to you? She never met you before this week. We didn't even know you and Veronique existed.'

At the mention of Veronique's name, Baptiste trembled. 'One of you did,' he said. His words sounded cold, undeniable. 'George knew her. He knew her well.'

'But he went away.' Lucy struggled to retain her composure. 'He went away and married my mother in England. He's got nothing to do with you any more. Leave us alone!' Despite her efforts to control herself, her voice rose in a hysterical shriek.

'Yes, he went away,' Baptiste agreed. 'And we would have forgotten about him. I could have forgiven her, even after—'

'Why didn't you?'

'Because after he went away, that was when the letters started. She hid them from me. She thought I didn't know. But I read them, every one. So one day I brought her up here on the mountain and burned them all, right in front of her eyes.' His shrill laughter sounded like a scream of pain. 'She cried when I burned them! And after that . . .' He paused, lost in memories. 'She had to die.'

Lucy did not need to ask how she had died, or at whose hand.

'It was a long time ago,' she pleaded.

'Oh yes,' he agreed. 'We were living here together in peace for a long time. Until the letters started again. He wrote to her at the post office. Did he think I had stopped watching for him? That I had forgotten? Did he think time would dull my desire for revenge? He wrote that he was coming back and I knew it was time for vengeance.' He stared at Lucy. 'This is all his doing. George.' He spat the name, his lined features twisted in loathing. 'He did not have to come back. Even now, we did not intend to kill you, his daughter.' He waved his gun at Lucy. 'You were not even born when Veronique . . . We tried to warn you.'

'Warn me?'

'In the water, and on land, we tried to frighten you away. We shot a girl like you, to show you we were serious. How were we to know you would not see the signs?'

'It was you in the sea, pulling me under. And you threw that rock at me on the beach.' Lucy frowned, understanding. 'You killed Judy, just to warn me off?' She could hardly believe what she was hearing. She struggled to concentrate on the immediate danger. 'Baptiste, you've got this all wrong. My parents are happily married. He didn't want Veronique—'

The old man interrupted her. 'He wanted my dark angel,' he shouted. 'They all did. He should never have come back. He stole my wife. Now it is his turn to suffer.'

He turned to the skull he was holding. 'Now you see George as he really is, a coward who sends his daughter to face danger in his place. Such a man does not deserve the love of the dark angel.'

He turned and pointed his gun at Angela. Frantically, Lucy looked around. There must be something she could use as a weapon. As she scanned the ground, she noticed a faint gleam. Something metallic was lying by her feet, almost hidden in petals. It could be a knife. Wincing at the prospect of plunging a blade into the old man's flesh, she bent her knees and reached down to feel the circular rim of a metal bowl. She picked it up. Grains of dried up rice were sticking to the sides. Seeing what Lucy was clutching, her mother attempted to keep Baptiste's attention on herself.

'Come closer,' she said. 'I want to see Veronique. She has looked after me and given me water when you weren't here. Let me speak to her and thank her for her many kindnesses to me.'

'See how beautiful she is,' he replied, holding up the skull.

As he took a step forward, Lucy leapt at him, bringing the rim of the bowl down on the back of his head with all her might. Metal hit bone with a loud retort, shattering the momentary silence. Lucy was faintly surprised when Baptiste collapsed without protest. For a second his arm twitched as he reached for the skull that had slipped from his grasp. Then he lay motionless. A few petals, disturbed by the movement, came to rest on his face.

For a moment nothing happened, as though time had stopped in that dark place.

'Oh my God, have I killed him?' Lucy asked, horrified yet curiously calm at the same time, her voice an intrusion in the silence of the hut.

'I hope so!' her mother replied. 'Hurry up. He must keep the keys on him. I've heard them jangling when he moves.'

Lucy hesitated, but she had to find the key if she wanted to rescue her mother. Cringing, she knelt beside his body, terrified that he would suddenly leap up and attack her.

'What if he's alive?' she asked.

Her mother closed her eyes and did not answer. Shaking, Lucy patted the old man's trousers. She had to force herself to slip her hand inside his pocket, but she found his keys. One of them looked as though it was small enough to fit the handcuffs. Her mother let out an involuntary sob as Lucy released her.

'I can't believe it,' she said, 'I can't believe it.'

'Come on,' Lucy answered gently, 'let's get out of here.'

Trembling so much that she could barely stand, Lucy was only dimly aware of her mother holding onto her arm, as they staggered out of the hut. Outside it was almost dark. In fading sunlight Lucy was shocked to see Baptiste's blood on her hand. Her arm shook as she held it up for her mother to see.

'It's only a smear,' her mother said, looking away. 'Wipe it off on the grass. And then let's get as far away from here as we can.'

'Rest here for a few seconds,' Lucy said, 'and breathe deeply.'

Snatching a handful of leaves from the nearest bush, she scrubbed her soiled skin. The stain did not disappear completely. Meanwhile, the fresh air seemed to revive her mother a little. Hanging on to each other, they tottered away from the foul den where Lucy had just killed a man.

38

'WHERE THE HELL HAVE you been?' Her father's voice seemed to reach her from a long way off. 'Oh my God! What happened to you?' he added, catching sight of her.'

'I've got Mum,' Lucy blurted out and burst into tears.

'What?'

'She's in the car.'

Without another word, her father turned and dashed to the lift. Lucy ran after him as fast as she could.

In the artificial light of the car, Lucy's mother looked dreadful. Her eyes seemed to have sunk into shadowy depressions, her cheeks were hollow, her hair looked like dead straw.

'Angela, what happened?' Lucy's father asked gently, his eyes filling with tears.

'Lucy saved my life on the mountain,' her mother answered feebly, as he climbed into the car beside her. 'But you mustn't tell anyone what happened. It stays between us.'

'Don't worry about that for now. You can tell me all about it later. But first we're taking you to the hospital.'

Lucy's mother moaned softly as the car began to move. On the way, Lucy told him a little of what had happened, how she had followed Baptiste and discovered her mother in the hut on the mountain, chained to the wall.

'We need to take the police up there as soon as possible,' her father said, 'show them the hut exactly as it is, with the chain fixed to the wall, before that maniac can destroy the evidence. The marks on your mother's wrists will match the shackles in there, and—'

'No,' Lucy's mother interrupted him urgently. 'We must never tell anyone about that place, never speak of it again.'

'Why? What happened up there, Lucy?'

As Lucy hesitated, her mother answered for her. 'Lucy saved my life. She saved all of our lives. He was going to kill us all.'

'So you said. And Baptiste?'

'He won't be bothering us any more.'

'He's—?' Her father broke off, his question hanging unspoken in the air.

Lucy's teeth were chattering. Her hands shaking. Her breath came in short rapid gasps.

'His sweeping days are over,' her mother said. 'If you take anyone there, it's going to stir up a lot of trouble for all of us, especially Lucy.' She broke off, gasping for breath and continued weakly, 'She had no choice. She had to kill him. It was us or him. She was acting in self-defence. He had a gun and was going to shoot us. But who knows what the police will make of it?

'I understand,' Lucy's father interrupted her. He glanced at Lucy in the rear mirror. 'Anyone would have done the same thing in the circumstances. I don't want either of you to worry about it. Everything's going to be all right from now on.'

'I had to do it,' Lucy burst out. 'I didn't mean to. I never meant to do it. I never meant to hurt anyone. But he was going to shoot Mum. I had to stop him. I had to. I didn't think about it. I just did it. Oh God, what have I done?' She began to cry hysterically.

'You did what you had to do,' her father said firmly. 'No one's ever going to go up there again. No one knows that place exists, and that means no one will ever find out what happened. Only the three of us know and we'll never tell anyone else.'

'You had no choice, Lucy,' her mother chimed in. 'It was him or us.'

'All of us,' her father agreed. 'He was armed. He would have shot us all, and he would have got away with it too, because he would have left our bodies up there on the mountain.'

'Like we're doing to him,' Lucy muttered uneasily.

'Do you think we ought to go back and bury him?' her father asked.

'He is buried, in the hut,' her mother replied.

'What I don't understand is what made us his target,' Lucy's father said, as they turned into the entrance to the hospital. 'I know he was mad, but why us?'

'He was married to Veronique,' her mother replied quietly.

George started at the mention of the name. 'Angela,' he stammered, 'I wanted to tell you – I can explain – it's not what you think – but first let's get you to a doctor. You're in a bad way, injured and probably dehydrated, and God knows what you might have picked up out there.'

Lucy thought about Baptiste in his remote hut on the mountain where his cadaver would become bone, like the precious skull he had guarded for so long. He had nearly killed her mother. Lucy had rescued her alive, but only just. During the journey to the hospital she had deteriorated, drifting in and out of consciousness. The excitement of her rescue seemed to have sapped the last remnants of her energy.

'We're here now,' her father said. 'Wake up, Angela. We're going get you some help. Look at me.'

Her mother groaned softly, and would not open her eyes.

'She'll be OK, Dad, once we get her to a doctor.' She hoped she was right.

Her father nodded without speaking. Gazing anxiously at her semi-comatose mother, her head lolling on her car seat, Lucy was almost pleased she had killed the animal who had reduced her mother to this breathing skeleton.

Lucy's father carried Angela, unconscious, into the hospital where she was rushed to an examination room in a wheelchair. Lucy and her father went with her and watched helplessly as a young doctor conducted her examination. Angela regained consciousness but could not even stand unaided, and was admitted at once for emergency treatment.

'What's happening?' Lucy's father asked in a trembling voice. 'Please, tell me what's wrong with her.'

'Your wife is seriously dehydrated. All her systems have shut down.'

The young doctor reeled off a series of medical details in jargon Lucy would not have understood even if the doctor had not been speaking very fast with a strong French accent.

'What does all that mean? Oh God, will she be all right?' her father asked. He looked close to tears.

'Oh yes, Mr Hall. We're putting your wife on a drip. She should begin to rally within twenty-four hours and then we can start feeding her. She's very weak but she should be fine in a day or two. We'll need to check all her vital organs, to check there's been no permanent damage, but there's every indication she's going to make a full recovery.'

The young doctor smiled at them. Crying with relief, Lucy hoped her mother would recover from the psychological trauma as easily as from her physical problems. With the crisis in Angela's physical state undergoing treatment, an older doctor wanted to question them. Pulling herself together, Lucy accompanied her father.

'What exactly happened to your wife, Mr Hall?'

'My wife was lost.'

'For how long?'

'Nearly a week.'

The doctor looked at him in surprise. 'It took you a week to find her?'

'Yes.'

Seeing her father looking exhausted, barely able to summon the energy to speak, Lucy forced herself to remain composed. It was hard to feel that anything else mattered now that her mother was safe, but she was aware that her father was somehow under scrutiny.

'Your wife has some strange marks on her wrists, Mr Hall. Can you account for them?'

Lucy took a deep breath. 'We reported my mother missing to the police nearly a week ago and they've been looking for her – but we found her – my father and I – we found her. She'd been—'

'She'd been lost for days,' Lucy's father cut in urgently. 'We found her on the beach, but we think she'd been wandering all around the island. The police have been searching for her ever since she disappeared.'

His interruption came just in time to prevent Lucy from blurting out that her mother had been taken up the mountain. She met her father's eye and nodded, recalling the conversation in the car on the way to the hospital. Under no circumstances could her mother's reappearance be linked to the body in the hut. No one must even know it was there. By the time anyone discovered it, if they ever did, Lucy and her parents would be long gone.

The doctor shrugged and stepped back. 'Oh well, if the police are investigating . . .'

He opened the door and ushered them out into the corridor. The nightmare was over.

39

Lucy saw her father stagger as he was led away by a grey-haired man in a white coat. She hoped the doctor was going to check he was all right. He looked dreadfully drawn and shaken. Meanwhile, she was left alone in the corridor. Sitting on a plastic chair she waited anxiously, telling herself that her mother was receiving the attention she needed and her father was in good hands. The trauma of the evening was over. It was uncomfortably warm and she wondered if there was anywhere she could get a drink of water. She walked along the corridor but the only nurse behind the desk was jabbering on the phone, and she could not see anyone else to ask. Hearing her name, she turned to see Adrian standing in the corridor looking pale and bewildered.

'I came as soon as I heard,' he said. 'How is she?'

Lucy shrugged. 'OK, I think. How did you know?'

He gave a tense smile. 'They told us at the hotel. Word travels fast here.'

As briefly as she could, Lucy gave a vague account of what had happened. She did not mention Baptiste.

'What luck that you found her,' Adrian said after she had explained how she had found her mother quite by chance, wandering on a deserted beach. Lucy's father reappeared. He went over to the desk, where the nurse was still on the phone. In a loud voice he demanded to know where his wife had been taken. With a nod, the nurse finished her call and ushered them into a noisy ward. Lucy's mother was lying on a bed with her eyes closed. Attached to a drip and very pale, she had been washed, and no longer stank of excrement. Her father sat on the only chair and Lucy stood beside him watching a young doctor supervise adjustments to her mother's drip. The patient's heart rate and blood pressure were monitored but Lucy did not like to ask how she was and her father looked too tired to speak, so they watched in silence as the medical staff bustled around. The doctor left and a couple of nurses remained fiddling with equipment until Adrian put his head round the door. They joined him in the corridor.

'How is she?'

'They've put her on a drip. She'll be OK, won't she, Dad?'

'Yes, the doctor said she should rally within twenty-four hours. She's going to be fine. The main problem is dehydration.'

'Thank goodness I – we – found her in time,' Lucy said with a shudder.

Her father nodded his head wearily. 'Another twenty-four hours and the doctor said she might not have made it. But there's no need to worry any more. It sounds like she'll be better very soon, and well enough to fly home.'

'I told Adrian how we found her on a beach,' Lucy said quickly.

Her father nodded at her then turned to Adrian. 'We think she was attacked by a drunken maniac, but we don't want to start a whole police investigation into what happened. You understand, don't you, we just want to enjoy the rest of our stay quietly from now on.'

Adrian told them not to worry. The police would be only too pleased to close the case on Angela's disappearance. 'By the time the police look into it, you'll be back in England.'

'I'm going to stay all night,' George said. 'I'm not leaving her on her own in here.'

The ward sister was initially reluctant to allow George to remain with his wife overnight, but he insisted he would not part from her.

'What if she asks for me? I'm not leaving her alone.'

After a brief discussion in Creole with Adrian, the staff nurse agreed to let George to stay on a chair at his wife's bedside.

Adrian drove Lucy back to the hotel.

'I'm so grateful to you,' she burst out. 'You've been such an amazing help with all this.'

He did not answer.

'Are you sure you'll be all right on your own overnight?' Adrian broke the silence as they approached the hotel. 'I could always stay with you.'

'I'll be fine,' she laughed.

'Well, you can't blame me for trying. Tell you what,' he went on as they drove into the car park, 'how about something to eat? I don't know about you, but I'm hungry.'

'That sounds like a great idea. I'm ravenous.'

With a guilty pang she remembered her father, stuck in a ward at the hospital.

'We should've asked Dad if he wanted us to get him something before we left. He must be hungry too.'

'He's quite capable of looking after himself,' Adrian told her. 'Stop worrying about your parents. They're going to be fine. And in the meantime here we are, it's late and we're both hungry. So let's have something to eat.'

'What did you have in mind?'

Parking the car, Adrian turned to scrutinise her. Wrinkling his nose, he laughed. 'Maybe a romantic dinner for two isn't quite the thing tonight.'

Lucy glanced down at her filthy jeans and her hands covered in green muck and smiled. 'It's a bit late anyway, isn't it?'

'How did you get so dirty?'

She shrugged. 'Clambering on the rocks and through the trees, you know.' As she spoke it occurred to her that she would be leaving the island in a few days anyway. She wondered if the same thought had crossed Adrian's mind. 'Actually, something to eat sounds great. I promise not to sit too close to you.'

'Damn, foiled again,' he said, and they both laughed.

Ignoring her dirty state he took her by the hand, and led her across the car park. He took her into the deserted dining room where the tables were laid ready for breakfast, and told her to sit down.

'Wait for me here. I won't be long.'

'I'll just go and have a wash and change.'

He glanced down at her feet and trousers and nodded. 'That's a good idea, and it will give me time to ferret around for something to eat. Tell you what, meet me here in half an hour.'

When Lucy returned, Adrian was waiting for her. He refused to let her see what was in the bag he was clutching.

'Grab a couple of glasses and follow me.'

He led her down to the patio and they sat together at a table overlooking the sea. Under the light of the stars he displayed the contents of his bag on the table: small fresh bananas, papaya, bread rolls, smoked fish, cheese and a bottle of wine.

'Tuck in. I'm sorry it's nothing very exciting, but it was the best I could rustle up at such short notice, without preparation.'

'It's a banquet,' she replied, grinning. 'A midnight feast!'

It was late by the time Lucy went up to her room. Laughing and joking with Adrian, she had felt intoxicated with wine and relief about her mother. Once she was on her own she could not help thinking about the hut up on the mountain, replaying that dreadful scene in her mind, with her mother chained to the wall. She almost regretted having declined Adrian's offer to spend the night in her room, and double checked her door was locked and the window to her balcony was securely fastened before she went to bed. Putting her mobile phone by her pillow in case her father called, she lay down, but could not sleep, wondering how her mother had been affected by her ordeal on the mountain.

40

LUCY CALLED HER FATHER first thing in the morning. She could tell he was reluctant to leave her mother.

'Tell you what, Dad. You stay at the hospital and sit with Mum. I'm sure she wants you there with her. It can't be fun, stuck in hospital in a foreign country. Adrian and I can go to the police.'

'Isn't he working today?'

'No, he's taken the day off. We want to spend some time together before we leave. He's meeting me here around eleven, so leave it to us. Give my love to Mum and tell her we'll be there as soon as we're done at the police station. Adrian can drop me off and I'll come back with you, whenever.'

She glanced at her phone. It was already half past ten.

'If you're sure . . .'

'Just stay there, Dad, and stop worrying. Adrian and I will speak to Inspector Henri. Leave it to us.'

She promised to give her father a detailed account of the police response to her visit and he rang off after anxious exhortations that she should call him if there was any problem at the police station.

'They're the police, Dad. It'll be fine. And Adrian speaks Seychellois and French. There won't be a problem. We can sort it.'

Despite his pallor, and the grey bruising still evident around his nose, he had recovered his characteristic air of authority. But while her father was reverting to normal, Lucy had changed. They would never return to the simplicity of the relationship they had enjoyed before this strange and terrible visit to the Seychelles.

As soon as she had hung up, Lucy got ready to meet Adrian, showering, fluffing up her short hair and applying subtle make-up. Despite the recent trauma she looked well, her normally pale complexion tanned and glowing with health. With only three days left, she was determined to make the most of her remaining time on the island. She was also a little excited at the prospect of spending the morning with Adrian. To begin with she had been convinced he was not her type, but she had fallen for Darren and where had that got her? Perhaps a short holiday romance would be the perfect way to end a trip that had hardly gone well so far. It was a pity the Seychelles were such a long way from England.

She waited for Adrian in the lobby, unaccountably nervous about seeing him again. At exactly eleven o'clock, he walked through the entrance.

'You're very punctual,' she said.

'Punctuality is a good thing,' he answered solemnly. 'It shows I'm reliable, and trustworthy, and responsible . . .'

She could not tell if he was poking fun at her. They wandered outside and she told him about their proposed visit to the police.

'I hope you don't mind my volunteering you,' she concluded, wishing she had asked him first. It was hardly a pleasant way to spend their limited time together. He must have had other plans for their day. 'It's absolutely fine if you'd rather not. I didn't mean to presume. I can easily go by myself, or with my dad—'

'Don't be daft, Lucy. Of course your father should be with

Angela, and we have to report this whole crazy situation to the police. The sooner they close the case the better.'

Remembering what she had done, Lucy nodded nervously.

The inspector's face creased into a grin when Lucy told him her mother had been found and he held out his arms as though to wrap her in a hug. She wondered how he would have treated her if he had known she was a murderer.

'That is wonderful news,' he beamed. 'And your father is well?'

He glanced enquiringly at Adrian. Lucy explained that her father was with her mother in hospital and the inspector started forward in consternation.

'Please tell me your mother will make a full recovery.'

He could not have sounded more concerned if the patient had been his own mother.

'Yes, thank you. She was severely dehydrated, but they put her on a drip as soon as she was admitted, and she's already much better.'

'Ah yes, it is important to drink plenty of fluids. I am sure your mother is a careful woman and it was only a temporary mental aberration that caused this problem. When you are not used to this climate, it is easy to forget, and with your mother—'

'It wasn't the sun,' Lucy interrupted. She took a deep breath and glanced at Adrian. 'My mother didn't have sunstroke. She was attacked by a drunken maniac.'

'Probably harmless as a rule, but drunk enough to get violent,' Adrian added.

'Ah, that is always a problem,' the inspector replied easily. He did not appear unduly perturbed by her hazy account. 'It was a tourist who attacked her, not an islander?'

'We think so,' Adrian said, with a glance at Lucy.

'We don't know really. I'm sorry, we'd be more specific, but unfortunately my mother can't remember much about what happened.

We think she was knocked out and then very confused. We found her wandering about on the beach—'

'On an empty beach,' Adrian concluded her rambling account. 'It looks as though she somehow crossed the island, because from what I can make out, they found her past North Point, on this side of the island, nowhere near Beau Vallon.'

The inspector leaned his elbows on his desk and drummed his fingertips together as he asked exactly where the missing woman had been found. Lucy glanced uncertainly at Adrian.

'On a beach,' she repeated.

'A beach?'

'Yes, she was lying by the sea, near some rocks. I can't tell you exactly where. It's all a bit muddled.' She smiled at the inspector. 'We were so relieved to find her, alive, we didn't make a note of where we were. We just rushed her to the hospital.'

The inspector looked at Adrian, then back at Lucy again. 'You were all together?'

'Not Adrian. I was with my father, out searching for my mother.'

The inspector frowned. 'The Australian girl's body was also found on a beach.'

'I don't suppose you know what happened to her?' Lucy asked. 'Only I kind of knew her, and I'd really like to know who killed her, and why, before I leave for England, if that's possible. It's just that I met her and we became sort of friends.' Aware that she was talking too much, she hoped it was not obvious that she was keen to change the subject.

'As it happens, we have a lead.' Inspector Henri leaned forward suddenly. 'Do you know of an old man called Baptiste?'

The point-blank question scared Lucy so much that she could not speak. She let out an involuntary cry. This was it. The body had been discovered, just as she had predicted. She was facing prosecution, defenceless in her guilt. There was no way of glossing over what she had done. She had crept up behind an old man and killed him with her bare hands.

'I – I . . .' she stammered.

Unwittingly, Adrian came to her rescue. 'Do you mean Baptiste who sweeps up leaves at the Garden of Eden Hotel?'

Inspector Henri nodded. 'The very same.' Lucy stared from the inspector to Adrian and back again, too terrified to speak.

'Yes, I know him to speak to,' Adrian said, 'although I don't think Lucy knows him. Why would she?'

'Why would I?' she echoed stupidly.

Every muscle in her body tensed as she waited for the policeman to slap handcuffs on her before throwing her in a cell. The sentence for murder would be a long one. She would spend years and years in an island prison for murdering a defenceless old man. Not even Adrian could help her now.

'Well,' the inspector continued, addressing Adrian, 'it may interest you to know that we have reason to suspect Baptiste may be implicated in the death of that poor Australian girl.'

'Really? Baptiste, a murderer?' Adrian's surprise sounded genuine.

'You may find it hard to believe, but I assure you the most unexpected people can turn out to be killers.' The inspector turned to Lucy with a resigned smile. 'Yes, even an old man like that. I can see you are very shocked, but it is a long time since anything surprised me. We have several witnesses,' he went on, 'local lads who saw the victim getting into a boat with Baptiste six days ago. That was the last time she was seen alive. Of course the old man may be blameless, but we will see. And if he did not kill her, at least we will learn from him where it is she went on the night she was killed.' He nodded solemnly.

'So what does Baptiste say about all this?' Lucy asked.

'We are looking for him. He has not been seen at the hotel since the girl was killed.'

'That's suspicious,' Adrian said. 'Do you think he's done a runner?'

'We are keeping a look out for him,' the inspector replied. 'He may be innocent of any wrongdoing, but—' He broke off with a shrug. 'He was seen returning to shore later, alone in his boat. Yet the girl was seen going out to sea with him. What can I say? The family have been told.'

The inspector beamed at Lucy suddenly. 'Well, I am delighted that you found your mother.'

'Thank you, sir,' Adrian said. 'We came here straight away to let you know that she's no longer a missing person.'

Lucy was touched by his support. This mess had nothing to do with him. It had been generous of him to offer to help out at all, and now he had become entangled in the madness that had threatened to destroy her family.

Leaving the police station, they returned to the hospital to find out how her mother was progressing. She was fast asleep. Lucy's father was seated at her bedside, holding her hand. His eyes were shut too, but he looked up when they entered the room. Lucy suspected they had woken him, but he jumped up and followed them into the corridor, keen to know what had happened.

'So he didn't say anything about investigating any further? He didn't want to know what had happened?' her father asked, staring anxiously at them.

'There isn't really anything to look into,' Adrian replied. 'To be honest, the whole account of her discovery is rather vague, but it's hardly surprising you can't remember much about it. You must have been really shocked, finding her in such a state.' He stared at Lucy so hard, she wondered if he suspected she was hiding the truth. 'But I hardly think the police are going to spend time looking for a beach, with rocks,' he concluded with a shrug.

'What's that?' her father sounded confused. 'A beach with rocks?'

'That's how Lucy described where you found Angela, lying on a deserted beach somewhere near North Point. That is where you found her, isn't it?'

'Well anyway,' Lucy interrupted him, 'once we told the inspector that Angela had been attacked by a drunken tourist, he seemed happy enough to close the case, so that's that. There's nothing more to say about it.'

41

Smothered in sunblock, Lucy was kneeling under a parasol, engrossed in building a sandcastle. Scooping up sand, she patted it firmly yet gently in place. Apart from a few handfuls she managed to dig up from deep beneath the surface, the sand was dry and her edifice threatened to cave in at any moment. Her father was spending time with Lucy before he returned to the hospital to be with Angela. He twisted his head round, shielding his eyes from the sun with one hand.

'You should get a bucket and spade if you want to play at sandcastles.'

'I'm not a child. I know what I'm doing.'

'A child would know the sand's too dry for sandcastles. You need a bucket to carry water up so you can work with the sand.'

'If I need your advice on building sandcastles, I'll ask you.'

Smiling, he lay back in the sun, mumbling to himself.

'I heard that,' she fibbed.

Aware that her stress was misdirected, she delved down into the sand, relishing the cool dampness on her finger tips. She dug up as much wet sand as she could, slopping dollops of it around the base of her structure, but it was slow going and the sand dried out in minutes.

'Do you think he believed us?' she asked, leaning back on her heels, scowling at the side of her castle which was slipping slowly downwards.

'Who?'

He obviously knew what she meant, but she told him anyway. 'Inspector Henri. He did believe us, didn't he?' She paused, but her father did not answer.

Returning to her sandcastle, she worked furiously to construct a barricade around it, hollowing out a narrow trench.

'It's going to have a moat.'

'How are you going to fill it without a bucket?'

With a flash of anger she swiped at her painstakingly constructed fortress. Sand flew everywhere. Her father swore and sat up, spitting, brushing sand from his face, and shaking his thick white hair.

'I'm sorry,' she muttered, 'it's just all such a bloody mess.'

'Don't blame me if you can't make a sandcastle,' he replied, smiling, his good humour restored.

He lay down again and closed his eyes. Lucy stared at the top of his head, his hair speckled with sand. It was all right for him, recovering from the horrors of the past week and lazing around in the sun on his holiday, without a care in the world. He had not just killed a man. She closed her eyes and shivered despite the heat of the day. Baptiste had been an old man, frail and defenceless against her attack. As soon as she struck, he had fallen without a sound, not even a groan or a cry of protest.

To her shame, the fear of discovery troubled her even more than her guilt. Sooner or later someone would stumble upon the hut, hidden though it was in mist and trees.

'People go hiking up there, don't they?' she asked.

Her father grunted. He sounded half asleep. She pictured a troupe of ramblers in khaki shorts and hiking boots, trekking up a steep narrow path. They could pass the red moped without noticing it concealed among the bushes, but they might notice the hut. Sooner or later someone must come across it. Curious, they would peer inside. Perhaps the stench would deter them from entering, but they would wave a torch around from the doorway. With a sickening lurch, she realised she had left her prints all over the metal bowl. It lay on the floor beside the old man's cracked skull. A forensic team would arrive on the mountainside, perhaps flown in from a distant city. Within hours they would be busy gathering evidence, like a scene from CSI on the television. Along with the dead man's blood, the hut would be covered with her fingerprints. Her DNA would be present, along with her mother's. Any amount of proof establishing her mother had been chained in there, like an animal, would not wipe out the evidence that Lucy had murdered Baptiste. When they arrested her, she would be unable to deny it.

A plan began to form in her mind, foolhardy but necessary. She could not just sit back and wait for the body to be discovered.

'I'm going up there to bury him,' she announced, sitting back on her heels.

Her father murmured something without opening his eyes while she outlined her plan. His eyes remained stubbornly closed but she noticed his expression change, his lips pressed tightly together, his eyebrows lowered. She reached the end of her proposal and paused.

'Well?' she prompted him impatiently. 'What do you think? Be honest with me.'

'Honest?'

'Yes.'

He did not answer.

'Well?'

He raised himself up on one elbow and flicked sand at the ruins of her fortification. 'Do you really want to know? Honestly?'

She nodded. 'Yes, I really want to know.'

'I think it's one of the worst ideas I've ever heard.'

'Why?'

'It's stupid on so many levels, I don't know where to begin.'

Lucy pouted and prodded his leg with her toe. 'Are you going to come with me or not?'

'Of course I'm not going up there, and neither are you. Listen,' he leaned forward and lowered his voice, 'all you have to do is hold your nerve and do nothing. It's over, Lucy. He's gone. No one will ever find him. A small heap of bones in a vast forest. Who's going to notice? You only discovered your mother because you followed him. If you hadn't, no one would ever have found her. The hut itself's going to fall down soon. It can't stay up for long without any maintenance. It sounds like the whole thing was on the verge of collapsing already. But once you start going back, digging around, you're going to risk drawing attention to the place. For all we know, the police are already keeping an eye on us. So please, don't be a fool. Let it go. It's over.'

Lucy opened her mouth to deliver an angry riposte but thought better of it. 'Yes, OK, you're right.'

He shrugged and lay down again, closing his eyes. 'I know it's hard, but you just have to try and forget about it and move on.'

Hearing that advice many times over the past few weeks, she had done her best to overcome her preoccupation with Darren. She had never anticipated his place in her thoughts would be replaced by a gnarled and withered old man with a curved spine.

42

Lucy was woken from a deep sleep by a loud knocking at her door. Initially startled, she was relieved to hear her father's voice calling her.

'Lucy! Are you up yet? I'm going down for breakfast. Are you all right?'

Sleepily she told him to go ahead. She would join him soon. Resisting the temptation to turn over and go back to sleep, she rolled out of bed.

'I just spoke to the hospital,' her father beamed as she sat down. Although his nose was still swollen it was no longer red. With his sunglasses on, his injuries were barely evident. 'The doctor has done his rounds and it sounds like we'll be able to bring her back to the hotel with us today, all being well.'

After a late breakfast, they set off for the hospital. Lucy was relieved her father was in such high spirits that he did not remark on her being so quiet.

'I can't believe she's coming out,' he kept saying. 'I just can't believe this whole nightmare is over.'

Lucy felt anxious when she saw a policeman leaning on the counter chatting in Creole to the receptionist, and was shocked when the woman nodded in their direction.

'Here's the husband now,' the receptionist said in English, as though she had just been talking about them.

The policeman straightened up and smiled politely at them. 'Good morning, Mr Hall, sir. The inspector has been here making enquiries in person, and he would like to question you and your daughter again, and also to offer you his congratulations on the safe return of your wife who went missing. They told us at the hotel that you were on your way. I am stationed here to look out for you.' He smiled complacently, his eyes flicking sideways to gauge the receptionist's reaction to his officious speech. 'The inspector asks that you go and see him at your earliest convenience,' he continued, his air of self-importance escalating.

Her father thanked the policeman and assured him they would go and see the inspector before the end of the day. But first, they had to attend to Angela.

'I will tell him,' the policeman said, before turning back to flirt with the receptionist.

Keeping very quiet, Lucy stood behind her father. It was silly to worry that her face would betray her guilt, but she could feel her legs shaking as she followed her father along the corridor to the ward. In the doorway, they were accosted by an eager young man clutching a camera.

'Mr George Hall? And Miss Lucy Hall?' he enquired, blocking their access to the door.

He introduced himself as a reporter for the online news channel, Seychelles Live.

'I know the BBC want to interview you,' he said, 'but as the number one Seychellois site for ex-pats we would like to be first to post the real story behind your wife's disappearance. We understand the police conducted a massive search, after she was taken hostage by a drunken tourist. Can we kick off with how you're feeling right now?' He grinned first at George, then Lucy, then back at George again. 'You must be very relieved?'

Her father looked slightly bemused as he shook his head and answered that he had no comment.

'Now, if you'll let us pass—'

'Yes, of course, but first can you just spare a moment to tell the public—'

'I said no comment,' her father repeated, irritated by the journalist's persistence. 'We're busy.'

'How about you?'

The reporter turned to Lucy. Itching to tell him exactly where he could stuff his expensive camera, she repeated her father's statement.

'So you're not relieved?'

'No comment,' she snapped, insulted that he judged her stupid enough to rise to his pathetic attempt to goad her into giving a response.

'Can I take a picture of you and your wife, reunited?' he asked.

George pushed past him. The reporter hovered on the threshold but did not follow them into the ward. Lucy suspected he had already tried his luck in there and had been banned from making a further nuisance of himself. She closed the door firmly behind her.

Her mother was sitting up in bed, pale and drawn, but alert. She smiled when she saw them and they had yet another emotional reunion. Lucy could not help crying. Even her father had tears in his eyes again.

'Stop it,' her mother scolded them with a hint of her customary bossiness.

She told them the doctor had seen her and she was free to leave. 'There's nothing wrong with me,' she said, 'so you can stop fussing.'

Lucy could see that was far from true. She hoped a few days of rest and good food would restore her mother's strength. For now, she struggled to get out of bed unaided and Lucy looked away as her father assisted her in dressing.

'I'm not an invalid,' her mother grumbled.

'Just put your other leg in,' her father replied patiently, and Lucy felt like crying again.

Lucy walked slowly to the car with her mother while her father had a word with the policeman in the entrance hall. He caught them up as they made their way past a row of parked cars.

'I told him we're leaving,' he explained quietly to Lucy. 'He said we can go along the station later on this afternoon. They're just going through the motions,' he added. 'All they want to do is tick the boxes and close the case. I'm sure it's all fine,' he reassured her, too elated at his wife's return to consider how Lucy might be feeling. 'Don't worry, Lucy,' he added, catching sight of her expression, 'everything's going to be all right from now on.'

She hoped he was right. It made her feel sick that her paranoia was stronger than her guilt over taking the life of another human being, but she could barely control her terror at the prospect of being arrested on a murder charge. She would feel better once the interview at the police station was over. The sight of anyone in uniform scared her. She avoided the eye of the security guard at the hotel. He did not appear to be paying her any attention. A waitress stopped to chat to him and they shared a joke before she sauntered away. The guard watched the girl appraisingly, her hips swinging as she walked. Before Lucy and her parents reached the lift, the same reporter who had accosted them at the hospital approached them, camera flashing. Her mother covered her face in her hands and Lucy leapt at the reporter, and grabbed his camera out of his hand. The security guard came hurrying over.

'What is the problem here?'

'This man has been harassing us,' Lucy announced. 'He's a reporter on a local newspaper and he's trying to get a story.'

She turned to the journalist who was glowering at her, red-faced.

'Give me my camera!'

'Leave us alone!'

'Just give him back his camera and let's go up to the room,' her father said wearily. 'He's only doing his job.'

Lucy handed the camera back. As she scurried after her parents she was aware of the camera flashing behind her and moved to screen her mother from the lens.

'It won't be much of a picture,' she said.

A hotel-guest relations manager sat with Angela while Lucy and her father went to the Central Police Station in Victoria to speak to Inspector Henri.

'Here we are again,' her father said cheerfully as they parked the car. 'Off to the police station for the last time.'

When Lucy did not answer, he turned in his seat and placed his hand gently on hers. 'Come on, Lucy, this is nearly over. Just stick to the story. We found her on the beach.'

'Yes, I know.'

'And don't look so worried. Your mother's back, she's going to be fine, and it's all over, a nasty worrying incident that we can go home and forget about. That's all it was. Nothing else happened. OK? Nothing.'

She glared at him. Her voice shook. 'How can you say what I did was nothing?'

'Lucy, you have to get it into your head that you had no choice. Now, are you ready for this? Say if you're not, and we can go and get a coffee or something and go over our story again. We don't want to say anything that might upset the apple cart, do we?'

Her father was right. Whatever happened in the interview, she could not afford to betray her true feelings. The inspector was a detective, trained to know when people were lying. Somehow she had to convince him they were telling the truth. In a way, they were. They had found her mother. It was only the details they were fudging, and that was more a question of keeping quiet than actually telling lies.

She nodded miserably and climbed out of the car. 'I'm ready.'

Inspector Henri greeted them like old friends. Nothing in his demeanour hinted at even the slightest suspicion that anything was amiss. He was almost overbearing in his congratulations.

'We scoured the beaches around the island,' he told them, as they all sat down. 'We would have scoured them again. We had not stopped looking, I assure you. It was only a matter of time before a patrol discovered your missing wife, but it is a happy coincidence that you found her first.'

'We were looking everywhere,' George said.

'As indeed were we, only not in the right place, it seems.' The inspector smiled broadly.

Lucy wondered if he was making a barbed point, suspicious that she and her father had succeeded where the police search team had failed. But the inspector was showing no signs of hostility towards them. On the contrary, he was being really friendly.

'So we can now close this case, as the drunk tourist who attacked your wife has presumably left the island.' The inspector shrugged, still smiling. 'Regrettably, there is nothing we can do to apprehend him now.'

Lucy felt as though a cloud had lifted from her mind as they left the police station.

'Well, he was busy covering his arse,' her father commented as they reached the car.

'What do you mean?'

'He was very keen to point out they had not stopped looking for her. He was worried we were going to complain. After all, if we were able to find her, just lying on a beach, how the hell did their massive search team miss her? He thought we were going to kick up a fuss. That's why he was so busy telling us they were still looking. That's why he wanted to see us, I think. Plus he was genuinely pleased that she's safe. He seems like a nice guy.'

'You don't think he was at all suspicious that we managed to find her when they didn't?'

'No, not in the slightest. He just wanted to close the case without any bother. If there's one thing they want to avoid here, it's bad publicity. It's fair enough. Their economy depends on tourism and they're terrified of disasters that might put foreigners off holidaying here. He's on a strict agenda to hush up any unnecessary bad press. Privately, I've no doubt he thinks we're too embarrassed to admit she went off and came back of her own accord. Now stop fretting, Lucy. You heard what the inspector said. The case is closed.'

Her parents ate in their room, and Lucy accepted an invitation to have dinner with Adrian. He drove her inland from Beau Vallon to a restaurant on a hill overlooking the sea, which he claimed served the best fish on Mahé. Sitting outside, they watched the sun set over the ocean as they stuffed themselves: smoked sail fish tasting like smoked salmon, soft red snapper cooked in an exquisite sauce, tuna steaks, and other fish Lucy could not identify, followed by more fruit than she could possibly eat. Adrian seemed to have no trouble, and willingly helped her out when he had finished his own.

'Where do you put it all?' she asked, smiling.

They held hands across the table and after dinner drove down to the beach to walk hand in hand on the sand. Swept up in the romance of the moment, lightheaded at the return of her mother, and more than a little inebriated, Lucy allowed herself to forget they were not involved in a relationship. She would be returning to England in a few days' time, after which they would probably never see each other again. As they kissed, Lucy struggled to suppress an overwhelming sense of regret for what might have been. She did not want anything to spoil this beautiful evening.

'Adrian,' she whispered. 'I'm sorry.'

'About what?'

'Everything, really.'

'Are you sorry about this?' he asked as he leaned down to kiss her again.

43

Tired and agreeably tipsy, Lucy thought about Adrian's kiss when she went to bed that night. The touch of his lips on hers had been so light, she almost doubted if their lips had touched at all. Romantic rather than rousing, it was a demonstration of an underlying intimacy, a recognition that if she had not been leaving in a couple of days, their relationship might have developed into something deeper than friendship. She was going to miss turning to him when she had a problem. They had discussed no long term plans, although he had promised to look her up when he next visited England. She hoped he would. They already shared a closeness she had rarely experienced with anyone other than her parents, and she could genuinely claim to trust him with her life. Her relationship with Darren had been constructed around future plans. They had talked a lot about what they were going to do with their lives, without ever actually doing anything. On reflection she realised that their plans had focused entirely on his ambitions. They had never really discussed her role in the life they were planning together.

Opening her window, she stood listening to the sea washing up on the shore. In little more than two weeks, she had grown to love that sound. It seemed to be a part of her, as though resonating with some primeval memory passed into her genes from when life first began. She wondered how her father had been able to tear himself away from the island. It had taken her only a few days to fall in love with the place. Despite the distraction of her mother's abduction and all the dangers she had faced on sea and land, she had succumbed to the allure of the island, surely the most beautiful place on earth. She wondered about Veronique, whose beauty had driven Baptiste wild, and wished she could have seen her, just once. Thinking about Veronique, she drifted into sleep.

It might have been the smell that disturbed her, or perhaps a faint noise, a soft breath carried on the still night air. The instant she opened her eyes she was fully alert, aware that someone else was in the room with her. She bit her lip, listening. Silence. But she knew there was an intruder in her room. She could smell him. Her mind raced, turning over possibilities. They had been so convinced that it was Baptiste who had broken into her father's room, they had not even considered the possibility that there might be a thief targeting the hotel. She tried to recall what had happened regarding her father's intruder, but she could not remember the hotel security taking any action. It had been dismissed as a random incident. Her father had been too preoccupied to press the hotel to take any further action.

Now Lucy was alone in her room with a stranger, and she was helpless. She had no rape alarm, not so much as a cricket bat for protection. All she had within reach was a pillow, hardly a powerful weapon for a slight girl to wield against a man. She strained to see him, but she slept with the curtains closed and the room was completely dark. One minute sliver of light pierced a paper thin gap between the curtains, insufficient to illuminate the blackness. She turned her head, trying to sniff silently so she could pick up the smell of beer and work out the direction it came from. It was no use. She had a horrible feeling he was circling the bed, like shark.

The wait was unbearable. With a sudden burst of energy, she sprang from the bed and made a dash for the door. The intruder was too fast. Strong hands gripped her wrists and she was flung face down on the bed, her head forced forward into the covers to mask her screams. She thought he was going to suffocate her. She imagined her parents coming into her room and seeing her laid out on the bed, dead. She pictured Adrian's sombre face as he viewed her body. Mustering all her strength, she kicked at her assailant's legs, making contact with sinewy flesh. He did not flinch. Without warning he yanked her backwards until she was almost upright, one of his hands firmly over her mouth.

With a gentle grunt he lifted her off the bed and began dragging her backwards. Twisting her head round she saw the tiny thread of moonlight between the curtains and realised he was pulling her towards the window. She pictured herself plummeting from the balcony two storeys down to the ground and writhed, desperate to escape his grasp. It was no use. He was too strong. After all they had been through, her parents were going to suffer the loss of their beloved daughter. It would destroy them. As she struggled, her captor swung her in a semicircle so he was dragging her away from the window and she felt a flicker of hope as he pulled her in the direction of the door. He was not planning to hurl her from the balcony, but she trembled to think what he might intend to do with her.

Her bare feet slid across the floor, scuffling for leverage. He was behind her, holding her under her arms with her legs stretched out, pulling her along so fast that she could not even try to stand. She tried beating at him with her fists, but the angle was awkward and she was unable to hit him with any power. Most of her punches did not even make contact with him. She gave up wasting her energy on waving her arms around to no purpose. She tried throwing herself forwards, out of his grasp, but he was holding her too tightly. She thrashed about, twisting her body sideways. It slowed their progress but he clung on and continued remorselessly dragging her towards the door.

All at once she felt herself lifted right up off the ground. He slung her across his shoulder, holding both of her wrists in one fist. With his other hand he opened the door then grabbed her mouth to stifle her screaming as he carried her out into the corridor. All she could do was kick him repeatedly, as hard as she could. He took no notice but hurried along the corridor.

44

Over the intruder's shoulder, Lucy felt herself tilt backwards as he reached forward to unlock the door of her father's bedroom. She felt a violent jolt as the door was kicked open. They staggered in. The instant she slipped to the floor she was jerked onto her feet. Too shocked to react, she stared into the wild dark eyes of Baptiste. Still alive, he had returned to finish what he had begun. On the side of his head she noticed a livid wound where she had hit him. She heard her mother whimper. Her father's gaze was fixed on her. She stared helplessly back at him. Beside her she could hear the old man's chest wheezing. The door swung closed. Her father froze in the act of sitting up, as Lucy felt the hard round edge of a gun at her temple.

Baptiste took a step forward, pushing Lucy ahead of him. 'If you make a sound, I will kill her.'

Lucy saw her parents' bed shake as her mother began sobbing hysterically, recognising the low guttural drawl. Her nightmare had returned. Lucy's eyes flicked to her mother.

'Don't, Mum,' she whispered. 'Please don't. It doesn't help.'

Her father glanced down at his wife who was clutching at his arm, her nails digging into his flesh.

'Do something, George, do something.'

There was nothing he could do, with the barrel of a gun pressing against Lucy's head. The pulsating tissue that formed her personality, her words, her thoughts and emotions, would be splattered on the carpet as a bullet pierced her skull and exploded inside her brain. Lucy wondered if he would shoot her between her eyes, just as he had shot Veronique.

Her father could barely speak, his teeth were chattering so violently. 'What are you doing in my room? What do you want? What are you doing with my daughter?'

'You know why I am here.'

Baptiste's low voice was steady, only his pounding heart betrayed his excitement. Lucy struggled to control her trembling. She could not go to pieces, not until her father had talked this maniac out of his lunacy.

'Look, Baptiste, I understand you felt you had a grudge against me and my family. You've terrified all of us nearly to death. You almost did kill my wife. Our lives will never be the same again.' He sat forward, warming to his exhortation, his voice clear and strong as he fought for his daughter's life. 'You've given us nightmares enough to last us for the rest of our lives. Surely you're satisfied? What more do you want? Put down the gun, Baptiste. You don't need it. Put it down and let my daughter go. She's just a girl. She doesn't deserve to die, not here, not like this. Put the gun down, Baptiste. Put it down and go away and we'll say no more about it.'

'I waited many years for you to return. I knew you would come back for her.' His voice rose in a shriek. 'She was mine! Out of all the men on the islands, the dark angel chose me. But then you came to the island and stole her from me.' His voice shook and he pressed the gun harder against the side of Lucy's head.

Her father could not contain himself any longer. 'Don't shoot her, Baptiste. Please, not my daughter. Not my daughter.'

Fear of losing her overwhelmed him and he broke down, his shoulders heaving with sobs.

'That is for you to decide,' Baptiste replied in his guttural drawl. 'You must choose if your daughter is to live or die.'

Shocked into stillness, Lucy's father stared at the old man. 'What in heaven's name are you talking about?'

Lucy yelped as Baptiste dragged her sideways until she was standing in front of him. At the periphery of her vision she could see him leaning forward to glare at George from behind her. He moved his gun under her chin, pointing upwards.

'If she moves, I will shoot her.'

He tossed a second gun onto the bed and withdrew to hide behind Lucy again.

'Your daughter will live – if you kill your wife, just as you killed mine.'

'What are you talking about? I never killed anyone. You've got this all wrong. I didn't kill your wife, you've got to believe me.'

'You stole my wife and with her my honour. It was because of you that she had to die.'

'You mean you killed her?' Lucy's father stared in disbelief. 'You shot Veronique?'

'Do not mention her name!'

Her father looked down at his wife, lying flat on her back, eyes closed, sobbing quietly.

'This is impossible,' he protested. 'Of course I'm not going to shoot my wife.'

'Do it,' Angela cried out suddenly. 'He means what he says. He killed her and he blames you. Don't you see? This is what he's been planning all along. This is his revenge.'

She reached up and laid her hand on her husband's arm, her eyes streaming with tears as she implored him to shoot her. 'You can't reason with a madman, George. Just do it. He'll kill Lucy if you don't.'

'I can't,' he answered, shaking his head. 'I can't.'

'It is the only way to satisfy my honour,' Baptiste insisted calmly. 'You stole my wife. Her blood is on your hands, not mine. It was because of you that she had to die. Now you must kill your wife, as I killed mine. Veronique has been waiting for you for a long time, George. Now the time has come to show her you are no better than me. Blood for blood. It is the only way.'

'I just can't,' Lucy's father repeated, his voice rising in panic.

'Don't let him kill Lucy,' her mother pleaded. 'How will we ever live with the consequences if you do?'

'Either way, you must live with the consequences,' Baptiste crowed.

Lucy watched her father gingerly pick up the gun. She suspected he had never handled one before. He studied the metal instrument lying in his hand. It looked quite old and terribly complicated. Perhaps he was holding the very gun that had shot a bullet into Veronique's skull. If this was CSI, ballistics would be able to prove it one way or the other. Wild notions flashed through her mind of her mother in a bulletproof vest using a small bag of pig's blood to fool Baptiste. But her parents were not actors putting on a show. This was real, and her father was about to shoot her mother.

Her father's hand shook. He dropped the gun and scrabbled to pick it up again. Then a slow smile spread across his face. Curiously composed, he turned to Baptiste, who was still hiding behind Lucy.

'I can't shoot my wife,' he said quietly. 'I'll kill myself instead. I accept my guilt and am prepared to die for it. But first you have to let my daughter go.'

Behind her back, it was difficult to tell if Baptiste was laughing or spluttering with rage.

'Baptiste, did you hear me? I'm going to kill myself instead.'

He raised his hand, pressing the gun against his temple as he fumbled for the trigger.

'No, shoot me,' her mother cried out. 'Do what he wants. Shoot me.'

'I'm going to shoot myself, Angela.'

'Shoot me,' her mother begged.

'Unbelievable,' Lucy burst out, aghast, as she listened to her parents compete to sacrifice their lives to placate a maniac. 'This is unbelievable. The whole world's gone mad. I can't listen to any more of this—'

'Shut up.' Baptiste jabbed her beneath her chin with his gun.

She fell silent, her eyes stretched wide in fear.

'If you kill yourself, I will shoot your daughter,' Baptiste said. 'I could have killed her at any time. I kept her alive to persuade you to shoot your wife. The decision is yours, George. You stole my wife, now it is your turn to kill yours.'

'This is insane,' her father replied quietly.

He too was calm as they settled into a surreal negotiation over who was to die.

'You know what you must do to save her life.'

'My wife is a gentle, kind and decent woman. She's done nothing to deserve this. Let her go. Punish me instead.'

'This is your punishment, George.'

'So you're killing my wife to punish me?'

'I am not going to kill her, George. You are. Only then can you understand what it feels like to destroy the one person you love most in the world. That is your punishment. Then you can kill yourself, if that is what you want. What you do afterwards is of no consequence to me. Now, enough talking. It is time to finish it. There is only one way it can end.'

'I'm not going to shoot my wife, and that's final. It's insane. I can't do it. It's over, Baptiste, your little charade is over. You've succeeded yet again in scaring us all half to death. You can leave us now and don't come back. I don't want any part of your sick games. Here, take your bloody gun and I hope it fucking kills you.'

Lucy gasped as he flung the gun away from him in disgust. Her mother wailed as it skidded across the carpet.

'I hope I've made myself clear.'

'Say goodbye to your daughter, George.'

'No!' her father cried out.

Lucy closed her eyes. She was not ready to die, but she had seen the anguish in her father's face, and her mother was crying. If she was about to die anyway, for their sakes she would not weaken.

'I love you!' she called out, her voice steady and clear.

With her eyes closed she could feel the barrel of the gun pushing against the soft flesh beneath her chin, forcing her head back.

'You've made your choice, George. Now watch your daughter die.'

Her mother's voice was shrill with alarm. 'Do something George, do something. Stop him.'

Her father must have shut his eyes, unable to watch, because Baptiste began shouting at him to open his eyes. 'See what you have done, George. Look deep into her eyes as the bullet hits, and remember her blood is on your hands.'

'It's OK, Dad,' Lucy cried out in a choked voice. 'It's not your fault. He's given you no choice.'

'Yes, you had a choice!' Baptiste cried out. 'There is always a choice. You could have saved her life. Her blood is on your hands.'

Her father's next words showed he understood Baptiste was no longer talking about Lucy. 'I'm sorry. I'm sorry. I didn't know she was married. She never told me. I didn't know.'

'The time for regret is past. Honour must be satisfied. Open your eyes, George. Open your eyes and watch your daughter die.'

45

It occurred to Lucy that Baptiste might not be intending to carry out his threats after all. He certainly appeared to be enjoying the melodrama of the situation, his language overly theatrical, his gestures exaggerated, but it was impossible to judge what such a deranged and erratic man might do. She twisted her head slightly and opened her eyes a slit so Baptiste would not see her looking round at him. All she could see was the grey stubble under one side of his chin, and beyond that the edge of the door.

She had thought the door had closed behind them when they entered the room, but she could now see that it was in fact ajar. A wild hope struck her that if she screamed loudly enough someone might hear her and alert a member of staff who would summon the police. But her scream might startle Baptiste into firing. She pictured a security guard running in, too late. By then she would be dead, shot through the head at close range. As she watched, she thought the door opened a fraction. She kept her eyes glued to it. Was someone opening the door very gradually to avoid being noticed? It was probably the wind, but there was just a chance a security guard had overheard them and was out there, assessing the situation, waiting for a chance to intervene.

In the meantime she could try to stall Baptiste, and make sure the situation was clear, in case someone else was outside, listening. She turned her head away, afraid Baptiste would notice her looking over his shoulder.

'I know you're going to shoot me,' she cried out as loudly as she could. 'But first you need to tell me why you're doing it. I don't understand.'

'I refuse to watch any more of this,' her father said, closing his eyes.

It was torture, not daring to look at the door and see if it was indeed slowly opening. She pictured a security guard, preparing to fire a gun.

'Open your eyes and watch,' Baptiste repeated stubbornly.

'I'm not looking.'

A sudden crash, like gun fire. Lucy was propelled forward. Flinging her arms out to break her fall, she landed on the floor with a horrible jolt. For a moment she must have blacked out. When she came to, it felt as though a heavy weight was pressing down on her back. A hard sharp object was digging into her stomach. She could not seem to shift away from it. Her nose was squashed against the carpet, but she could not raise her head, nor could she move her legs. Either her spine had been broken when she fell, or else she had been shot in the back. Either way, she was paralysed. Her ears were filled with the sound of someone screaming. As she was wondering if she would be a paraplegic for life, she realised she was the one screaming. She could see her own fingers groping at the carpet, so at least she could still move her hands.

Miraculously, the pressure bearing down on her lifted and she felt a sudden lightness. Then someone gripped her under her arms and began pulling. She yelped. A moment later, her father was dragging her out from underneath Baptiste, who had landed on top of her when they fell. Paralysis had not been the cause of her immobility. It was Baptiste. Crying with relief, she let her father lift her gently onto the bed to lie beside her mother. Propped up on pillows, Lucy looked around the room and was surprised to see Adrian standing over Baptiste.

'How did he get here?' she asked. No one answered.

Baptiste lay sprawling in the floor. His nose was bleeding and his eyes were closed. Suddenly he sat up and pointed his gun at Adrian who backed away, his face tense with fear.

'No!' Lucy yelled.

Baptiste took no notice of her. His face was bruised and bloody, his left arm hung limp and one of his ankles was swollen, probably broken. He was physically shattered, yet he held all the power in the room, concentrated in that one small black device in his hand. Painfully he straightened up, blood dripping from his bottom lip.

'Now you all get it,' he hissed. 'Who will be first?'

He waved the gun around, pausing when he pointed at Lucy, then her mother, and Adrian, before coming to rest on her father.

'How about you?'

No one moved. Out of the corner of her eye, Lucy noticed Adrian staring pointedly past Baptiste. Then, with an unexpected yell, her friend flung his hands up in the air. Shouting at Baptiste, he began waving his arms above his head in an absurd parody of balletic movements. It seemed the pressure had proved too much for him.

'How about this?' he cried out, executing a bizarre gesture and pulling a fantastic grimace. 'I'm a gargoyle!'

Baptiste stared at him, bemused by the display.

'You think this will save your skin?' he asked. 'This dancing of a desperate man?' He spat blood on the carpet. 'It is not even a good dance.'

While they talked, Lucy glanced at the point Adrian had indicated with his eyes and looked away quickly. The gun her father had thrown off the bed was lying on the floor, their only hope of salvation an instrument of death. She caught her father's eye. He nodded. He had seen it too. Adrian continued playing a dangerous game. His efforts to distract Baptiste would probably get him killed. But they were all likely to die at the hands of the madman anyway.'

'Enough. Now I will kill you first,' Baptiste said, still looking at Adrian.

Lucy's heart pounded as she watched her father edge silently across the floor towards the gun. Behind Baptiste's back, he lunged forward and seized it. Pointing it straight at Baptiste's head, he wrapped his other hand around the gun to keep it steady. Shutting his eyes, he squeezed the trigger. At once the room exploded with a noise that made Lucy's ears ring painfully. Through a haze she watched Baptiste pitch forwards, shooting at Adrian as he fell. Her father flung the gun from his hand and sank back against the bed, rigid with shock, as Adrian screamed and slumped to the floor, his blood spurting onto the carpet.

46

Momentarily stunned, Lucy stared the scene of devastation in her parents' hotel room. Her father was leaning back against the side of the bed. His eyes were closed and he looked very pale. Baptiste was lying on his side, staring straight ahead, an expression of astonishment on his face, as though surprised that his long awaited revenge had backfired. The pool of blood around his head had almost sunk into the carpet and he appeared to have stopped bleeding.

She turned her head away from the body and gasped. Adrian was lying on his back on the floor, blood pouring from a gunshot wound to his shoulder.

'Call an ambulance!' she yelled at her mother. 'Get a doctor here right now. You see to Dad!'

Snapping into action, she ripped a pillow from its case. She folded the fabric into a thick square as she jumped down from the bed, and ran over to Adrian. His eyes were shut, but she could see he was breathing. Tentatively she raised the improvised pad to his shoulder. There was blood everywhere. Her hands were soon coated in it. Normally squeamish, she took no notice of the slimy blood oozing down her arms. She just wanted Adrian to be all right. She thought he was unconscious but his eyes flickered open as she lifted his head gently onto her lap. It felt very heavy.

'That's three times,' he muttered as his eyes closed again.

'Now it's my turn,' Lucy replied. A tear dripped from her chin as she smiled down at him. Gently she wiped it off his cheek, leaving a smear of blood behind. 'Keep still and try to stop bleeding.'

Adrian's lips curled in a smile that changed to a grimace as she bent forward, pressing the folded pad of material against his injured shoulder.

'Ow! Stop doing that, will you? It hurts.'

'Well, if you really want me to let you lie here and bleed to death . . .'

She shifted her position, moving her legs under his head, while he winced, grumbling at her to keep still.

'You keep still,' she retorted. 'Every time you move, the pillow case slips.' In the background, she could hear her mother's voice, explaining that an ambulance was required urgently.

'No, it can't wait until the morning. There's a man bleeding to death up here. He needs medical assistance now. And there's another man—' She broke off. 'Look, we need an ambulance, and we need medical assistance up here straight away.' She paused, listening to the person at the other end of the line. 'Shot and bleeding to death, yes. It's an emergency . . . Yes, tell them it's an emergency. The injured man is a Seychellois. He's the hotel accountant . . . That's right, Adrian . . . Yes, Adrian's been shot . . . Thank you. Honestly, George, you'd think I was asking for a space shuttle to the moon. George? George? Are you all right? George?'

It was Angela's voice, calling her father. Lucy looked up and saw she was shaking him by the shoulder. He opened his eyes.

'Are you all right, George? Are you hurt? George, answer me!'

He smiled weakly and assured her he was fine.

'But it's all my fault,' he mumbled. 'All of it. My fault.'

Lucy's mother sat back on her heels and launched into one of her lectures. 'Listen to me, George. If you hadn't shot that animal right between the eyes, we'd all of us be dead right now, you, me, Lucy and Adrian. It's only because of you that we're all still alive.'

'All?' her father repeated, as though he did not understand the word. 'Did you say all?'

'Adrian's still alive, but he's bleeding a lot,' Lucy said. Adrian shifted in her arms and moaned with pain. 'You've got to keep still, Adrian. Help will be here soon.'

Her father's head fell back against the side of the bed.

'I did it,' he announced to no one in particular. He sounded dazed.

His head jerked as Lucy's mother pulled a sheet off the bed. Lucy watched her drag it over to Baptiste and throw it over him. Twitching the edges, she covered the dead body completely.

'There,' she said, brushing her palms together in a washing motion. 'We don't have to look at him.'

Before she walked away, she stamped viciously on the hidden corpse. The body jolted beneath its shroud. Lucy flinched at the sadistic expression on her mother's face. She wondered what unspoken atrocities had been committed against her in the name of revenge, while she had been chained to the wall in Baptiste's stinking hut. Still pressing the bloody wad of material against Adrian's wound, she closed her eyes to shut out the sight of her mother's face contorted with loathing. When she opened them again the room was full of people. Two men lifted her father up onto the bed and he lay immobile for a few seconds, observing the bustle that was going on around him.

'The ambulance is on its way,' a porter told Lucy.

As her father sat up, her mother bent down to plant a kiss on his cheek.

Lucy turned back to Adrian. He looked dreadfully pale. His head was resting on her lap and her flimsy nightshirt was drenched with blood. He seemed to be losing a lot of blood. She shivered. After the stress of her mother's disappearance, she was not sure she could cope with any more grief.

'It's all right now,' she repeated. 'It's all right.'

She could feel the tension in her shoulder as she pressed the pad against Adrian's wound. As far as she could tell she had stemmed the bleeding, but it was not clear if Adrian had lost consciousness or had just closed his eyes.

'The ambulance will be here soon,' someone said, and a buzz of muted voices rippled through the onlookers.

A stout sunburned woman strode into the room.

'I'm a doctor,' she announced in a strident English accent. 'Where's the injured party?'

'Thank God,' Lucy breathed.

One of the porters lifted a corner of the sheet to reveal Baptiste's face. The doctor lowered her bulk to kneel on the blood-soaked carpet beside him. As she wriggled around the body in a vain attempt to avoid staining her dressing gown, Lucy grabbed her by the arm and yanked her away.

'Never mind about him,' she cried. 'Adrian's injured. He's bleeding to death and I can't stop it!'

With a helpless shrug at Baptiste's corpse, the doctor turned her attention to the living. As she moved away, Lucy's mother darted forward to flick the sheet back over Baptiste's face. Once again, her mother's expression gave Lucy a cold sensation, she looked so malevolent. Gently the doctor lifted the blood-soaked pad off Adrian's shoulder and he groaned.

'You're doing the right thing,' she announced, with a nod at Lucy. 'Keep pressing the pad against it. Hopefully the bleeding will have washed the wound out, but he'll be put on antibiotics to prevent any infection and he might need a tetanus shot.'

'He's going to be all right then?' Lucy's voice shook so much she could hardly get the words out.

'I should think so,' the doctor replied. 'He seems healthy enough and it's just a flesh wound, despite all this blood. You're not a haemophiliac, are you?'

Adrian shook his head and winced.

'How did it happen?' the doctor continued. 'It looks like . . .' She glanced back at Baptiste, concealed once more beneath the sheet, and frowned. Standing up with a grunt, she addressed the hotel manager. 'This chap needs to go to hospital as soon as the ambulance gets here, to check everything's as it should be and there's no further injury, and you'll need to notify the police if you haven't already done so. As I was first on the scene, you know where I am if you need a death certificate for our friend under the sheet.'

'He's not our friend,' Lucy's mother snapped so ferociously that the doctor looked round at her in surprise.

47

THE SUN SHONE FIERCELY on the sparkling water of the pool. Not far away the shouts of holidaymakers could be heard from the beach, just a short walk away through lush gardens. Her father was lying on a lounger by the pool where Lucy was taking a dip with her mother. Neither of them fancied going in the sea. Lucy doggy-paddled past her mother who laughed and chased feebly after her across the pool. The events of the past few days seemed impossible to believe, as they splashed around in the water. From his seat in the shade, her father called to them not to stay exposed for too long. The only danger now was from too much sun. Aware that her mother was still physically weak, Lucy called to him she was getting out.

Lucy's mother followed her up the steps out of the pool. She looked emaciated. Since she had been discharged from hospital she seemed barely able to eat, but they had given up nagging her for now. It was bound to take time for the effects of her ordeal to fade. Tired out after her swim, she went up to the room for a rest. Lucy's father went up with her. After a while he came down again to sit by the pool with Lucy.

'She's fast asleep,' he said. 'It's probably the best thing for her right now.'

In her mother's presence, Lucy and her father were keeping up a pretence that everything was fine. When her mother was not around, Lucy's father made no attempt to hide his anxiety. He confided his fears that the unseen consequences of her mother's experience would prove more tenacious than any physical signs. Her mother refused to talk about her confinement in the hut. Lucy had noticed how her mother recoiled from any physical contact with her father, but now she said only that she wished there was something she could do to support him, and help her mother.

'I'm not sure there's anything we can do, other than to be there for her,' he said. 'Once we get home I'll take her to the GP and insist she's referred to a counsellor, maybe a psychiatrist, someone trained in helping people suffering from post-traumatic stress. Perhaps all three of us ought to go?'

Assuring her father she would do whatever he thought was best for her mother, she lay back on a sunbed. Adrian came and sat beside her, a large dressing taped to his shoulder the only visible reminder of the crisis they had survived. The brisk English doctor's diagnosis had been confirmed by a hospital consultant. Adrian had suffered a nasty flesh wound which they expected to heal quickly. In the meantime, they had advised him not to drive for a few days – advice which Lucy knew he was ignoring – and he had been signed off work for two weeks.

'Two weeks,' Lucy wailed. 'But we're going home tomorrow!'

'I'll just have to find some other way to pass the time while I'm off work,' Adrian replied, laughing.

'Well, you'd better not go rescuing anyone else. Damsel in distress is my role.'

'Next time I see a girl drowning, or having rocks thrown at her, or being shot at, I'll look the other way,' he assured her solemnly.

When her parents joined them, Lucy went to the bar. She walked past a few holidaymakers sitting in the shade around the pool, young couples probably on honeymoon, and older couples celebrating anniversaries or retirement, all of them relaxed and contented. It was hard to believe anything sinister could ever happen in this lovely setting. Eddy, the blond barman, obligingly brought a tray over to them.

'How's the injured hero?' he asked, with a wink at his colleague.

Adrian shrugged, then grimaced. 'Bugger, I keep forgetting about this damned dressing. It's more uncomfortable than the wound itself. Every time I move my shoulder, it pulls.'

'You shouldn't drive then,' Lucy retorted.

Overhearing her, Eddy grinned as he set their drinks down.

'That's right, Lucy. You tell him. By the way, did you hear the news?' he sat on the edge of her lounger.

'What news?'

'About Judy.'

Lucy sat up. 'What about her?'

'They think Baptiste's gun was used to shoot her. It's not definite yet. The police are still waiting for confirmation. But apparently he was seen taking her off in his boat, so if it was his gun that shot her, well, that's going to wrap it up, isn't it? She was a great girl. It's a tragedy, what happened to her.'

With a sigh, he stood up and wandered back to the bar where a young girl was waiting for him. Lucy gazed at a few petals floating on the surface of the pool, blown there by the wind.

'It's better to let them fall,' she said. 'More natural. They don't need to be swept up.'

Her mother shuddered and pulled her sarong over her bony knees.

'Health and safety wouldn't let them lie around on the flagstones like that in England,' her father replied. 'Someone could slip over and sue the hotel.'

'That's ridiculous,' Adrian said.

They sat for a moment, sipping lemonade and beer, each absorbed in their own thoughts.

Lucy's father broke the silence. 'Thank God you came along when you did. Although I don't understand what you were doing in the corridor outside our room.'

Adrian looked embarrassed. 'I told you, I happened to be passing. I'd been working late – that is, I'd been drinking with some of the hotel staff and – I heard a commotion from the corridor,'

'But what were you doing up on our floor in the first place?'

Adrian looked away, flustered. Lucy caught her mother's eye and Angela put her hand on her husband's arm.

'Never mind,' she said. 'He was there when we needed him and that's what matters.'

'Exactly. So stop going on about it, Dad,' Lucy added.

'I'm hardly going on—'

Lucy jumped up. 'Come on, Adrian, let's go for a walk. It's my last day. Let's go and frolic in the sea.'

'Not sure about frolicking with this,' he said, raising his injured arm a fraction and wincing. 'But I might be able to manage a sedate stroll.'

He stood up and took her hand, and they walked down to the beach together.

Before dinner, Lucy joined her parents on their balcony to watch the sunset. Her mother must have had a word with her father. Lucy was mortified by his awkward attempt at an apology.

'It hadn't occurred to me that there was anything going on between you and Adrian. If I'd known, I would never have asked him what he was doing in our corridor, at night.'

'Please, Dad, there's nothing going on.' Lucy felt herself blush. It was embarrassing, knowing her parents must have talked about her private affairs. 'And there's no holiday romance. Adrian's a friend.'

Her parents must have discussed her break up with Darren a lot when she was not around. She wondered if she would ever understand how much they must have suffered, witnessing her misery. She was only twenty-two. Deep down she had always known that she would carry on with her life and forget about Darren. Carried away by the drama of her own grief, she had been cruelly self-centred. In the bright light that exposed every wrinkle and crease, her mother's face looked tired and old. Her hair was turning white. Lucy wondered if her own problems had added lines to her mother's face.

The sky began to flare orange and they all turned to watch the sun set.

'I think it's going to be a good one tonight,' Lucy's father said.

'You say that every night,' Lucy answered with a smile.

Her mother's words dropped so softly on the quiet air, Lucy thought she must have misheard. 'Tell us about Veronique.'

It was a while before Lucy's father answered. When he did, he spoke very slowly. 'What it all boils down to is that I had an affair with a woman back in the seventies, while I was working here.' He gazed past them at the ocean shimmering with pink light. 'I didn't know she was married.'

'Would it have made any difference if you had known?'

'Yes – no – I don't know. Yes, of course it would. But I was very young. It never occurred to me to ask her, and she didn't tell me. I suppose I assumed she was free. Why would I think otherwise?' He shrugged. 'I wasn't much older than Lucy.'

'Old enough to know better,' her mother said, tartly.

Lucy thought that was unfair. It was not her father's fault that he had unknowingly fallen in love with a married woman, or that his letters had betrayed their affair to her jealous husband. She looked at her father, who seemed bowed under the weight of his misery. Perhaps he had never cared for another woman with a devotion equal to his love for Veronique. She might have reciprocated his feelings with equal passion, her love for George goading Baptiste beyond endurance. But all that had happened before he met Lucy's mother.

'I told you,' he repeated wearily, 'I didn't know she was married. It was just an affair. I was young, and I was lonely, and like you said yourself, it's natural.'

Her mother spoke. 'Did you love her?'

The answer lay in his hesitation. 'Yes,' he replied heavily at last. 'I did. I loved her.'

'Why didn't you tell me about her? She was a part of your life before we met.'

She sounded so hurt, Lucy began to understand her mother's anger. It was not her father's love affair but his silence that had been a betrayal. Her parents seemed to have forgotten she was sitting there. Feeling uncomfortable, she wondered whether to get up and leave, but she did not want to draw attention to herself.

'I didn't think it mattered. It was over such a long time ago.'

Her mother's voice was cold as she repeated his words. 'A long time ago.' Her voice rose as she continued. 'Why did you write and tell her we were coming here, if it was all over?'

His reply was halting, as though he found it difficult to speak. 'It was a long time ago, but I did care about her once. I just wanted to see her, to know she was all right. When I left, the island was a dangerous place. I always felt guilty about leaving her and worried about how she had coped. I just wanted to check she had been all right over the years. I wanted to see she was happy in her life, as happy as I am with you. Was that so very wrong?'

He waited but her mother did not respond. 'We are happy together, aren't we?' he blurted out. 'Angela, please don't shut me out like this. I know I was wrong to write to her without telling you, but I only wanted closure on that chapter of my life by making sure she was all right. She never answered my letters when I first returned to England, and I always wondered why, whether she'd forgotten me, or if something had happened to her. Once we decided to come back, I had to try and find out.'

Angela turned to face him. Her eyes were burning with an anguish she struggled to express. 'She couldn't write to you, could she? Because he shot her. Right between the eyes. I can't stop thinking about that poor woman, George, killed because she loved you all those years ago, and I knew nothing about it.'

George bowed his head and took his wife's hand. Lucy could see his eyes were filled with tears. They had survived Baptiste. Veronique had not. She had been a young woman, perhaps the same age as Lucy was now. They had both fallen in love with the wrong man, but Veronique had suffered a terrible fate as a consequence. In all the time Lucy had been distraught over Darren, it had not once occurred to her to appreciate how lucky she had been. Her relationship with Darren was over. Her life was not.

48

When Lucy's parents retired to their room for a siesta, she walked out of the hotel on her own. Without having told anyone what she was planning to do, she drove towards Victoria. When she reached the track that led into the forest of Morne Seychellois, she turned off the road. It was early afternoon. With five hours of daylight left, she had enough time to complete her task and be back in the hotel before her parents realised she was missing. Her mother would never need to find out where she had gone. The journey did not take as long as she had expected. Spotting the flattened patch in the bushes where the old man's moped lay, she climbed out of the car and continued on foot. She had brought some red beads with her. Every few yards she dropped a bead to help her find her way back to the car. After all the trouble she and her parents had suffered, she did not want to add to it by getting lost on the mountain.

On foot, she climbed for such a long time that she thought she must have followed the wrong path. She was wondering whether she ought to turn back when the hut appeared in front of her. Half hidden in overgrown moss and ivy, the door wedged open with the wooden shrine, it looked abandoned. Dismissing a mental image of her mother chained to the wall, she entered the hut. The white curtain had been ripped off the wooden box which still lay across the threshold, where she had left it. The floor was covered in a thick layer of shrivelled petals, their delicate scent overpowered by a foul stench. Suspended from one wall, her mother's manacles remained fixed to the hut. In a corner where the shrine had stood, the small white curtain had been draped over the skull.

Stepping over petals, avoiding the place where Baptiste had fallen when she hit him, Lucy made her way across the hut. Peeking beneath the curtain to make sure she had found what she wanted, she picked up the skull, still wrapped in its cover, and left the hut. Unless some stray hiker on the mountains stumbled across it, no one would ever enter that hut again. She turned and began her trek back down the mountain. Following the trail of beads, she found the car easily and placed the skull, still in its wrapping, in a bag.

Arriving back at the hotel, she hid the bag inside her wardrobe. Before dinner, her mother went up to her room to shower. As her father stood up to accompany his wife, Lucy put her hand on his arm.

'Come for a walk on the beach with me, Dad,' she said, adding in an undertone that she needed to speak to him alone.

Her father nodded. 'I'll be up in a bit, Angela. I'm just going for a short walk with Lucy, down to the sea and back.'

Lucy led him through the gardens down to the beach where they sat on a wall. Gazing at the serenity of the ocean, she told him how she had gone back to the hut to retrieve Veronique's skull.

Her father turned to her, visibly shocked. 'You did what?'

She was taken aback by his expression. 'I'm sorry,' she faltered, 'I should have asked you first, but it was difficult, with Mum around. I just thought you might not want to leave it up there in that dreadful place. You were wrong to write to Veronique without telling Mum, but I think I can understand why you did it. And even if I can't, Veronique still deserves to be treated with some decency.' She hesitated. 'I thought you might want to bury her.'

Her voice trailed off. Her father sat perfectly still, staring at the sea, making no sign that he had even heard her. When he turned to her, she saw tears glistening on his cheeks.

'I'm sorry,' she mumbled. 'I thought . . .'

Her father reached out and put his hand on hers.

'It's in a blue bag in my wardrobe,' she muttered. 'You can go and get it any time you want.'

With a nod he turned away, his shoulders shaken by silent sobs.

Over breakfast next day, her mother announced she intended to spend the morning packing. Her father said he wanted to drive down to the airport to print out their boarding passes, which the hotel had explained could only be done there.

'Why make a special journey?' Lucy's mother said. 'You can do all the checking in when we get there later.'

He insisted he wanted to make sure everything went smoothly.

'Let him go if that's what he wants to do, Mum,' Lucy interrupted.

'I just want to look after you, and make sure everything goes smoothly,' her father repeated, leaning down to kiss his wife on the cheek.

Lucy accepted her father's invitation to accompany him. 'Are you really sure you want me to come?'

'He's only going to the airport, Lucy,' her mother said.

Lucy knew that was not true. She was surprised to see her father looking cheerful as they set off. It seemed to her to be quite a grim undertaking. But as they drove away from the hotel, he fell silent and his features set in a stern expression, as though he was steeling himself for the task ahead.

Before they reached the road to the airport, he turned off onto a track that meandered between tall palm trees and masses of shrubs covered in flowers, pink, white, yellow and purple, stunning against the dark green foliage. He had brought Lucy and her mother there once before. The flowers were even more lovely than she remembered. Leaving the car in a passing place beneath the overhanging branches of a takamaka tree, he took the blue bag from the boot and started to descend the incline. A short way down he stopped to look at the view. Lucy thought he had forgotten about her, walking a few paces behind him, but he turned and beckoned her. He put his arm round her and side by side they gazed out over the sparkling ocean, far below.

'I remember dreading your mother had drowned,' he said. 'I don't know how I ever dared fall in love for a second time.' He paused. 'Wait here.'

She watched him walk down the path towards the property where strangers had lived for thirty years. He did not even glance at the two-storey white house with its verandah where he used to sit as a young man, looking out at the ocean. She knew he had been happy there, perhaps happier than he had been at any other time in his life, but the building was just stone and cement. The only warmth he would find there now would come from the sun beating down on him. Halfway down the path he stopped under a frangipani bush, its white flowers delicate against the dark foliage. Opening the blue bag, he lifted out the skull wrapped in white fabric. Laying it gently on the ground beside him, he began to dig.

He had brought an assortment of children's spades, designed for the beach. Lucy guessed that was all he had been able to find, without making a special trip into Victoria. The first spade was not up to the job of digging earth and after a few jabs the delicate wooden handle snapped. He threw it to one side and picked up a red plastic spade that looked more robust. Rhythmically, he dug until he had cleared a hole in the earth. The handle of the spade kept juddering as the end hit against woody roots of the frangipani bush. In the end he abandoned the spade and gouged the earth out with his bare hands, shovelling it from the slowly deepening hole. It took a long time, but he persevered. Lucy wondered what the residents would think if they returned to find him digging beneath the bushes like an animal. He toiled on, until his shirt clung to his sweating body, and at last the hole was deep enough. Reaching up to gather fresh frangipani petals from the living bush, he lined the hole with them.

In the shade of the frangipani she had loved, he let go of the woman he had lost a long time ago.

'I would have come back,' he whispered, 'but I don't know if it would have been enough.'

Lucy knew what he meant. There was no way of knowing whether he would have been able to return in time to save her from Baptiste's bullet. It was strange to think that if his passion for Veronique had turned into a long-term relationship, he would not have married her mother, and she would never have been born.

She watched him sprinkle the skull with more frangipani petals, before shovelling earth into the hole. Walking over to stand next to him, she placed a flower on the spot where Veronique was now buried.

'I'm sorry,' he muttered as he knelt and patted the earth down. 'I'm so sorry.'

'None of this was your fault, Dad.'

He sighed. 'Rest in peace, my dark angel.'

49

LUCY TOOK HER LEAVE of the barman, Eddy. He gave her a wink before turning his attention to a girl, slim and blonde, with the telltale pale skin of a new arrival. When they were ready to leave, she went round with her father, saying their goodbyes. Her father disagreed, but Lucy had the impression the manager was relieved to see them go. They even stopped to speak to the reporter from Seychelles Live in the lobby. Hovering beside them, the manager brightened up when Lucy's father praised the Garden of Eden Hotel for its first-rate accommodation, food and service.

'We couldn't fault it,' her father said.

'How did you feel when you saw your wife again, after she had been found?' the reporter asked.

'We were happy with her stay in hospital, and of course very pleased when she was able to leave hospital. She's been well looked after here. Like I said, we can't fault it here.'

'They even sweep away the petals outside so no one can slip,' Lucy muttered to her father.

The reporter turned to her eagerly. 'I'm sorry? I didn't catch that.'

'It's nothing,' her father answered, ushering her away.

Lucy drove to the airport with Adrian, her parents following behind in the hire car. Adrian had insisted on coming with them, despite Lucy's protestations that he should not drive all that way.

'You really don't need to do this, Adrian.'

'You know you're turning into your mother?' he laughed. 'It's not far.'

'You're not supposed to be driving at all yet.'

'If I only did what I was supposed to do, I would never have tried my luck that night, and come up to your corridor just in time to save you from a maniac with a gun.'

She smiled and turned to gaze out of the window. The scenery was so beautiful, it would be a wrench to leave it all behind for the grey skies of England.

'I'm going to miss all this,' she said.

'I'll take that as a compliment.'

A building blocked her view. They rounded a bend in the road and a clear panorama of a deserted beach opened out below them. Turquoise water sparkled in the bay beneath a glaring sun, and far away tiny white boats bobbed in the water, like toys.

Lucy turned to Adrian. 'I don't want to leave.'

'I'd love you to stay,' he replied seriously, 'but I don't think my nerves could cope with looking after you for longer than two weeks. You need to get on to Superman, or perhaps James Bond would be up for it, not some dull accountant who isn't even supposed to risk driving a car.'

She laughed. She was going to miss his sense of humour. 'There's so much I don't know about you.' All at once she was steeped in regrets, conscious their time together had almost run out.

'Ask me anything you like. If you find out anything remotely interesting, please let me know. I could do with a good chat up line. Not every girl I meet gives me so much scope to play the hero.'

'OK, here goes. Twenty questions.'

'Fire away.'

She learned that unlike his peers in the shanty town where he had grown up he had worked hard at school, and he did not regret the time he had spent studying. He had no siblings, or at least none that he knew about, did not know who his father was, spoke three languages fluently, and had never been in love. He told her he did not know what that meant, and she dismissed his remark as typical of a man. When she had finished questioning him he admitted she had seen little of his real existence.

'Man of mystery then?'

'No, what I mean is, the time I've spent with you wasn't in any way typical. This has been the most exciting time of my life. It's been incredible. Think about it, Lucy. I'm an accountant. I spend my days at a desk, checking figures. Meeting you has been a real adventure for me!'

'For me too. I've only ever read about other people's adventures in books. I never had one myself before this.'

They smiled at one another.

'My turn to ask the questions,' he said.

Lucy agreed reluctantly. She was taken aback by his first question but Adrian had answered her questions honestly so she tried to be truthful.

'I loved him, I suppose.'

'I'm glad you put that in the past tense. So you're over him now?'

'I guess so.'

'Good. I know we only met a couple of weeks ago, but we've been through a lot in that time, more than most friends go through in a lifetime. I think of you as a real friend, Lucy.'

He paused as though expecting an answer.

'Me too,' she replied. 'I'd say right now you're the best friend I've got on Mahé.'

'I'm being serious,' he reproached her. 'We won't see each other again for a while, and I'd hate to think of you being miserable.'

Touched by his concern, she was not sure how to respond. 'From now on, I'm going to appreciate every minute of every day,' she promised him. 'I'm lucky to be alive, thanks to you.'

'Yes, I'd like to think you're going to make the most of your life. You're young and intelligent, and beautiful. There's no knowing where you might end up.'

'Young, gifted and talented?' She laughed. 'Thanks for the vote of confidence. I just wish I knew what I wanted to do with my life. I feel like I'm drifting.'

'Well, you're highly intelligent, you see connections other people miss, you never give up, and you've definitely got more guts than anyone else I've ever met.' He paused. 'And I suspect you can pick locks.'

'So you're telling me I'd make a good burglar,' she laughed.

'You could be a spy!'

She thought back over the adrenaline rush of the past sixteen days, and the dangers she had faced.

'I don't think a life of adventure is for me,' she laughed. 'Two weeks was enough.'

'I know what you mean. It's been quite an adventure though, hasn't it?'

'Normal life is going to seem dull after everything that's happened.'

'You could join the SAS?'

'Too many rules and regulations for me. And I'd need to be fit.'

'You could be a private detective.'

'Like Miss Marple,' she said and they both laughed.

They said goodbye in the car park of the small airport with its runway bordering the ocean. Before she followed her parents to check in, Lucy ran back and threw her arms around Adrian's neck one last time.

'Ow,' he complained. 'My shoulder!'

'Sorry.'

Her mother was calling her.

'Make sure you keep in touch,' Lucy called out as she ran after her parents.

Adrian shouted in reply but she did not hear what he said. By the time she realised she did not have his email address, it was too late. Her mother found them seats in the waiting area and they sat looking out at the runway and beyond that the ocean stretching away to the horizon. Her father put his arm round her.

'Nearly there,' he said. 'We'll soon be safely home, and then no more hair-raising escapades for you, young lady. From now on I'm going to be keeping a close eye on you and your mother, taking care of you both.'

Despite his well-meaning words, Lucy knew that he was no longer responsible for her. She was ready to take control of her own life. Thinking about what had happened, she was more determined than ever to forget about Darren and move on with her life.

With a roar, the plane gathered speed. Lucy stared at low white buildings and lush green hills flashing past the window. A granite mountain peak towered above the forested slopes. Concealed in that idyllic landscape a dilapidated hut sheltered a wooden shrine, surrounded by heaps of dry petals. Those that were not blown away on the wind would be consumed by insects, or rot into the forest floor. The plane rose rapidly, the ruffled turquoise surface of the sea far below them now. They turned and a green island appeared, framed in the window. She could not be sure but thought she recognised the curve of the coastline before the plane wheeled once more and the island disappeared. Her parents were laughing together, finding a way back to their quietly affectionate relationship. Smiling, Lucy returned to the email she was writing. She would send it care of the hotel, knowing Adrian would reply as soon as he was back at work. When she next glanced out of the window, they were flying above the clouds. Along with the island, the time she had spent with Darren was already fading into memory. On her own for the first time in her life, she felt ready to face whatever challenges the future might hold.

Acknowledgements

Producing a book is a team effort, and I am fortunate to be supported by many talented individuals. I am particularly indebted to Emilie Marneur and Sophie Wilson. No author could wish for more consummate expertise and sensitivity from editors who are not only brilliant, but inspiring to work with.

I would also like to thank the Seychellois Police and the British High Commission in the Seychelles for their assistance and generosity with their time, and my contact in UK Ballistics Intelligence for his advice.

Finally, I am lucky to be represented by Annette Crossland, a fantastic agent and a true friend.

About the Author

Photo: © Phillipa Leigh, 2014

Leigh Russell is the author of the internationally bestselling DI Geraldine Steel and DS Ian Peterson crime series, both of which are currently in development for television. She studied at the University of Kent, gaining a master's degree in English and American literature. After many years teaching English at secondary school, she now writes crime fiction full-time. Published on both sides of the Atlantic, as well as in translation throughout Europe, Russell's books have reached top positions on many bestseller lists, including #1 on Kindle and iTunes. Her work has been nominated for a number of major awards, including the CWA New Blood Dagger and CWA Dagger in the Library. As well as writing bestselling crime novels, Russell appears at national and international literary festivals and runs occasional creative writing courses across Europe.

About the Author

[illegible]